Behind in the Count

by

Kent Krause

Behind in the Count

Kodar Publishing
ISBN 13: 978-0615791777
ISBN 10: 0615791778

This is a work of fiction. Apart from the well-known actual people, places, and events mentioned in this novel, all of the characters, names, and events, as well as all places, organizations, and dialogue in this book are products of the author's imagination or are used fictitiously.

To Jill

Other books by Kent Krause:

The All-American King

Men Among Giants

Acknowledgements

Thank you to my wife Jill for her estimable work as proofreader, editor, and promoter of my books. Dave King, Sam Judge, Boo Carter, and Zane Fischer owe their existence to Jill's ongoing encouragement of my writing. Even when my faith wanes, hers remains.

And many, many thanks to the following good people for helping me along in my journey with this novel and my previous book, *Men Among Giants*.

Jim Ballard
Patty Beutler
Kevin Burton
Richard Clarence
Cindy Conger
Ron Kalkwarf
Jeff Korbelik
Keith Larsen
Mark Piro
Benjamin Rader
Patrice Reynolds
Hilary Sire
Jean Tennant
Homze's Heroes

And finally, I wish to thank all those who have read and shared a kind word about my novels. Your encouragement is much appreciated.

Prologue

I had never seen grown men act like such idiots. Nor had I ever seen grown men so happy. Champagne and beer sprayed everywhere as howls and shouts filled the clubhouse. I toweled off my head to find a microphone thrust in my face. I didn't hear most of the ensuing question, but I still tried to respond. Just as my mouth opened, the contents of another bottle anointed my head. After my fingers rubbed the stinging liquid from my eyes, Rob Dibble wrapped me in a massive bear hug. "We did it, Fish," he shouted. "We did it! Woooo!" He bounded off to share discourse of a similar nature with someone else in the crowded room.

The reporter repeated his question to me. Something about how it felt to finally win it all. After a short period of reflection, I offered my eloquent response. "It feels great. Yeeaaaaah!!!" To support this profundity, I stuck out my tongue like Gene Simmons and pointed at the "Cincinnati" written across the front of my drenched jersey. Deep stuff, I know.

Like my esteemed colleagues, I had good reason to celebrate and act like a fool on national television. It was October 1990 and my team, the Cincinnati Reds, had just won the World Series. I had pitched the night before, our third win in what was a four-game sweep over the Oakland A's. That victory capped off my best season in the majors, a 20-win campaign that earned me the Cy Young Award. I was 33 and still in the prime of my career. Many baseball experts considered me the top lefty in the National League, and my agent was negotiating a fat contract with the Reds to reflect

1

that lofty status. Yep, I had plenty of reasons to smile for the cameras that night. To the millions of fans across the nation watching on TV, I had it all.

But in actuality, I had nothing. My world was falling apart.

My wife Toni was in the process of leaving me. Didn't seem that long ago, we'd been hopelessly in love and ready to conquer the world. We had a daughter and a son and a tighter bond than any couple I knew. The future and our happiness knew no limits. Then in the fall of '89 our boy Luke died—an accidental drowning in our pool. He'd just turned three. Toni shut down. For weeks she could barely pull herself out of bed. I checked out too, seeking refuge in a river of booze and a mountain of cocaine. Yet, even while subjecting my body to this untold abuse, I threw myself into baseball like never before. That became my other escape from the pain—wreaking havoc on the mound. Though I still won at the ballpark, I drifted away from my wife when she needed me most. After a year Toni couldn't take it anymore. She took our daughter and left me—same week as the World Series.

As for baseball, it proved to be a temporary shelter. After my Cy Young season in '90, I gave Cincinnati another decent year, but then the drug and alcohol abuse finally started affecting my performance. Two mediocre seasons later, the Reds released me and I signed with Kansas City. After a couple years with the Royals, I ended up in Pittsburgh. Not much went right in the Steel City. The team sucked and so did I. In April I couldn't get much on my fastball. By May I couldn't get much on my changeup. And the pain got worse with each outing. At the end of June, the doctors told me I had a torn rotator cuff. If you're curious about what that feels like, just take a poker that's been heating in the fireplace and jam it through your shoulder. Then leave it wedged in there and try to throw a baseball. That's what it was like for me the summer of '96.

That fall I hit rock bottom. My life became a blur of liquor, drugs, and strippers. Got myself arrested a couple times. Once for DUI and once for pissing in the Ohio River. In the latter instance I thought it was dark out so nobody could see me. It was actually around noon. You probably read the articles about that, and a few other incidents that made the news. Sportswriters had plenty of fun with me that off-season. They seemed to reach a consensus that I'd become an over-the-hill, broken-down drunk who'd never pitch again.

They weren't the only ones with that opinion. One night rotting in the drunk tank, I overheard a couple cops talking about me. "That's Zane Fischer, the pitcher. He used to be great. Man, look at him now. What a bum." That opened my eyes. I couldn't let it end this way. A fire still flickered inside me—I had to prove I was still worth something as a man and as a ballplayer. That very night, I vowed to get sober and to get back to the big leagues.

With the help of a sponsor and a lot of meetings ("Hi, my name is Zane and I'm an alcoholic"), I made good progress cleaning up my act. Unfortunately, my shoulder injury kept me off the mound the entire 1997 season. Not a problem, I thought. I was an eight-time All Star, so there will be plenty of teams wanting to sign me in '98. I'd have to call the general managers myself though because my agent had dropped me by this time. No biggie, I figured. I'd played for five major league teams over nineteen years, so I knew plenty of people in baseball front offices. But I couldn't get a single GM to give me the time of day. So I contacted independent teams not affiliated with the big league franchises. Still no takers. Then I moved on to leagues in other countries: Canada, Mexico, Japan, Turkey, and a couple other places I've since forgotten. Nothing. Surprisingly enough, a 40-year-old pitcher with a recently shredded rotator cuff and a history of substance abuse problems is not a prized commodity.

It wasn't looking too good for the Fish. Then one day in February '98 the phone rings. It's from the owners of the Lincoln Giants, an indy team in the Central States League. Giants ownership had told me "we'll keep you in mind" when I had contacted them weeks earlier. I figured that response was another way of saying no. Well, they apparently got to thinking that a former big league star might be good for attendance, even if the chump couldn't throw anymore. So they tell me they're interested.

But first I have to meet their manager. Turns out, this guy is Curtis Glass, my former teammate from when I played for the Texas Rangers in the '80s. I'm thinking what a great break. My old buddy will definitely get me in the door. Sure, the Lincoln Giants were a no-frills indy operation. But they're in the United States (definitely better than Turkey in my view) and there's some good talent in their league. At least AA level, so I'd heard.

And there was one other not so insignificant detail about Lincoln, Nebraska. That was where my ex-wife and teenage daughter were living. I couldn't believe how the stars were lining up. I'd found a place to start my comeback and I'd get the opportunity to see my kid. She and I talked on the phone fairly regularly, but my ex had full custody so I usually only saw her one weekend a year. I was psyched that I'd get to spend a little more time with my daughter, and hoped she would feel the same way. On the other hand, I knew Toni would be less enthusiastic about the Fish coming to town. Things got a little ugly during the dark days at the end of our marriage. Divorce is tough on everybody, and Toni made it clear at the time that putting distance between the two of us was the best plan for all involved.

So even though I'd told the Giants I was on my way, I had to pause and think about whether this was a good idea. After adding it up, the plusses seemed to outweigh the minuses. And if everything went according to plan, I'd be in Nebraska for only a few weeks anyway. That's how long it would take to show the baseball world that Zane Fischer was back.

So I thought …

Chapter 1

Even though they said they were interested, Lincoln ownership sent me mixed messages. I talked to the VP and he made me think it's a done deal. They'll have a uniform with my old number 33 waiting for me when I arrive. But then this other guy, the Giants president, tells me if I get the manager's approval, there will be a tryout. And if things go well there, then maybe I can come to spring training. So I'm getting a big noncommittal runaround. I just hate that kind of crap. No way I would've put up with that BS back when I was on top. Especially from bush league exec wannabes like those clowns. But my stock had fallen and I didn't have many options. So in April 1998, a week after my 41st birthday, I packed a couple suitcases, got behind the wheel of my Chevy C/K, and headed for Nebraska.

I'd been living in a condo in Cincinnati. At one time, I'd owned three residences, including this sweet mansion in a ritzy Louisville suburb. But all I had left in '98 was the condo (which was up for sale) and some junk in a storage unit. By this time I was what you might describe as "cash deficient." Actually, I'd filed for bankruptcy. You probably think that all your sports heroes are multi-millionaires and set for life. Well, I suppose I should've been. But things changed in a hurry after I hired a financial manager who managed to transfer most of my finances from my bank account to his. I'd tell you more about this crook, but there's a lawsuit pending and I'm not supposed to talk about the case. And there were other leeches who did what they could to bleed me dry. Yes, I admit I squandered plenty of money myself. Blew a mountain of cash on booze, coke, women, and a bunch of expensive toys I didn't need. It happens.

The trip west from Cincy to Lincoln took forever. I usually don't mind driving, especially when I'm in my truck, but twelve butt-numbing hours is a bit much. Makes a guy really appreciate the wonders of air travel. Not long after crossing the Mississippi the CD player went on the fritz, so Garth Brooks and George Strait no longer accompanied me. Then I got a speeding ticket somewhere in Missouri. Finally, not long before midnight on a Tuesday, I reached the bustling metropolis of Lincoln. I checked into the first motel I spotted and crashed for the night.

So there I was in the capital of Nebraska. I'd watched a few Cornhusker football games on TV, but I'd never been to this place before. Omaha was as close as I'd gotten. I must admit, my first day in Lincoln did not get off to a promising start. The drive to the ballpark included two wrong turns and a lengthy delay at a train crossing just a half-block from my destination. The urge to turn around and head back to Ohio grew stronger as each railcar rattled by. Finally, I made it to Sherman Field. The parking lot was gravel, of course. After stepping around several pools of grey water, I approached a weathered white structure at the front gate that reminded me of the four-stall garage at my grandparents' farm. A sign just below the overhang of the slanted roof proclaimed in purple, "Sherman Field, Home of the Lincoln Giants." On the side of the building was a closed window under a sign that read, "Admittance." I passed through the unlocked gate in the chain link fence and surveyed the grandstand rising before me in all its bush league glory. I had to remind myself, *Eyes on the prize, Fish. Eyes on the prize.*

After a short walk down the concourse, I reached another building, a beat-up wooden shoebox with the words "Giants Clubhouse" above the door. My first thought was that someone had mislabeled an equipment shed. But this shack was in fact the team's clubhouse. I paused to summon what was left of the resolve that had pushed me to make the 750-mile drive to this place. Like ripping off a Band-Aid, I entered the building and marched forward, not allowing myself even a glimpse at the lockers on either side. I found a half-opened door at the far end of the room. That had to be the office of the manager, my old teammate Curtis.

With a quick knock, I stepped through the doorway and again thought I had the wrong place. The man behind the desk looked vaguely familiar, but appeared to have been inflated two or three times beyond the size of the person I expected to see. I prepared to excuse myself, but then spotted the nameplate on the desk: "Curtis Glass, Manager."

"You're late." The man didn't bother to remove his eyes from the paper on his desk.

"Curtis? ... Hey buddy. You know I almost didn't ..." I stopped myself, realizing that completing my statement would take the conversation in a direction I did not want to go.

"Didn't what?" He looked up with annoyance in his eyes.

I forced a smile. "You know, man. What's it been, twelve years? We've all changed since Texas, right?"

"And how have I changed?"

I couldn't believe he was being such an ass. I felt like yelling: *Really? You want to know how you've changed? Last time I saw you, you looked like Eddie Murphy. Now you look like Fat Freakin' Albert!* But being the gentleman that I was, I said, "You know, sittin' behind that desk. You look managerial now. Very impressive."

"Mm-hmmm." Curtis shook his head ever so slightly. "Well, you gonna stand there all day or take a seat?" Through the irritation, his voice carried a deep resonant tone. Not quite James Earl Jones, but close.

I lowered myself into an old wooden chair. He didn't say anything right away, so I asked, "Will we be heading over to talk to Mr. Wright and Mr. Mendleson?"

Curtis's eyes narrowed with disdain. "That's Mendenhall. You might want to remember the name of the team's vice-president.... And no, they ain't comin' in today."

Biting my tongue, I glanced around the room wondering if some of my past locker stalls were larger than this sorry excuse for an office. "Oh … so, we'll be handling the paperwork right here, ourselves. Two old Ranger pals takin' care of business, just like the old days."

Curtis glared at me. "I ain't yer pal. Not then. Not now."

"Aw c'mon, Cruiser." That was his nickname during his younger, speedier days. "We were teammates for three years at Arlington."

"Two-and-a-half years. You left us for Cincy right after the All-Star break in '85."

"They traded me."

"Some say you forced that trade. Didn't leave the Rangers any choice."

His attitude threw me off my game. I shifted in the hard wooden chair and sent my eyes over to the bulletin board on the side wall. I had to avoid saying something I'd later regret. "That was business, Curt. Things got a little messier than they should have. My agent was pushing for a big payday. You know how it gets. I would've been okay with stayin' with Texas. I liked all you guys. Ward, Heathcliffe, you."

"Mm-hmm. Liked all of us, huh?" His eyes returned to his desk. "I know you liked the white boys. Real tight with them. Rest of us, you didn't have much to do with." He scoffed. "What was that you called your crew? Oh yeah, the Texas Rebels. Even put up a Confederate flag in your locker."

"Hey, we were young. Just havin' fun, man."

"Yeah, fun. Remember when I told you that flag was offensive and politely asked you to take it down? Remember what you told me I could go and do with myself?"

"Oh, Cruiser. You know what it's like in the locker room. We all gave each other a hard time. Was I an idiot sometimes back then? Yeah, sure. But hey, I always liked you. I appreciated all those great plays you made behind me at second base. Your glove work lowered my ERA by at least a half-run, I bet."

"Hmpf." Curtis scribbled something on his paper. "So you did know there were fielders out there backing you up. The way you talked back then you were gettin' everybody out all by yourself."

I decided to ignore that jab. "And man did you have the wheels. Watching the Cruiser leg out a triple was a thing of beauty." *Never mind that you probably can't jog to first anymore without an oxygen mask.* "And now you're a skipper. That is too sweet. I'm really lookin' forward to pitching for you this season." I had to keep laying it on.

Curtis was quiet for a few seconds. "How old are you now, Fischer? Forty? Forty-one? I thought you retired a couple years ago. Pittsburgh, right?"

I nodded even though he wasn't looking at me. "Pitched there in '96. Had a little problem with the shoulder, so I missed last year. But I never called it quits. I'm ready to get back on the hill."

"Is that so?"

"Just need a chance, Cruiser. I've got something left. I can still do this." I noticed that the paper that continued to hold his attention was a crossword puzzle.

"Gonna dazzle us here in Lincoln and get back to the Show, right?"

"That's the plan."

"Hmm." Curtis fixed his charcoal eyes on me. "I'm guessing that the great Zane Fischer has never played for a team like this one. See, this is the Central States League. No big league affiliations. It's an independent league—"

"I know that."

He paused, annoyed at being interrupted. "It's a different world than what you're used to, Fischer. We play in front of hundreds of fans, not thousands. We travel in broken down busses. We change in cramped locker rooms. And don't even ask about the bread.... I just don't think you're a good fit here."

Wow, he was pissing me off. "I've played in the minors, Curt. I remember what it's like. If the mound is sixty feet, six inches from the plate, I can pitch."

"It remains to be seen whether you can still pitch or not. But even if you can, what I'm talking about is the mental side of things. That, I don't think you can handle."

"What's that supposed to mean?"

9

He held his glare on me for several beats. "You're arrogant, Fischer. This league here is beneath you. That's how you'll see it. And I will not have that attitude poisoning my team."

My temper boiled hotter, but I had to keep it in check if I wanted this opportunity. I also remembered my sponsor's advice to avoid using so much profanity. Pulling back on the reins, I chose a different set of words than what had first lined up to exit my mouth. "F—orget about who I was, okay. If I was a jerk to you in the past, I'm sorry. I'm here now ready to pitch for the Lincoln Giants. I'll be a good teammate and I'll win ballgames for you. Just give me a chance."

After lingering on me for a while, Curtis's eyes returned to his puzzle. "I don't know."

"Please, I just need a chance. Let me come to tryouts." Yeah, that's what I was reduced to—begging for a tryout in the bush leagues. Hello, rock bottom.

Curtis's expression softened slightly. "Well, it's a long shot, Fischer. The bosses here like the young guys. But I'll take it up with the honchos again, see what they got to say. Leave me your number."

Great, more runaround. I gave him my cell number and the business card from my motel. "This is the number of where I'm staying. The front desk answers, so you'll have to tell them my room number—nineteen. I wrote it on the back."

Curtis examined the card and scrunched his brow. "You're stayin' here? What the hell you doin' at a dump like this? After all the scratch you made, don't you got a couple million stashed away somewhere?"

"No ... when you end up with an idiot for an agent and a crook for an accountant, the money disappears in a hurry."

"At least you didn't blow it all on booze and hoes."

"Well, that didn't help either."

"So you're wiped out?"

"Pretty much."

My Chevy plodded up a street lined with low dirty mounds of rapidly-melting snow. Each car that passed added more slushy grime to the layers already caking the sides of my once maroon pickup. A thick blanket of clouds concealed the sun, leaving the city under a dismal shadow. The only color to speak of came from the changing traffic lights. To return to my motel, I should have continued north. I instead turned right on O Street to explore the downtown area. My truck rolled past one bar, and then another. An open parking space beckoned.

One drink won't hurt, I thought. After the day I'd had, I figured I'd earned it.

The Chevy rolled into the open spot. As my fingers gripped the key to turn off the engine, I felt my gut tighten. Old demons started to slither out from their hiding places.

Not yet. Fight it, Fish. Fight it. I'd been sober for ten months and didn't want to blow it. If I stumbled here, my comeback could be over before it even started. I took a deep breath and drove to my motel.

I couldn't find anything on TV. Finally the remote stopped on ESPN, but the documentary on European soccer failed to hold my attention. My thoughts churned as I lay on the bed reflecting on how I'd gotten to this point. With the afternoon light seeping in through the frayed olive curtains, I passed the time seeing how close I could toss a baseball to the ceiling without hitting it. The heater knocked and rattled. My nostrils inhaled the room's aroma— a cocktail of coffee, dog food, and desperation. I thought about calling my daughter, but decided I should wait until I knew what was going on with the Giants.

Finally, the phone rang. It was Curtis.

"Alright Fischer. You got a tryout. Friday. That's in two days. Get to the ballpark by eight. You gotta get registered first."

"So I'm gettin' a shot?"

"You goin' deaf in your old age? Like I said, you're getting a tryout."

"Alright. I'm glad you reconsidered about me fitting in here."

"The honchos made the call. Guess they couldn't pass up the chance to sign a living legend. Anything to grab publicity, you know."

11

I paused to breathe. "Okay … Friday. I'll be there."

"Eight o'clock, Fischer. And stay outta trouble, alright?"

"Hey Curt, thanks for going to bat for me with the owners."

"I didn't do no battin'. They'd already decided about you last week."

After hanging up, it took me a second to realize it—that jerk knew all along I was getting a tryout.

It was about a quarter till 5:00. I figured I'd call my daughter and let her know her old man was going to be in town for a while. Since it was a weekday, I was hoping she would be home from school and her mom would still be at work. Fortunately, that turned out to be the case.

"Yeah." She answered with her typical teen enthusiasm.

"Hey Buddy." Yes, that's what she went by, just like Kristy McNichol on *Family*. But that's not who my daughter was named after. Her real name is Leslie, after her mom's mother. When she was a baby, I started calling her Buddy. I was on the Rangers at the time and one of my pals was third baseman Buddy Bell. It surprised me as much as anybody that the name stuck. Her mother was not pleased.

"Hey Dad."

"Thanks for the birthday card."

"Sure."

"I got a surprise for you."

"Cool …"

"Don't you want to know what it is?"

"Cool … I mean, yeah."

In the background I could hear clicking, gunfire, and explosions. "You playing video games?"

"Yeah. Stick's over. We're playing Resident Evil." Stick was this goofball she'd known since elementary school. He wasn't her boyfriend, but they hung out a lot.

"It's warm enough today. Couldn't you guys be doing something outside, like shooting baskets or something?"

"Well, after school we threw mudballs at a few cars and busses."

"That sounds like a mature activity. You know you're in high school now?"

"We had to run away from the bus driver. That counts as exercise, right?"

"Delinquents."

"How do you know what the weather is in Lincoln? It could be raining here."

"But it's not."

"How do you know? You're in Cincy."

"Nope, not in Cincy. I'm in Lincoln. That's my surprise."

"No way. Now?"

"Yes, genius. Now. I'm at a motel by the airport."

I heard shuffling. She must have turned away from the phone, because her voice sounded distant. "Hit pause, Stick ... yes, pause it ... dumbass." She spoke into the receiver again. "What are you doing here?"

I told her about my upcoming tryout with the Giants.

"Can you still pitch?" she asked. "I mean, didn't you retire?"

"Did I ever tell you I retired?"

"No, but some guy at school read on the Internet that you retired."

"Well guess what, the Internet got it wrong. I'll be pitching in Lincoln for a while this spring. Then I'm going back to the majors."

"Where you gonna be stayin' in town?"

"Don't know yet. I'll figure something out."

"Oh."

"Hey, you think your mom is gonna be cool with this? Me livin' in Lincoln for a few weeks."

She paused. "I don't know. Yeah, maybe ... she should be alright. It's not like you'll be coming over for dinner or anything."

"Would you tell her that I'm in town?"

"Fine."

"I'd call her myself, but ..."

"I understand, Dad. I'll tell her."

"Thanks." I paused before asking, "So how's school?"

"Fine."

"Are you playing softball this spring?"

"No. Haven't played since seventh grade."

"Are you a cheerleader then?" I knew better. Buddy was not into that crowd.

"Shut up."

"Just having some fun. Can't I tease my little girl?"

"I'm not a little girl anymore."

"Well, okay then…. Got a lot of homework?"

"Yeah."

"Should you be doing it now?"

"Probably. But I don't understand any of those stupid Algebra problems, so the PlayStation seemed a bit more appealing."

"Hmmm." I probably should've said something fatherly at that point about the importance of education, learning, and whatnot. But I was never that great in math either, so I moved on. "Got a boyfriend?"

"No."

"How's that science club thing going?"

"Dunno. Quit going last semester."

"Really? Aren't you still into biology and nature and all that?"

"Yeah, I still like hanging out in the woods, but that club was weak. Bunch of lame-ohs."

"Hmpf. Still thinking about taking guitar lessons at the music store?"

"Nah. That's not my thing."

The video game resumed in the background as my hold on her attention weakened. So I wrapped up the conversation by saying we should get together soon. She said "sure" and that was it.

Like I said before, Toni had full custody of Buddy. So after the separation—she was seven at the time—I didn't see her very often. When she got older we started talking on the phone. I'd call her about once a month, or at least every other month. We'd talk for maybe a half hour. I know it wasn't much, but I was thankful we at least had that. Yes, I could've fought for more time in the custody hearings, but I didn't. My presence would've stirred up bad memories and prevented my wife from moving on. And that would've been bad for our daughter. So I agreed to what seemed best for everybody at the time.

Given that I hadn't been much of a father to Buddy (other than paying child support and giving her that great nickname), I was hoping we could spend some time together while I was in town. And I hoped the eight years that had passed was long enough so that Toni wouldn't mind me being in our daughter's life a little more. Overall, I felt optimistic that things would work out okay with me moving to Lincoln.

I sure didn't see the curveball that was coming my way.

Chapter 2

I've never had problems sleeping before a big game. Even the night before my start in the 1990 World Series, I was in bed by 11:30 and asleep a few minutes later. But before my tryout with the Lincoln Giants, I tossed and turned all night. Don't know why. It could have been the finality of it all. I'd been playing baseball since age six and for the first time faced the possibility that it could be over. Think about it, finding out you can never again do something that you love. Pitching was the only career I'd ever known and I didn't know what else I could do. As one of my former managers told me, "Aside from throwing a baseball, you have no marketable skills." So at 3:30 AM, I'm sitting in a dark motel room watching a couple idiots on TV rave about the DVD players they were hawking. When one of them would finish his spiel about the amazing product and how insanely low it was priced, the other guy would exclaim, "No! They can't do that! The price is too low! They'll go out of business!" Great entertainment, those two. I wondered if they might ever need an ex-ballplayer to help them sell those DVD machines.

On the way to Sherman Field the next morning, I stopped at QuikTrip for a 32 oz. hit of Mountain Dew. My adrenaline was already flowing, but I wanted to make sure I had plenty of caffeine to compensate for the lack of sleep. Curtis put me third on the list of pitchers trying out. While waiting my turn, I stood near the first base coach's box and rotated my arms like airplane propellers. Though I wore a long-sleeved cotton shirt under my old Reds practice jersey, the frigid air bit my skin and threatened to revive the pain in my shoulder.

"There's the Fish!"

I turned to see two men approaching from the visitors dugout. Both appeared to be a few years older than myself. They wore navy sweat suits, though neither looked like he'd been recently exercising. The chilly wind turned their clean-shaven faces pink, but had no effect on their heavily moussed hair.

"Hello Mr. Wright ... Mr. Mendenhall." I made sure I got their names right.

Both men seemed pleased at being addressed with such deference. They extended their hands, neither suspecting that I didn't know which name went with which face.

"Ready to start your big comeback?" The guy with the salt and pepper hair grinned, darkening his crow's feet.

I blew on my hands and rubbed them together. "Oh yeah, I'm ready."

"Probably a little colder than the spring trainings in Florida you're used to," the man with the blond hair commented. He reminded me of the preppies I used to beat up in junior high.

"Yeah, little bit."

"Oh, you're going to be great. It wasn't too much warmer than this when you threw that no-hitter for Toronto in April of '82. That was against the Red Sox, right?" Blondie grinned, obviously pleased with himself for recalling such details in my presence.

I glanced back at the diamond. The kid on the mound looked barely old enough for Legion Ball. "Yeah, that was a cool one. I think the batters had trouble seeing past their own breath that night."

The two men chuckled a little more than the comment warranted. "Boston had some good hitters on that team. Boggs was in the lineup, right?"

I nodded. "Boggs was there."

"That was a true masterpiece," salt and pepper hair said. "You know ... I did a little pitching myself." He drew a snorting inhale through his nose like Don Knotts on *Three's Company*. "Started at Emporia State, then had a stint with the Tigers organization."

"Is that so?" I asked, wondering where the state of Emporia was located. Out on the field a ground ball rolled through the legs of a husky guy at third base.

"Yeah, yeah. Had to hang it up after I tweaked the shoulder though. Then I transferred my pitching skills from the mound to the boardroom." He snickered in amusement with himself.

I wondered how much longer it would be before my turn to throw.

"I played too," said blondie. "Starting second baseman for Wayne State." The sentence came out as if it had been practiced in front of a mirror. "Then the Astros came calling. But like Grant here, I got bit by the injury bug. But hey, it's all good. We're more involved with baseball now than we ever were in college. You know, since we bought the Giants five years ago."

Grant nodded. "Yes, it's a lot of work running a baseball team … in addition to our responsibilities with our consulting firm. But Kevin and I love it, being the president and vice president of a professional baseball club. That's way more exciting and fulfilling than just being a player." Smugness oozed from both of their faces.

The response going through my head at that moment was, *Wow, you guys are jackasses.* Fortunately, my mouth translated that into "I appreciate the opportunity you both are giving me here today. Thank you, again." The words resisted coming out, like a big dog that must be pulled to the car before a trip to the vet.

The two executives grinned at each other. "Don't mention it, Fish. Happy to have you here. We look forward to you leading us to a championship, just like you did for Cincinnati."

"Well, I'll do my best." I watched an outfielder drop a routine fly ball.

"Ouch!" Kevin laughed at the misplay. "Won't have to worry about measuring that guy for a uniform."

"Yes," Grant said, "these open tryouts attract some real stinkers. We have to do them though. It's good for community relations." They both chuckled.

I tried to recall the last time I'd been to a baseball tryout. Must have been my freshman year of high school. I remember watching *The Partridge Family* when I got home.

"Well look at that." Kevin pointed to a man sitting in the stands behind home plate. "The press is here. The media usually doesn't cover these proceedings. Wonder what's different about this time." He winked at me.

I had not previously noticed the man in the red windbreaker scribbling something in a notepad. "That guy's a reporter?"

"Yes. That's Brian Carter. He covers the Giants for the *Lincoln Journal Star.*"

"He doesn't usually come to open tryouts though," Grant added. "Must have heard a tip that we've got a hot prospect here today."

"Speaking of which," Kevin said, "looks like your time has come."

Curtis approached. "Okay Fischer, you ready?"

I pounded my fist into my glove. "Yeah."

"Snowman is your catcher." He gestured toward the plate. "Just throw a few easy ones at first. Then work up to some harder stuff."

The catcher, mask and helmet in hand, joined me at the mound. The mop of hair atop this kid's head reminded me of the Beatles. Except for the color, which was almost completely white. Guess that solved the mystery of his nickname. "Shall we go over the signs, Mr. Fischer?" Snowman asked eagerly.

"How about I just tell you what I'm gonna throw?"

"Yeah but, you're gonna be facing some hitters later on, so I thought—"

"How old are you?"

"Uh … twenty-one." Acne craters dotted the kid's face. When not forming words, his jaw vigorously chomped on the wad of gum in his mouth.

"Great." I wedged my glove into my armpit and rubbed the baseball with both hands. "Well, Snowman, let's keep it simple.

19

One for a fastball. Two for a curve. Three for a slider. Then, four for my out pitch."

The kid scrunched his brow and counted to four with his fingers. "Your changeup?"

"Actually, I've got something else I'll be using today."

"Oh, what's that?"

"You'll find out."

Snowman's chomping slowed before he turned and trotted down the dirt path between the mound and home plate. He probably didn't top 150 pounds, even with all his catcher's gear on. *So much for pudgy catchers.* I glanced up at the stands. They were maybe ten rows deep, extending from shallow left around to shallow right. A typical ballpark roof canopied the stands and a shoebox-sized press booth nestled above the rows behind home plate. If you counted the standing-room-only areas beyond the outfield foul line fences, maybe three thousand could squeeze in to watch a game. Riverfront Stadium, it wasn't.

"Alright, Southpaw," Curtis bellowed, "let's see what you got." He leaned over the crouching catcher like an umpire ready to call balls and strikes. Wright and Mendenhall lingered near the visitors dugout.

I kicked the dirt in front of the rubber and nodded at the catcher's single finger. Not so long ago that sign meant that a laser beam in the mid-90s would follow. But I knew I could never again approach that kind of velocity. Not with all the cutting and rearranging those doctors did in my shoulder. *But there are other ways to get hitters out.*

My hands swung over my head as my left foot pivoted and my right knee rose. Rotating my hips, I drove off the rubber and let the ball fly. It zipped over the center of the plate. Man, that felt good. Until …

"Sixty-six." The words came from a bespectacled man with a radar gun in the front row of the stands. I hadn't noticed him there before. He reminded me of my least favorite math teacher.

I glared at him. *Unbelievable. This geek thinks he's going to time my warm up pitches.*

"Don't pay him no mind," Curtis said. "That's Lawrence Lutgens, my assistant coach. Forget about the gun and keep throwing. Easy at first."

I tossed in a few more batting practice-speed strikes. No pain flared in my left arm or shoulder—a welcome change from two years ago. After about a dozen easy ones, Curtis told me to amp it up. "Gimme a little heat now, but don't go full bore yet."

I dealt a couple pitches with a little more cheese. The arm still felt good, so I let one fly with all I had. An old pain flickered in my shoulder. "Eighty-two," announced Lawrence Lutgens.

I felt like firing the next one at his face. It was bad enough that my once-feared heater had lost its heat. It was worse that the Chess Club president was the one bringing me the news. Resisting the urge to try to knock Larry the Geek's glasses off, I delivered a few more three-quarter-speed fastballs.

"Alright," Curtis said, "let's see the hook."

I adjusted my grip and unleashed a curve ball that didn't get the memo that it was supposed to change directions at some point during its flight. The following succession of so-called breaking balls similarly did not have much break. I heard muttering from the wannabe players who had gathered behind me to watch the exhibition. One of them bragged that he now had better stuff than the no-longer-great Zane Fischer. I glanced over at Wright and Mendenhall, who muttered to each other with grim faces.

Focus Fish. They haven't seen it yet.

"Okay, gimme some sliders now," Curtis said. He sounded tired.

"Actually, I've got a new pitch I'm going to be using."

Curtis cocked his head. "The old dog's got a new trick, huh? Alright, let's see it."

I rolled the baseball around in my hand. My thumb found the lace. The tips of my index and middle fingers dug nails first into the cowhide just below the red-stitched horseshoe. It was a grip I'd practiced a thousand times for a thousand practice throws over the past several months. It still felt strange holding a baseball this way. I mumbled a familiar mantra. "Don't spin. Don't spin. Don't spin."

Following the wind up, my hand set the baseball in flight. It followed a lazy arc toward Snowman. But as it neared the plate, the ball shuddered like the steering wheel in a car with bad alignment. Then it dropped with a late swerve to elude the catcher's mitt. Not until it bounced against the backstop did the ball finally roll to a stop.

The players on the field chuckled. "Boo-yeah," one of them exclaimed.

Curtis placed his hands on his hips and shook his head. "So you think you're Phil Niekro now?"

I nodded while waiting for the return throw from the catcher. Zane Fischer's new pitch, the knuckleball, had been unveiled. For nearly two decades, I'd made my living with the four standards: fastball, curve, slider, and changeup. Occasionally I fooled around with other stuff, like a sinker and a cutter. But the big four remained my bread and butter. Charlie Hough taught me how to throw a knuckleball in the mid-1980s when we were teammates on the Rangers. After a few dozen tosses with him, I could make the ball dance. Not as much as Charlie of course, but I had a decent knuckler. Never used it in a game though. No need to mess around, since my other pitches were getting the job done. That was then, before I had my shoulder carved up like a Thanksgiving turkey. Now I was 41 and the knuckleball seemed like the perfect weapon for a guy who couldn't throw so hard anymore. But it's a devilish pitch that often turns on its master. Could I control it? Can anybody?

I threw about fifteen knucklers to Snowman. They had some wicked movement, if I do say so myself. The poor kid caught maybe a third of them. He looked like he was trying to use a leather cereal bowl to trap a housefly. Curtis didn't have much of an expression. Neither did Larry the Geek, his radar gun lying in the seat next to him.

Curtis called in three of the players standing in the field. "Okay, let's see what Niekro can do against some hitters." He pointed at one of the kids. "Sid, yer up."

Snowman, fatigued from his frequent trips to the backstop, put down one finger. I took pity on him and fired in a straight one. Though it came in shoulder high, the batter took a cut and fouled it back to the screen. The catcher next called for a curve ball. I knew that wasn't the pitch that would get me back to the majors, so I shook him off. Snowman reluctantly dropped four fingers. I nodded and sent a big white butterfly dancing toward the plate. The hitter stepped forward with a mighty swing, but his bat came nowhere near making contact. Neither did Snowman's glove. My next knuckler brought another swing and a miss.

I was so pumped after getting the strikeout that I didn't focus on the second batter. He lined my first pitch, a lazy fastball, foul into the bullpen down the left field line. I followed with a weak curve that he popped into the stands behind the visitors dugout. The third pitch, a knuckler, died ten feet in front of the plate for ball one. The kid then waved in vain at a fluttering moth that dropped just before crossing the plate. Good stuff.

The third hitter followed with three straight whiffs. Yeah, I was all sorts of jazzed after that. The players on the field shouted and clapped. So did Wright and Mendenhall. The three strikeout victims approached with baseballs for me to sign.

"Are you kidding me," Curtis snapped at them. "You guys are supposed to be competitors. Would you ask a pitcher on another team for an autograph? Get on outta here. Y'all run to the centerfield fence and back. The rest of you join them." He gestured at the other Giant hopefuls, setting the herd in motion.

"Little hard on them?" I asked. "They've never faced major league pitching before."

"And they still haven't," Curtis retorted.

"Oh, c'mon now. Three strikeouts against the first batters I've faced in almost two years. You gotta admit, that ain't bad."

"Don't book your flight back to Cincinnati just yet. Those guys you faced are no better than your average high schooler. And they were eager. Just dying to get a hit off the great Zane Fischer, so they have something to tell their folks when they get home tonight."

"Yeah, okay. But those knucklers were really moving."

"Oh, they was movin' all over the place. You threw ten pitches. Maybe two of 'em would've been called a strike. That's it."

"Hey ..."

"Hey nothin'. The umps in this league ain't gonna widen the plate, even for you. If you'd have been facing three real hitters, you'd have walked the bases loaded."

I watched the kids smack the centerfield wall and start their trek back to the infield. "So what are you saying? I didn't make the team?"

"Ain't my call." He nodded at Wright and Mendenhall, both of them still beaming. "Don't worry, Fischer. I'm sure we'll be seeing plenty of each other this season."

After the tryout, Snowman talked me into going out with him and a couple other guys to a place called JK's. My condition for going was that he stop calling me Mr. Fischer. As if I didn't feel old enough already. Snowman agreed and told me the joint was located in the Haymarket District. I didn't know where that was so I just followed him there. Once inside, I felt at home. The establishment was kind of a cross between a modern sports bar and an old speakeasy. Not too much light. A few TVs up high. Some old movie posters on the brick walls. There were a few framed pictures of sports heroes too, including an autographed portrait of Joe Namath. None of yours truly though. We'd have to work on that.

The three guys with me looked young, and they sounded young too. I wondered what I was doing there, especially when they started ogling some girls at the bar who didn't look much older than my daughter. I did what I could to direct the conversation back to baseball. Turned out that Snowman was the starting catcher for the Giants. How he'd ever survive a collision at the plate, I did not know. The other kids were two of my strikeout victims. They'd told me their names, but I couldn't remember either of them.

"Saw the big shots talking to you before we left," said the guy with the shaved head. "They give ya anything?"

I wanted to tell him to lose the earring—it made him look like a punk. "Yeah, they said some things."

"Well, you make the team?"

"They told me to show up at spring training."

"Like they were ever going to cut Zane Fischer," the other nameless kid said. His fuzzy red facial hair resembled something on a map. A continent maybe. "No way that was ever going to happen."

Snowman spoke. "You guys find out anything?"

They both shook their heads. "Nah," said the shaved head. "Just have to wait for the phone to ring."

"I don't think the manager likes me much," said mapbeard.

I snorted. "Eh, that's an act. Curtis is just playing the tough guy manager. He wants to keep you on edge so you'll respect him."

"Is it true you guys were teammates in the bigs?" Snowman asked.

I imagined taking a pair of electric clippers and shaving off all of his Edgar Winter hair. The thought made me smile. "Yeah."

"So what's it like in the Show?" asked one of the nameless guys. "I mean, how is it different from here?"

I rubbed my chin. The bottom felt like sandpaper. "You remember your first year of Little League when you were a kid?"

All three nodded.

"Compare that to what it was like playing ball your senior year of high school. The difference between here and the majors is something like that."

The trio furrowed their brows in contemplation as if I had just asked them to analyze the themes of a Faulkner novel. Yes, I know who William Faulkner is. In high school I'd even read *The Sound and the Fury*. Well, part of it anyway. Actually it was probably just the Cliff's Notes version. But the point is, I've heard of William Faulkner. Anyway, while the kids were pondering my wisdom, a waitress came over and set a pitcher of beer on the table. She placed a Roy Rogers in front of me.

The young guys looked inquisitive, but none of them verbalized a comment about my beverage of choice. That suited me just fine. The less conversation about me, the better. A period of drinking and bantering followed—mostly about girls and bands I'd never heard of. Midway through the second pitcher, the shaved

25

head with the earring turned to me. "So man, what are you doing here?"

I just looked at him, trying to use my Jedi mind control powers to get him to shut his trap. Didn't work.

"I mean ... you've done it all. You've made the millions, won hundreds of games, got the ring. Why try to keep going after blowing out your shoulder? Why not just call it a career?"

"And miss the chance to strike out guys like you?"

"I'm just sayin' ..." The kid flung his arms out. "Look at all the great athletes who hung on too long. Mantle. Namath. Even Muhammad Ali. Man, it's just painful watching once-great athletes embarrass themselves." He stifled a belch. "Not sayin' that's you. But what's the point of trying to come back?"

I swallowed a gulp of soda and leaned back in my chair. "I got my reasons."

Mapbeard swatted the guy's arm. "Dude, the Fish has 290 wins. Just needs ten more and he's a lock for the Hall of Fame."

I be lying if I said winning 300 hadn't crossed my mind. It's an important number for pitchers. Not many get there. Go ahead and check the list of names. I have them memorized.

"Ahhh, so that's it," the shaved head slurred.

"You guys are both off-base," Snowman said. "Zane Fischer has still got it. He can still get batters out, like you both found out today. A bunch of pitchers kept it going into their forties. Look at Ryan. Look at Niekro. Hough too. Fish is gonna get it done just like them."

"I hope you're right," the shaved head said. "I'd just hate to see another great one tarnish his reputation."

My eyes roamed the room until fixing on a picture of Willie Mays in a Mets uniform. I hoped it wasn't an omen.

That evening I picked up Buddy to go out for pizza. It was strange driving up to her house, a place I'd never seen before. And yeah it was strange watching the windows wondering if Toni would be peeking through the curtains. She didn't, but I knew she was inside.

Buddy burst out the front door and raced forward to throw her arms around her beloved father. Alright, that didn't actually happen. She shuffled down the driveway as if she were playing charades and trying to act out the word "lackadaisical." And to complete the effect, she wore a ratty red-hooded sweatshirt with a faded University of Indiana logo on the front.

It had been about five months since I'd last seen my daughter. Seemed like she'd grown a little taller. Still skinny though. Needed some meat on those bones. Her hair was short, like a bob those flapper girls wore in the '20s. It looked cute, though I always liked her hair long with a ponytail. At least it was still the light brunette she'd been born with, and not streaked with green or pink or whatever the latest trend was among teenage girls.

Buddy directed me to a place south of downtown called daVinci's. Good pizza. My girl may have been a buck-ten soaking wet, but she did alright keeping up with me. We had no problem knocking down a large pie between the two of us. While we ate, she asked about my tryout. I said it went well. Then I described the knuckleball and how one goes about throwing it. She pretended to listen, even though I knew she didn't have much interest in baseball. It bummed me out when she quit playing softball. I liked to think that if I'd been around, she would've stuck with it. Because she was good. No surprise there. You gotta figure she had some of my ballplayer genes. Toni was athletic too—a gymnast and a cheerleader in high school. But there's no use moaning about the athletic potential Buddy was wasting. If she didn't like sports anymore, there wasn't much I could do about it.

I asked her how school was going. She said she had to do a report on this Harry Potter book, but she hadn't started it yet because all her friends picked different titles from the list their teacher had given them. Buddy found it easier to read a book if she had someone to discuss it with. She also told me she was thinking about trying out for a play at school. Gesturing at her hair, I asked if it was "The Great Gatsby." She said I wasn't as funny as I thought I was. She then pointed out my crow's feet and the grey flecks in my otherwise dark brown hair.

"Hey," I said, "I still resemble Paul Newman, right? And that hint of grey up top just makes me look more distinguished, like Bill Clinton. I bet Hillary still thinks he's foxy." My daughter rolled her eyes.

After we'd finished discussing my movie star good looks and the president's salty hair, I asked Buddy about her mother. "Is she okay with me being in town?"

"Yeah, she's cool with it."

"What did she say when you told her?"

She shrugged and looked away. "Nothing."

"Nothing?"

Buddy tugged at one of her ears before running her hand through her short locks. "She said she didn't think you were still pitching."

"A lot of people seem to have made that assumption. She's not mad?" I examined the handful of tiny freckles dotting her cheeks—cheeks that were round like a doll's. I used to call her dollface when she was little.

"Don't think so." She shrugged again. "Said you gotta do what you gotta do."

"Oh … well, good. I'm glad this isn't a problem." I waited for a response that didn't come. "Thanks for telling her."

"No biggie."

"She okay with us meeting up tonight?"

"Yeah. I told her we might be hanging out a little more now that you're in town. And if she don't like it, tough. I'm old enough to make my own decisions. What's she gonna do about it?"

That struck a nerve—I did not want to cause any trouble between my daughter and Toni. "Watch the attitude, Buddy. She's your mother. You listen to her. Don't give her any grief."

She seemed startled at the sharpness of my tone. "Fine."

Neither of us spoke for a while as we finished off our pizza. "What's she doing tonight?" I finally asked.

"Mom?"

"No, Hillary Clinton. Who do you think?"

"I was just asking." Her blue eyes narrowed into a glare. "Don't bite my head off."

"Well, who were we just talking about?"

"She's got a date."

I had just taken a drink and some of the soda streamed into my lungs. Man, that hurts. After I'd finished hacking, I coughed out, "Your mother has a date?"

"No, Dad, Hillary Clinton. Don't tell Bill, alright?"

Smartass. Wonder where she got that from. "Who's your mom dating?"

"Cole Hagler." The name came out with a sneer.

"Who's that?"

"Some loser she met at the music store where she works. He started taking guitar lessons there last fall. He is so lame."

"So they started dating last fall?"

"Yeah, but she broke it off in December. Thank God."

"You don't like him?"

"Not really."

"Why?"

"I dunno. I just don't." Buddy's expression shriveled like she'd eaten a lemon. It reminded me of when she was a baby and was about to get fussy.

"So she started up with Cole again this spring?"

"Actually, tonight's their first date since they broke up."

"Oh." As I pondered that bit of information, my eyes roamed the murals covering the restaurant walls and ceiling. Clouds, blue sky, and scenes from Italy. Something like that. I wasn't exactly focusing on the details.

When we were about to leave, she reached into the pocket of her sweatshirt. "Hey I brought something for you." She slid a small envelope across the table to me. I opened it and pulled out a wallet-sized photo. It was of Toni and Buddy. Mom was sitting and daughter was standing behind her, like how a professional photographer sets up a pose. "We got these taken at Sears last October," she said.

My daughter actually looked like a sweet little lady in her flower-print dress. Her hair was still long at the time. And Toni, seeing her in that photo hit like a punch in the stomach. A wave built up inside me. I told Buddy I had to go to the can.

You may think my reaction to seeing my ex was strange, given that we hadn't been a part of each other's lives for so many years. Some people who get divorced end up hating each other. Well, that wasn't me. I was married to this woman for fourteen years and we'd dated for two years before that. Toni and I were high school sweethearts in Terre Haute. It's like we were meant to be together. I certainly believe we were. That opinion didn't change after the divorce.

Some of you are probably now wondering about all the women who were linked to me in past years. Yes, the rumors about me and that Fly Girl from *In Living Color* were true. And I did date a *Baywatch* actress thirteen years younger than me. No it wasn't Pamela or Yasmine. This girl was an extra who appeared in only three or four episodes. The other women I got with weren't even that famous. I can't recall most of their names and none of the "relationships" lasted more than a few weeks. Okay fine, most of them were one night stands. But here's the important point: I wasn't with any of those ladies before Toni and I separated. I never strayed while we were together. None of the womanizing (as the press liked to call it) happened until after my wife left me.

So yes, Toni still meant something to me. That shouldn't come as such a surprise. The bad stuff at the end of our marriage didn't erase all the good times we'd shared before. We were happy together for a long time. I never forgot that, and I hoped she didn't either. When my daughter gave me that picture, it had been several years since I'd seen Toni. And she had never looked more beautiful.

Chapter 3

A couple weeks after my tryout, the Lincoln Giants opened spring training. Don't confuse that with Major League spring training. You know, hanging out in sunny Florida or Arizona in February and March. I did that for twenty years, and I have to say both places were pretty wonderful. Well, the Giants held their spring training in Lincoln, Nebraska, in late April and early May. The weather wasn't so bad, but it sure wasn't the Grapefruit League. No matter. I was there to get ready for baseball. And that's what I did. Drills, calisthenics, running, throwing, the whole nine yards. My teammates seemed alright, though young. Some of them played it cool and didn't say much to me. Others showed no such restraint, gushing about how great I was and asking for autographed baseballs for their brothers, fathers, nephews, uncles, etc.

Two weeks into training the Giants scheduled an exhibition game at Sherman Field against one of the other teams in the league—the Topeka Titans. Curtis told me I'd be starting. Awesome, I thought, now I've got the chance to mow down some bushers. Get an early start on showing what I can do.

The game also gave me the opportunity to don my Giants game uniform for the first time. It was white with my name and a purple 33 on the back; the front featured a cursive purple L. It also had purple pinstripes. I'd worn a lot different uniforms in my career, but never purple pinstripes.

Things were rolling along okay until the third inning when I walked a couple guys with one out. Ran the count full on the next batter, so I had to throw a strike or the bases would be loaded.

Snowman wanted a fastball. I wanted the knuckler. To get back to the majors, I had to be able to rely on that pitch in tight situations. Plus, the hitter would be expecting my not-so-hot heater. So I shook off the sign and delivered a knuckleball. Ball four.

It was actually a pretty good pitch, barely an inch off the plate. The man in blue wasn't giving me anything though. Maybe he wanted to show up the big leaguer. Or maybe he'd never called a game pitched by a knuckleballer. Either way, I didn't get any of the borderline calls. Curtis waddled out of the dugout. While waiting for him to arrive, the team mascot caught my eye. It was supposed to be Abraham Lincoln on stilts, but big Abe's mask didn't look quite right to me. I made a mental note to check a five-dollar bill after the game.

Glass finally arrived. Snowman too. "How ya doin?" Curtis asked.

"Peachy. Just peachy. That damn ump."

"Don't worry about him. Just throw your stuff. Nothin' hurt."

"Yeah, right." I glared at the umpire standing behind home plate with his hands on his hips.

"Just an exhibition game, Fish. A glorified practice, nothin' more."

I spat at the ground and kicked dirt over where it landed. "I'm here to win, okay."

"Is that really what's eatin' you?"

"The sacks are jammed with one out and I can't get any calls. Isn't that enough?"

Curtis's face wrinkled into a contemplative expression. "Hmmm … could be worse."

"Yeah, the next guy could hit a grand slam."

He chuckled and gazed at the half-empty stands. "You know I went to the doctor yesterday."

"Huh?" I glanced at Snowman who returned my confused look.

"Yep," Curtis continued. "He said I got diabetes."

It took me a few seconds to process that. "I'm sorry, man."

"Yeah, so in the big picture, Fish …" He waved his arm at the runner on third. "This here ain't much of a problem."

The umpire approached. "Are we done here? I got *Seinfeld* taping on the VCR. I'd kinda like to get it watched before midnight."

Curtis nodded at him and looked at me again. "Just hit the mitt." He clapped my arm. "You'll be alright."

I'd experienced my share of depressing mound conferences, but never anything like that. As Curtis ambled back to the dugout, I felt bad for him. Then the crowd suddenly erupted. Over by the on-deck circle, stilted Lincoln had tripped and planted his face into the ground. I didn't think things like that ever happened to those circus guys. Someone from the grounds crew and a ball boy helped him up and off the field. The fans' laughter seemed a bit mean-spirited, but at least it distracted them from the potential disaster I faced.

The batter dug in from the left side. He watched a knuckler that caught the inside corner. I then snuck a slider past him for strike two. With an 0-2 count, I tried to waste a fastball high. But it didn't get high enough and the batter lofted it to left field for a sac fly. The next guy drilled a spinning knuckleball to the wall to drive in two more. The Giants trailed 3-1 when a groundout finally ended the inning.

Snowman sat next to me on the bench chomping his gum and spouting the usual clichéd encouragements. I know he meant well, but I just wanted him to shut up. All I needed was the knuckler to get over the plate. That's it. And in the fourth inning that's what happened. Topeka went down 1-2-3. I found the plate again in the fifth. But the knuckleball stopped moving that inning—it just floated up there in a lazy arc. Two solid doubles and a single plated two more for the visitors. Curtis came out to get the ball and I trudged to the dugout amid a smattering of indifferent cheers.

When I reached the dugout, I glared at Larry the Geek. He didn't even bother looking at me. I felt like going over and knocking off his math teacher glasses. Just because. Yeah, I knew my problems weren't his fault, but he still bugged me. Especially when things weren't going my way. Exiting the dugout, I trudged across the concourse to the clubhouse. A few young fans asked for my autograph, but I brushed them off. "Sorry boys, not tonight."

Inside the empty locker room, I flung my glove and cap to the floor. Our trainer Jerry wasn't there yet to ice my arm because he was still in the dugout tending to another player. I could've gotten the ice myself, but didn't feel like it. So I just sat on a stool, head in hands, contemplating my recent disaster. Replays of all my pitches flashed before me. If blue had given me a couple calls, it might not have been so bad. That strikeout I should've had in the third would've saved at least one run, maybe all three. But the stupid *Seinfeld*-loving ump kept squeezing me. No matter who was calling balls and strikes though, I needed to get a tighter rein on my knucklers.

I heard something, a cough maybe, from the shower room. I went in there and found a guy sitting crosslegged in his underwear on the tile floor. He had long straw-colored hair—kinda reminded me of Jeff Spicoli from *Fast Times at Ridgemont High*. The guy was just sitting there, not a care in the world, surrounded by a cloud of smoke—a product of the joint he held between his thumb and index finger. A strange sight, though not the first time I'd walked in on something like that in a clubhouse shower room.

"Woah, man." Spicoli stuffed his doobie into the floor drain and fanned the air around his head. Like that was going to help. What a criminal mastermind, this guy. He looked up at me, his half-closed eyes widening. "I didn't hear you come in. Crap. You alone?"

"Who are you?" I asked as the illegal aroma filled my nostrils. It had been a while since I'd had that pleasure. I'm not gonna lie, I kinda missed it.

"Um, I'm the mascot. You know, Big Abe, the Lincoln Giant." He scrambled to his feet and waved the air again. "My name's Bruce. Oh hey, you're that old dude pitcher we got ... I mean, not old ... um, a veteran. That's it. You know what I mean."

"Quite a spill you took out there."

"I know, right? Those stilts are tricky. Especially with that stupid mask. Can't see where I'm going with that thing on."

"You okay?"

"Yeah, I'm good." He examined his arms. "Couple bruises, nothing more. They told me to take the rest of the night off though. So I thought I'd light up a quick one before anybody came back here. Hey, you're cool, right?"

"Don't worry about it." I reflected on my early days with Toronto when a clubbie caught me doing the same thing. Fortunately, he didn't rat me out. He actually joined me for a couple tokes. "You oughta be more careful though. If Curtis catches you in here, you're finished."

"Right." He nodded. "Hey, my friends call me Weed." He extended a hand.

"You don't say." I didn't feel like shaking hands.

"Yeah, I used to pitch here. Not that long ago. Four seasons, relief mostly. I was even the Giants closer for a while." He stood up a little straighter. "Then I tweaked the ol' soup bone and had to give it up. Stan, he hired me for his grounds crew. But that wasn't really my thing. So when our mascot quit at the end of last year, I applied for the job. And whaddyaknow, now I'm Big Abe." His grin fading, he glanced down at his bare feet. "Wish I didn't have to do it on stilts."

"Alright, Bruce." I turned to go back to my locker.

"Call me, Weed. And hey, if you ever need hooked up, let me know."

I wished he hadn't said that. I'd been clean for a long time and knew I had to stay that way if this comeback was going to succeed. Being around a supplier would make it that much easier to fall off the wagon. With my history, I didn't need the extra temptation.

The fragrance of Weed's joint hung in the air before, during, and after my shower. The smell took me back to the good old days … and some not so good old days. I finished toweling off and returned to the locker area just as Snowman entered. "Game over already?" I asked.

"Nah. Just starting the eighth. Glass took me out. He wanted to give Cy some work behind the plate."

I nodded and started putting on my street clothes.

"You want to head over to JK's after the game?" Snowman asked. "A bunch of us are going."

I shook my head. "I don't want to be around a lot of people now." That especially included the drunken fans who would sometimes approach my table.

"Cool." Snowman shuffled at his locker. "Hey, you know what? Dirk and me are goin' over to Gale's later to play some cards. We could skip JK's and just head there after the game. Would you be up for that?" A pink bubble inflated from his mouth, before he sucked it back in.

"Don't think so."

"Aw man, he's got a sweet place. You gotta see it. New appliances. A big-ass TV. His parents are paying for it. They're loaded. And Gale makes these great nachos. You gotta try 'em." Snowman reminded me of a little boy asking his dad if he could go to the fair.

I tossed my uniform in the dirty clothes bin. "So who all's gonna be there?"

"Me, Gale, Dirk, and you, if you go."

Playing cards did sound better than sitting alone sulking in my motel room. "Alright, give me the address."

Gale McGrady's apartment on the other side of town wasn't quite the Park Avenue suite that Snowman had made it out to be. It wasn't bad though, given that players in this league averaged $6,500 a year. Most guys on the Giants lived with host families. The players who tried to live on their own usually had to triple up in some hole-in-the-wall apartment or stay at the Y. But Gale was different. Like Snowman said, his folks were rich. Old money back east. Their cash had bought Gale plenty of opportunities in life, as well as a generous helping of elitist confidence. After graduating with honors from Yale, he put off his inevitable lucrative business career to try his hand at the National Pastime, the sport he loved. He called himself "Gale Force," because in his head he could throw 98 miles per hour. In actuality, his pitches came in like a gentle breeze. As such, he bounced around the low minors before the Astros cut him last season. So, to stay in baseball, he had little choice but to sign with Lincoln, where he found himself in the bullpen. How do I know this? The man himself told me. More than once. Because if there's one thing "Gale Force" McGrady liked to do, it was talk about himself.

The four of us settled around an oak table to play some five-card draw. Gale dealt the first hand. Compared to the rest of us ruffians, he looked smug and aristocratic. Perfect posture, not a hair out of place. He wasn't wearing a smoking jacket and an ascot, but he might as well have been.

At the opposite end of the spectrum was Dirk Davis, a barrel-chested drinker who continually established new definitions for the word uncouth. Don't get me wrong, I liked Dirk … most of the time. At 33, he was the oldest player on the team (aside from yours truly). And he had played in the majors—three years with San Diego and part of another season with Florida. Big Dirk could hit for power, but oh man was he wretched with the glove. When his average dipped into the low .200s, he got shipped to the minors, where his struggles continued. Last winter he signed with the Giants, hoping to tear it up in Lincoln and attract the attention of an American League team in need of a designated hitter.

It didn't take long before the conversation shifted to my outing at Sherman Field. Dirk was the first to pipe up. "Nice of you to take it easy on those bums tonight, Fish,"

"Yeah." I examined my cards.

"Wish you would've thrown me one of those lazy knucklers back when we squared off," he continued.

"You batted against Fish in the majors?" Snowman asked.

"Yep, we had a few battles in the Show," Dirk said, raising one of his hefty buttocks to squeeze out a crisp fart. "I didn't get many good swings against this dawg, let me tell ya." He clapped my shoulder.

"Who'd you play for?" Snowman asked.

"Padres. Back then Fish was in his hey-day with the Reds. Struck me out five times in twelve at-bats. Right Fish?"

"Something like that." Actually it was eight times in twelve at-bats.

"But he had the advantage with it being a lefty-lefty matchup." Dirk punctuated his statement with a deep open-mouthed belch. "I gotta give it to this old man here, he had good stuff. And he could command it too. Wasn't easy picking up that nasty bender he'd throw."

"Sounds like the curve I unsheathed in the eighth tonight," Gale interjected with a patrician tone. "The poor devil at the plate hadn't a chance."

"Yeah, but I got ole Fish one time." Dirk's brightening grin nearly matched the overhead light gleaming off his bald head. "Remember in May of '92? I lined one of your sliders into left-center to drive in the tying run. We ended up winning that game, you know."

I remembered. "The left-center part is right, but it was more like a bloop that dropped between two outfielders and the shortstop."

"Call it whatever you want." He grimaced before unleashing another barrage of flatulence. "It was still a clutch RBI off the Fish."

"My word, Davis," Gale gasped, frantically waving the air in front of his face. "You reek worse than the interior of a horse's arse. Do you have any manners at all?"

"Eh lighten up, McGrady," Dirk replied. "Sorry if I don't meet the etiquette standards of your old charm school. I'm just relaxin' here. Ain't that okay?"

"It's one thing to relax." Gale disappeared into another room and returned with an oscillating fan, which he sat on the floor near the table. "It's quite another to empty your bowels in the middle of my dining room."

As the breeze from the fan dispersed the lingering foulness, I decided to change the subject. "So what's the deal with our mascot?"

"Oh, you've met Weed," Snowman said.

"The surfer dude who wears the Giant Abe costume?" Dirk asked.

Snowman smirked. "Yeah, but I don't think he surfs much."

"He told me he used to pitch for the Giants," I said. "Hard to imagine."

"I know he pitched," Snowman said. "Don't know if he was any good. The few times we talked, he spent more time bragging about his stash than baseball."

"Yeah. When I found him tonight stoned in his skivvies, he said he could hook me up."

Gale's face soured. "Our team mascot smokes marijuana in the clubhouse? In his underwear no less? You should tell Glass and have him banished."

"I don't know about that, McGrady," I said. "I was thinking I should try a hit of his grass before my next start. It's not like I can pitch any worse."

Dirk grinned as he scooped up the chips from the hand he'd just won. "You may have a point there, Fish. I heard there was a guy in the '70s who pitched a no-hitter while jacked up on LSD."

"Yeah, Doc Ellis." I chuckled while reviewing my cards. "Forgot about him. And here I've been trying so hard to stay away from all that stuff. That'll be one good thing about ending my failed comeback. I can start indulging again."

Snowman stopped chomping his gum and looked at me like his dog had just run away. "You can't give up, Fish. Those knucklers were really dancing tonight. Some of those curves were sharp too. You've got great stuff. I know you can—"

My raised hand cut him off. "Easy, Snow. I'm not serious about quitting. Not yet, anyway."

We were quiet for a while, before Gale cleared his throat. "Well Fischer, I'd be happy to let you observe my mound repertoire. Perhaps that would prove beneficial in helping you regain your proficiency. I know you didn't get to witness it firsthand tonight, but my arsenal proved quite formidable during the inning I pitched. Had a wicked break on my curve and the old fastball was really humming. They don't call me Gale Force for nothing."

I wasn't quite sure how to respond to that one, so I just stared at him. We all did. Then Dirk burst out laughing. "Seriously

McGrady? You think anybody else on this planet calls you Gale Force?" His head grew redder as the guffaws came harder. "And you think you're going to give pointers to a Hall of Famer? How many innings have you pitched in the majors?" Dirk laughed so hard he nearly fell out of his chair. "You do realize you're a dime-a-dozen middle reliever for an indy baseball team, right?"

"Shut up," Gale snapped, his face hardening with humiliation. "Just shut up. I was merely offering to help a teammate. Which is more than I can say for you, you corpulent oaf."

It took a while for Dirk to regain his composure, during which time Gale went to the kitchen to pour himself a brandy. Oddly enough, he didn't offer a drink to any of us. Finally we resumed playing cards. Snowman started chatting about nothing of significance. It wasn't significant to me anyway, because I was losing. After about an hour, I'd had enough.

"Alright gentlemen, I'm through." I pushed my chair back.

"C'mon Fish," Dirk said. "The night is young."

"I'm cleaned out. Thanks for helping with that, by the way."

"The house can float you some credit, right McGrady? Play a couple more hands, huh?"

What I said next just flowed out before I could stop it, the product of a losing night. "I don't want credit. Wouldn't be able to pay it back anyway. Not with what I'm making now. I can't even afford that crappy motel I'm stayin' at. Another week or two and I'll be out on the street. Unless I sell my truck, then maybe I can stay in that rat's nest a little longer. Either way, I don't need to fall any deeper in the hole tonight, okay?"

The buzzing of the fan was the only sound that followed my outburst. Snowman examined the table and Gale fiddled with his chips, while Dirk's pudgy face deflated like a balloon. Finally, he spoke. "Geez Fish, I didn't know. I figured you were set up okay. You know, after all them years in the bigs."

"Well, it's gone. All of it."

"That sucks, man." After a few moments of silence, he hammered the table with his fist. "I've got it!" The big man's face glowed like he'd just won the lottery. "You can stay here with McGrady."

Gale's eyes widened to the size of silver dollars. "What?"

"Sure. You got plenty of room here." Dirk stood and gestured down the hallway. "You've got two bedrooms there and then there's that thing up there." He pointed up the stairs to a loft that overlooked the living room.

"Yes, but uh ..." Gale stammered a bit. "All those spaces are occupied. There simply isn't room for a boarder here."

Dirk lumbered halfway up the stairs. "You ain't got much up here. Plenty of room for the Fish."

"My books are up there. And my golf clubs. And my cello. That's where I practice."

Dirk snorted. "Really, McGrady? A cello? Books? You think you're on a cricket team or something? You are a BASEBALL player, my friend. We don't read books and we don't play candy-ass instruments. Your hobbies should be drinking beer, chasing skirts, playing cards, drinking beer, pissing off your manager, and uh ... drinking beer. That's it."

Gale rose from the table. "I, uh ..."

"I'm not moving here," I said. "I can solve my own problems."

"Where you gonna stay then?" Dirk demanded.

"Don't worry about it."

"I'd bring you over to my place, but there's three of us living there already. Barely enough room for the cockroaches as it is. What's your situation, Snow?"

"I'm living with a retired professor. Cy and me share a room upstairs in his old house. I can ask Dr. Hornsby if he'd mind another ..."

"Don't worry about it." I stood. "It's not your problem where I stay. I'll handle it." My voice was firm, but I really didn't know what I was going to do for living arrangements when my last few dollars evaporated.

Dirk leaned over the stair railing with his palms out. "C'mon Gale. Fischer is your teammate. And just think, you could be a part of his big comeback story. When he's back in the majors, your name will be all over the press as the man who helped him get there."

Wheels turned inside Gale's head. I may have been called the Fish, but McGrady was the one who'd just been hooked. It took only a few more lines from Dirk to reel him in. I protested a little more about how this wasn't necessary. And honestly, I wasn't all that psyched about moving in with Gale Force. But sacking out next to a cello sounded a heck of a lot better than sleeping in my pickup, so I agreed too.

The next morning I packed up my belongings—all two bags worth—and threw them in the back of my truck. Then I went to the motel office to settle up. Dirk and Snowman gave me back what I'd lost the night before, so I had just enough to cover my bill. Good thing I didn't order any pay-per-view movies. Can't say the thought didn't cross my mind.

There was a family of four ahead of me at the front desk, so I had time to grab the Lincoln newspaper lying on a nearby table. The front page of the sports section featured an article about the Giants written by Brian Carter, the guy sitting in the stands during tryouts. From his piece, I learned the following:

- The Giants went 42-52 last season.
- The team hadn't made the playoffs since 1994.
- Expectations are high this spring due to several new acquisitions.
- Season ticket sales for the Giants have increased.
- Former major leaguer Zane Fischer will be starting the season opener.
- The hopes of Giants fans will be dashed by the third inning of the season opener.

Okay, the last one appeared only in my head, not the paper. Don't get me wrong, I appreciated being named the Opening Day starter. That is what I wanted here—opportunity. But after the previous night's debacle, I knew the decision to start me in the opener was more likely the result of front office pressure than a vote of confidence from Curtis. Zane Fischer was a recognizable name. The chance to see him on the mound would put butts in the stands.

But can he still pitch? I was as interested as anybody to find out the answer to that question.

It didn't take long to move my stuff into Gale's apartment. He tried not to cringe too much during the process. He even moved his cello and some other junk to clear out a space for me in the loft. There were still a bunch of books and a bust of Bach (or somebody like that) up there, so I didn't have a whole lot of room. No problem. I was just grateful to be out of that motel and its drain on my dwindling funds. Unfortunately, Gale did not have a bed or a sofa up there. So Zane Fischer, five-time 20-game winner, would be sleeping on an inflatable mattress under a picture of Ronald Reagan. Yeah I know, beggars can't be choosers.

After settling in, I gave Buddy a call to let her know I had a new address. I also gave her Gale's phone number, in case she couldn't reach me on my cell. Dropping my phone plan was an increasingly likely possibility given my financial situation. We talked for a while about the usual stuff. She seemed chipper, especially when describing the limericks she and Stick wrote at school that day. But later in the conversation, I noticed something wasn't right. A drag in her voice that usually wasn't there.

"Everything okay?" I asked.

"Yeah."

"You sure something's not bugging you?"

Silence. "It's nothing."

"Spill it, young lady. Something going on at school? Bad grades?"

"My math grade is in the toilet, but that's nothing new."

"So what is it?"

"Mom's still seeing Cole."

"Oh … well, maybe it'll fizzle out. That's what happened before, right?"

"No, this time's different. He's coming over more."

"At least he's not living there."

"Not yet."

"Come on, that's not gonna happen. I mean, your mom wouldn't … would she?"

"I don't know. She better not." Her words came with an edge.

"So you don't get along with him, this Cole?" Buddy said nothing, so I asked again.

"I don't like him."

"Why? Is he mean to you?"

A pause followed. "No."

"Really?"

"Yeah."

"Is it something with your mom? Does he treat her okay?"

Another pause. "I guess so…. It's nothing that he's done. I just don't like the guy. He gives off a bad vibe."

"Well, maybe they'll break up."

"Let's hope."

We moved on to other topics. She told me about Pioneers Park, how it had all these trees, a lake, and some huge pillars from an old building in D.C. where President Lincoln once gave a speech. Buddy liked to hike around that place on weekends. We made plans to hang out there the next Saturday with a Frisbee and some food.

After hanging up the phone, I replayed everything my daughter had said. Especially the part about Toni's budding relationship with her new boyfriend. A development I could've lived without.

Chapter 4

Spring training in the majors lasts about six weeks. In the Central States League, it's half that long. That was plenty for me. After two decades in the bigs, I knew how to get myself ready for a season. But things were different this time. Even though the owners wanted me, I still felt I had to prove myself worthy of a roster spot. I hadn't been in this position since my rookie year with Toronto in '77. All that I'd accomplished in my big league career didn't mean squat when I took the mound at Sherman Field for the Giants opener.

I spent the evening before the game up in the apartment loft listening to Warren Zevon CDs. Though Gale and I both had our doubts going into this arrangement, we'd actually gotten along fairly well. He even started leaving me home unsupervised. That was progress. The first few days I'd lived there, he barely let me out of his sight. Can't blame him I guess, given what had been written about me over the past decade. But I avoided the misdeeds of my past. No kegs, no strippers, and no military-grade explosives. To pass the time, I watched TV, listened to music on my Walkman, and flipped through baseball magazines. Once Gale realized that I was housebroken, he felt free to go out and mingle with Lincoln's polite society.

The other thing I did up in that loft was think. And I had plenty to ponder that evening before the season opener. Would this knuckleball experiment really work? Could I actually make it back to the majors? I thought about Buddy too. She and I had been getting along great since I'd moved to town. We'd gone out hiking, caught a couple movies, and ate a bunch of pizza. Would it last? I'd been less than a part-time father for most of her life, so I really didn't know. She didn't mention Cole much. Maybe her opinion of him was changing. Or maybe she wasn't telling me something about him. The situation still bothered me.

I pulled the picture of Toni from my wallet. My thoughts drifted back to happier times with her, like when we were engaged and took a trip to Niagara Falls. I could still see her eyes. They were usually hazel, but at Niagara they were green. And they spoke to me even when her lips were closed. In her hair that day she wore a white daisy, and her perfume, even two decades later, still made me dizzy. With the roar of the water cascading in our ears, we both thought we'd be in love forever. What young couple doesn't?

"Tally-ho!" Gale's return yanked me back to the present. He dropped his keys on the kitchen table. "Up in the loft, Fischer? My word, it's not even nine yet. Have you retired for the evening already?"

I rolled over on my inflatable mattress and glanced down at him. "Nah, McGrady. I'm just up here with a hooker. Once we settle up, she'll be on her way."

"What! … Oh, I see, another one of your silly jests. Very funny, Fischer. Very funny."

"How was the wine tasting?"

"Impressive, I must say. Brought home a few bottles. Care to partake? I could warm up some of that leftover nacho meat you seem to fancy. Could even make some chocolate chip cookies too."

"Gotta pass on the spirits, but I think I could knock down a few nachos. Some cookies too."

"Very well." He skipped into the kitchen. Yes, skipped. He had apparently found a vintage or two to his liking.

I plodded down the stairs and took a seat at the table. "So where'd you learn to cook, McGrady?"

"The product of fine breeding and a well-rounded education, my boy." He rummaged through the cupboards. "And I'm merely slumming it with these indulgences. One of these days, I'll cook a full seven-course meal to showcase the complete range of my culinary talents."

"That must have been one helluva charm school you went to back east."

"Ha ha. Again with the levity. You know you shouldn't mock a person whilst he prepares your food. When I was a lad, our family cook taught me that lesson in a most graphic manner."

He had a point. "I'm just messin' with you, McGrady. You know I have the utmost respect for your cooking skills."

"That's more like it." He started mixing sugar, butter, eggs, and brown sugar in a bowl. "And it was indeed one helluva prep school I went to in Pennsylvania. I'll show you my yearbooks sometime."

"I look forward to that." Yes, I lied. The things I'll say for food.

A while later, Gale presented his culinary creations. Good stuff. The man knew his way around a kitchen. I must have been feeling pretty good, because after my third cookie I dropped my guard and started telling him what had been on my mind. Didn't tell him everything, but he got an abbreviated report on Buddy, Toni, and the new boyfriend.

"Well," he said, dabbing his mouth with a napkin, "it seems to me that your course of action is clear."

"What's that?"

"You've got to call her, this Toni."

"Call my ex-wife?"

"Yes, old boy. Be proactive. At the moment, your perspective on this situation is limited to your daughter's cryptic revelations. By reestablishing communications with Toni, you attain a fuller view of the landscape. In the course of your dialogue with her, she will, inadvertently or not, reveal more information germane to the situation."

"I see." I reached for another cookie wondering how information about germs would help.

Gale's eyes widened. "You could even invite them both to watch you pitch tomorrow night. Then if Toni brings this Cole fellow, it gives you a chance to size him up. You can see first hand how the three of them interact."

The idea didn't sound half-bad. "Hmm. Maybe …"

"Yes, Fischer! Seize the moment. Do it now." He retrieved my cell phone from the coffee table. "I'll head outside for a bit of fresh air to give you some privacy. Good luck."

One minute, I'm devouring mountains of nachos and cookies, shooting the breeze with my eccentric teammate. The next minute I'm staring at my cell phone, preparing to talk to my ex-wife for the first time since ... I couldn't recall.

My finger dialed the number. She answered.

"Toni."

Silence. I expected to hear a click, followed by a dial tone. She finally said, "I'll get Buddy. It's getting late, so don't keep her up too long."

I glanced at the clock: 11:03. It was later than I realized. "Sorry about the time.... Um, I'm not calling to talk to Buddy."

"Oh. Well, is something wrong ... with Buddy, I mean? Is that what you want to talk about?"

"I want to, uh, see how things are going with you."

"With me?"

"Yeah, since I'm in town and hanging out with our daughter more I thought I'd see how things are with you."

She sighed. "I'm fine, Zane."

"Good. You still at the music store?"

"Yes."

"Teaching guitar classes there?"

"Yeah. That, the register, and some bookkeeping."

I'd forgotten how much I liked the sound of her voice. Not what people usually mean when they say that—that it's great to hear from someone. I'm talking about the actual *sound* of her voice. It had this melodic, even sensual, quality. Toni never liked her own voice. Said it was raspy and dull. She was wrong.

Our small talk continued with halting pauses and short answers. She opened up a little more when I brought up Buddy. After we lamented our daughter's lack of interest in math homework, Toni said the girl wanted a car.

"She's fifteen," I said. "She can't drive it yet anyway."

"That's what I told her."

"What did she say to that?"

"She said we could park it in the front yard until she got her license. She thinks it would be cute having a green Volkswagen bug sitting in front of the house."

"How's she gonna pay for this bug?"

"Beats me. She's too lazy for a paper route. Maybe she thinks she'll find a bunch of loose change in the sofa."

"That girl, she was always such a smart kid. Then she became a teenager and decided to start slacking off and thinking up goofy ideas."

Toni laughed. Not much though. Little more than a snicker, truth be told. But it was nice to hear. Made me feel like this call might have been a good idea. But that pleasant sound was followed by something not so pleasant. From somewhere in her house came a man's voice. Deep. Guttural. Impatient. Toni covered the phone and responded to the voice. Upon removing her hand from the receiver, she said, "I should go. It's getting late." Her tone was cold.

"Okay." I wanted to ask about the man I pictured glaring at her from across the kitchen. But I didn't.

"I'll tell Buddy you called."

"Oh hey, I almost forgot."

"What?"

"I'm pitching the opening game for the Giants tomorrow night. I was wondering if you and Buddy would want to come."

A pause followed. "I think Buddy's planning to go with Stick."

"And you?"

"I don't think so."

"Oh." I thought about suggesting she could bring her male friend. After all, that was part of Gale's plan. But I couldn't bring myself to say his name or even indicate that I knew he existed. "I hear it's a lot of fun at these games. You know all the stuff they got going on at these bush league parks."

"It's not going to work out."

"Okay … um, maybe some other time then. Nice talking to you, Toni."

"Yeah."

And she hung up. I noticed that my fist was clenched. I thought about slamming it into the oak table, but didn't want to cause any damage. Knowing Gale, the thing had been imported from Prussia in the 1800s or something.

So I ate another cookie and went to bed.

Opening Day at Sherman Field. Even though close to three thousand fans packed the ballpark, it was still the smallest crowd I'd pitched in front of since Jimmy Carter was president. Wait, I take that back. In one of my last starts for Pittsburgh in '96, Three Rivers Stadium was pretty much empty. Couldn't have been more than a couple thousand there that night. And they were quiet. The sound of the players' spikes hitting the dirt echoed throughout the desolate ballpark. Eerie.

At Sherman that wasn't the case. The crowd roared as we rode onto the field in vintage convertibles. The hollering and clapping continued during player introductions. I was warming up in the bullpen when my name cracked through the PA system. I must admit, the ovation made me feel good. I even paused to tip my cap. Then the organ cranked up, someone started ringing a cowbell, and Big Abe staggered across the field on his stilts. Gotta love minor league baseball.

My knuckler displayed some funky moves during the warm up tosses. And the pitches felt natural flying off my calloused fingertips. Like I could put them in the strike zone all night. Juices flowed inside me as I turned to the outfield and rubbed the ball. It felt great being on the mound again pitching in a game that counted. Zane Fischer's triumphant comeback was about to begin.

My first pitch bobbed across the plate for strike one. The crowd erupted. After throwing the ball back to me, Snowman pounded his oversized mitt and yelled something encouraging. He sounded like one of the fans. Many of them started chanting, "Fish! Fish! Fish!" I hoped that Buddy was among them. Since I usually didn't look in the stands while on the mound, I couldn't verify her presence. But she said she'd be there, so I figured she was. Toni, probably not. She could've been listening on the radio though.

My second pitch fluttered inside and low, so the count evened at 1-1. I sent in another knuckler that died in the dirt and rolled to the backstop. Then I missed again. With the count 3-1, I had to go with a fastball. It sailed high. Great. I walked the leadoff hitter. Not the auspicious beginning I was hoping for. To make matters worse, my feel for the knuckler was slipping away. The next four pitches missed badly, so the second guy also got a free pass.

I started the third hitter with a knuckleball that dipped low and bounced past Snowman. The runners advanced; the crowd groaned. I didn't know what was going on. Minutes earlier in the bullpen, I could put the ball where I wanted. Now it was like trying to toss a ping pong ball into a Dixie Cup sixty feet away. And behind the cup was a fan going full blast. It felt like a year's worth of preparation had been erased with just ten pitches. Baseball is a cruel mistress.

After walking the bases loaded, I had to go back to throwing fastballs, sliders, and curves. None of the pitches had much movement, so the batters knocked them all around the park. Four runs crossed the plate before our centerfielder mercifully caught the third out at the wall. When I reached the dugout, Curtis asked me if something was wrong. I shook my head and flopped onto the bench. There was plenty wrong, but I didn't know what. Though I'd had plenty of bad outings before, never had I felt so lost on the hill.

Nothing changed in the second. I tried the knuckleball again, but couldn't get it over. So I again went back to my old stuff. The pitches unfortunately still lacked confidence and zip. Until they met the bats, that is. Then the ball moved with plenty of velocity. When Curtis came out to end my beat down, the Cheyenne Mules led 7-0. Yes, that's what it had come to. After winning 290 games in the majors, the Fish was now getting kicked around by a busher team called the Mules. I'd been taken out of a lot of games in my career, but no walk to the dugout had had ever been longer. It turned my stomach thinking of Buddy watching this from somewhere in stands.

I trudged across the ballpark concourse toward the clubhouse, where a bunch of kids had gathered to get the Fish's autograph.

"Sorry, not tonight," was all I gave them as I brushed past their pens and hopeful faces. Yeah, I know, I'm the devil. Once inside, I changed into my street clothes. No need for ice or a shower, since I didn't even last two lousy innings. Plus, you don't work up much of a sweat lobbing in 65-mph knucklers. I checked the shower room to see if the mascot guy was there. No such luck. So I just lay down on the clubhouse floor. That's where I stayed for the next two hours, staring at the florescent lights above. Did some thinking, mostly about how to pull the plug on this ill-fated comeback attempt. The idea I liked best was to pack up my bags first thing in the morning and then hit the road. No goodbyes, no explanations, and no more Zane Fischer. Just me, my pickup, and the interstate.

When the game finally ended, I got up and planted my butt in a metal folding chair. I could tell by the players' unenthusiastic entrance that the Giants had lost. Not too many teams could've dug themselves out of the hole I'd left them in. I didn't have much to say to the guys and they didn't have much to say to me. Curtis gave us a few "rough night, we'll get 'em tomorrow" comments. Larry the Geek said something about tomorrow's practice. Then our left fielder fired up a rap CD in his boom box. I usually hated that crap, but this time I was glad for the distraction of a pounding beat. Brian Carter from the paper tried to ask me a few questions, but I just shook my head and exited the locker room.

Dirk and Snowman wanted me to join them at JK's. Against my better judgment, I went. Going out socializing wasn't a terrible idea. The mistake was placing myself in a high-risk environment while in a vulnerable mindset. To have any chance of making it back to the bigs, I had to stay clean and sober. And to do that I had to avoid placing myself in situations in which I'd be likely to take a drink.

I first came to that realization in the spring of '97 when I started one of those 12-step programs and got a sponsor. He was Tim Haines, one of my Pirates teammates. He put me on the right track and helped me stay committed during those early difficult weeks. And let me tell you, the first couple months were hell. A big breakthrough came when Tim taught me about avoiding temptation while in a "red flag mood." For example, going out to a bar with a bunch of free-drinking teammates while depressed about my big comeback going up in flames—that would be a big red flag. Definitely shouldn't do that.

You can probably guess what happened that night.

The first sip of beer tasted strange. It had been so long, the bitterness really hit me. I liked the second glass a little better and the third and fourth ones went down smooth. We were back in business. At this point in the evening, the old Zane would start ordering harder stuff. Whiskey sounded good. The new Zane, however, was too poor for shots. So were his teammates. That was for the best—I would've downed a lot more booze if we'd had the funds. As it was, I drove home with the barest hint of a buzz. My four beers at JK's ended a ten-month no alcohol streak, but I took solace in the thought that my sobriety streak remained intact.

Still, this was a setback. Sitting in my truck in front of Gale's apartment building, I figured I'd better call Tim. So I dialed.

"Hello."

"Hey, Captain Underwear." I called him that because his last name was Haines. Like Hanes Underwear, get it? That's right, with me the laughs never end.

"Fish, what's goin' on man?"

"You sound tired. Is it past your bedtime?"

"Well it is almost one."

I looked at my watch—five 'til midnight. "Oh crap! I forgot about the time zone thing. Your wife is going to kill me."

"Nah, she'll get back to sleep."

"Yeah, but our talking will keep her up."

"Nope. I'm out of bed and will soon be headin' down the hallway. We won't bother her."

"Sorry about this, Haines. You got school in the morning, right?" He taught biology at a high school just outside Pittsburgh. He was also the assistant baseball coach. "I should let you go."

"No way, Fish. Like I've told you before, you can call me anytime day or night."

"Thanks man, that's cool. I take back all the bad stuff I said about your pitching."

"Even the time you said Venus de Milo had a better arm than me?"

"Especially that. You can throw way harder than ol' Venus."

"Thanks. But I heard that after the Pirates released me, they brought her in to take my spot in the bullpen."

"Yeah, but her ERA was nearly a run higher than yours."

He chuckled. "Right … so what's up, Fish?"

"Had some drinks tonight."

"How many?"

"Four beers."

"I'm glad you called. Four beers, huh? Anything else?"

"That's it. Ran out of money."

"Four beers isn't so bad. How'd it happen?"

I told him about my evening at Sherman Field and JK's. "I know it was stupid of me to head to that bar in a red flag mood."

A brief pause followed. "It's good you're owning your mistake. You know what you did and you know why it happened. You'll be able to avoid falling into the same trap again. And don't forget about the great progress you've made. Ten months sober. That really didn't end tonight. So you've still got a great streak going, right?"

"Yeah, I guess."

"No guessing. You *know* you're still sober, so acknowledge to yourself that this thing you started nearly a year ago is still going."

"Yeah, okay." I mentally obeyed his command.

This was the first time we'd talked since my arrival in Lincoln, so he asked what else had been going on the past month. I told him about tryouts, spring training, Buddy, and of course Gale Force.

"So there have been a lot of positives since moving to Lincoln," he said.

"Um, you think so?"

"Sure. You're back in your daughter's life. She's at an age where she can really benefit from her father's presence."

"I guess."

"Again with the guessing? No, this is a fact. It's good for you and Buddy to be hanging out. And you're in the Giants rotation, so your comeback is on track too."

"I did tell you about my start tonight, didn't I?"

"That's one game, Fish. How many starts have you made in your career? Over five hundred, right? So you of all people should know better than to place too much emphasis on what happened in one game."

"This is different, Haines. I had no command. And there was nothing I could do to get it back."

"So tomorrow you go to practice and you start figuring things out."

"Don't think so, man. I hate to say it, but it's probably time for me to call it a career."

"You're quitting after one start? What have you done with Zane Fischer? Put him back on the line, will ya?"

"Don't know if I can do it anymore." The words came out in a mumble.

"Fischer, can I read you something from the Bible?"

"You wouldn't need to do that."

"Okay, great. This passage is from the book of Judges. It's about a man who had some big doubts when faced with daunting odds. Maybe you can relate."

Tim proceeded to read about this guy named Gideon who was supposed to save his people from these other guys who were busting their chops. So he rounds up a big army to go kick some ass. But God tells him to cut a bunch of the soldiers. Then God tells him to cut some more. Eventually all Gideon has left is 300 men to go fight this powerful enemy force. On the day of the battle there were some trumpets and broken jars, then Gideon and his boys beat up the bad guys.

"Thanks, Tim. Great story."

"You're welcome, Zane. I hope you'll stick it out with the Giants. Remember God can help you through whatever you're facing. No matter how bad it seems."

That may have been true for people like Tim, but I doubted the Good Lord wanted anything to do with the Fish. "Appreciate it, Haines."

"Hey, would you mind if I closed with a word of prayer?"

"Nah, that's not necessary."

"Excellent, I'll pray."

Tim started praying. Mostly about me and the stuff I was dealing with. He usually ended our conversations this way. His heart was in the right place, but I don't know that it did much good. It seemed to make him happy though, so I went along with it. And, I must admit, I felt better at the end of our talk than I did at the beginning. I was lucky to have Tim as a sponsor and a friend. There weren't too many old teammates I still kept up with, even though I'd played on five different teams. Funny how that goes.

I climbed out of my truck and dragged myself up the stairs leading to the front door of Gale's apartment. Still had a lot of questions bouncing around my head. And they all revolved around the one big question: *Should I keep pitching or should I quit?*

I looked up and imagined Luke standing at the top of the stairs. Usually in these instances I saw him as a three-year-old. This time he appeared to be around eight or so. I could see him watching me with that clever smile of his, like he knew what was going to happen next. I would've asked him, but he disappeared. Like always.

Chapter 5

After my Opening Day debacle, the Giants dropped two of the next three to the Mules. We then headed to the Dakotas for an eight-game road trip. The first step in that delightful journey involved getting up at the crack of dawn and driving to the ballpark. We took my pickup so Gale wouldn't have to leave his precious Lexus in the Sherman Field parking lot for a week. While filing down the narrow aisle of the idling bus, it was hard not to reminisce about how good I'd had it in the bigs—flying the friendly skies with comfortable recliners, cute stewardesses, and well-stocked beverage carts.

I claimed a window seat about halfway back in the long metal cattle car that would shuttle us to Bismarck, North Dakota. The stench of diesel fumes and body odor filled the air. Since it was an eight-hour trip, I'd hoped to keep the seat next to me vacant so I could stretch out a little. A few of the younger guys slowed as they passed by, but my glare encouraged them to keep right on going. Yeah, I know, I'm a jerk. Well, I got what was coming to me when Dirk plopped his fat posterior in the seat next to mine.

"Man, I am so hung over," he said. "Glad the seat next to you was open. I sure didn't want to listen to some kid chattering in my ear all the way to Canada, or wherever the hell we're goin'."

This turn of events did not meet with my approval. A few choice words lined up on my tongue, but I said nothing. Dirk convinced Gale to take me in, so I could at least try to deal with his girth pressing against my ribcage until the first stop, which hopefully wouldn't be too far down the road.

"Where's your pillow?" he asked.

"Didn't bring one."

"Well, well, looks like somebody's forgotten the joys of minor league travel." He chuckled. "Don't worry, Fish. When the time comes, you can use mine." He punched the stained off-white pillow in his lap.

"Thanks." *But no thanks.*

"Hey, whatcha got there?" He pointed at the book lying on my thigh.

"Harry Potter."

"Who'd he play for?"

"He's not a ballplayer. It's about this British kid who finds out he's a wizard."

"A wizard? You gotta be kiddin' me. You going through a second childhood or something?"

"My daughter's reading it for school. I bought a copy. Figured I could read it on the bus. Then me and her can talk about it when I get back."

"Shouldn't have let her talk you into that. Who knows what the girl will hit you up for next."

"She didn't ask. I'm doing this to surprise her."

A smirk cut across his round stubbly face. "Look at you being a Dad and all that. Maybe we should call you Ward Cleaver."

"Well, I ain't read it yet." I flipped the book over and glanced at the back cover.

"Probably a good idea not to tell her yet. You might not get much reading done on these trips. This bus may be an old rust bucket, but it does have a VCR." He pointed to the television screen at the front. "I offered to let 'em borrow a few titles from my collection of fine adult entertainment, but Glass wouldn't go for it. You believe that?"

"The hardships we endure for the love of the game."

"I know it. Someone said they're gonna be playing that crappy *Caddyshack* flick this morning."

"I loved that movie."

"Not the first one. Everybody liked that one. We're gonna be watching *Caddyshack 2*."

"Really? Why? Are we being punished?"

"Looks that way. Guess we're gonna have to start winning if we want to see anything decent."

The bus snaked its way out of town and onto the interstate. With all its rattles and hisses, the lumbering land-boat sounded like it could break down any second. I once again reviewed the tenuous status of my baseball career. Dirk was apparently having similar thoughts.

"Hey Fish, you ever think about what you're gonna do when this is all over?"

"You mean after I'm dead?"

"Nah, not that." He chuckled. "I know exactly where me and you is goin' when that happens." His thumb pointed downwards. "I'm talkin' about baseball. What happens when you finally decide to hang it up?"

"Haven't thought about it."

"Aw c'mon, you had to have thought about it." One of his bushy brows rose. "You were away from the game for a whole year."

I glanced out the window at the Nebraska farmland whizzing by. "Believe it or not, Dirk, I was focusing on my comeback. Stayin' in shape. Workin' on the knuckler."

"You disappointed the big league clubs passed and you ended up here?"

I kinda was, but decided to give him a positive spin. "Nope. I'm back playing professional baseball. Lincoln is a necessary step in my return to the majors. Just like for you."

"Yeah …" His word hung in the air, like it was waiting for something to follow. But nothing did.

"What?" I met his uncertain eyes. "You don't think we're getting back to the Show? Isn't that the whole point of these eight-hour bus rides?"

"I hope so, Fish. But we're in different boats. If I don't make it back, what have I got to show for my time the game? Not much.

And I don't know what I'll do after baseball. It's scary, man. That's why I'm here, rotting on this stinkin' bus with a metal spring wedged in my butt crack." His expression fell serious, not a familiar look with him. "But you, you're already a Hall of Famer. You can use your success to jump into a bunch of careers. Broadcasting, coaching, hawking tube socks ... whatever."

I glanced at our teammates in the rows in front of us. All of them hoping for that big break. "I don't want to think like that, Dirk. Don't get me wrong, I'm proud of my past successes. But I'm not ready to start trying to capitalize on what I once was. I'm still doing stuff in baseball right now." My open hand sliced the air in front of me. "Someday I'll leave this game, but it will be on my terms. And it will be my decision, not some doctor or team trainer. The Fish is still a pitcher, and he will be for a long time."

Dirk's big shiny head nodded. "Damn straight, Fischer. Damn straight."

My juices were flowing. For the time being, the doubts that had dogged me were gone. I knew they'd come creeping back, but I wasn't going to tell Dirk that. Like he said, thinking about life after baseball was scary. Something I didn't want to dwell upon.

"Hey Fish," he said a while later. "Remember in June of '94 when I just missed hitting a grand slam off you?"

"I don't think it was all that close to being a home run."

"Sure it was." He raised a butt cheek and released a long growling fart into the aisle. Unfortunately, few of our teammates heard it over the roaring bus engine and surrounding conversations. "Just missed the foul pole by a couple feet. Bases were loaded, you know."

"Yeah, the bases were loaded. But this foul ball you're talking about went straight up and landed ten rows behind the first base dugout."

"No, that's not where it landed."

"Yeah it is. And then you struck out on the next pitch, chasing a slider in the dirt."

"Hmph." He rubbed his chin. "That's not what's important about that at-bat though."

"So what is?"

"That I hit a ball off you that landed in the stands."

The guy across the aisle from Dirk pulled his shirt up over his nose and stared dry heaving. "Aw, man! ... Davis, is that you?"

Hours later we arrived in Bismarck, North Dakota. As a kid, I'd uttered this city's name dozens of times while reciting state capitals. And there I was at last—another dream realized in this magical season. We pulled up to some crummy motel. I thought Gale was about to cry, a sentiment I shared. After exiting the bus, my teammates grabbed their bags out of the storage compartment. That was another change from the bigs for me to remember—I'd have to carry my own luggage on these trips.

An enchanting array of stains decorated the walls of my room, which greeted my nostrils with a refreshing musty smell. I estimated the room's size as just a bit smaller than one of the walk-in closets at my former home in Louisville. I'd be sharing this spacious accommodation with Ryan McCormick, one of the other starting pitchers. He asked me which bed I wanted. I said the one in a Ritz-Carlton a thousand miles away.

McCormick was a young guy maybe a year or two out of college. Tons of potential on the mound. He could throw fastballs close to a hundred miles-per-hour, but he had no control. That seemed to be his approach to life in general. On the bus ride, he passed the hours by playing cards, telling stories about his exploits at Alabama State, belting out Lynyrd Skynyrd songs, spitting dip into a cup, and holding up signs encouraging women in passing cars to remove their tops. He was one of the few guys on the team— actually maybe the only guy on the team—who seemed to enjoy every minute on that wretched bus. Curtis must have thought that a "stable" veteran such as myself would have a positive influence on this young buck. It's amazing the ideas that people get in their heads sometimes.

McCormick usually hung out with Lee Rodgers, another southern kid. Guys on the team called him General Lee. And man, this dude could pitch—hard fastball with movement, nasty changeup, and an overhead curve that was almost ready for prime time. If I weren't around, the General would've been the Giants Opening Day starter. He was also the guy who looked most likely to be pitching in the majors by the end of the year.

After the game that night (a Giants victory), I went with some of the boys to grab some fast food. The team gave us five dollars per meal while we traveled. That amounted to $120 for the eight-day road trip. Back in the bigs, I could blow twice that amount in a single evening. Even more when we hit Dorrian's in New York. Oh, how things had changed for the Fish. Five bucks a meal. Good thing I kinda liked Wendy's.

When we'd finished eating, the guys migrated to a bar near our motel. I returned to my room, donned my reading glasses, and started that Harry Potter novel. Boy wizards and talking snakes weren't really my thing, but I must admit I got into it and looked forward to discussing the story with Buddy. I turned in at 11:30. Wanted to be nice and rested for my start the next night. McCormick and Rodgers woke me up an hour later when they stumbled into the room and flipped on the light. Annoying yes, but I was used to it. Actually, over the course of my career, I was usually the guy waking somebody up rather than the other way around. They bragged for a while about the all chicks they could've landed, before taking my hint that it was time for lights out. Rodgers went to his room and McCormick headed for the sink where he took a lengthy piss. I made a mental note to find somewhere else to brush my teeth.

The next evening, I toed the rubber for my second start of the season. Upon hearing my name over the PA, the Bismarck fans gave me a nice ovation. After I'd finished warming up in the bullpen, one of the ball boys told me there were twice as many people at the ballpark than on a typical night. That made me feel good. What didn't make me feel good were the Bismarck batters. They apparently didn't give a crap that they were facing a living legend who deserved their respect and admiration. The first batter drilled a sharp single into left. Things got worse from there.

A knuckleball, as mentioned earlier, is supposed to leave the fingertips with no spin. When that happens, the air currents hitting the laces of the ball cause it to move in an erratic manner. Very difficult for batters to hit. However, when a knuckleball leaves the pitcher's hand with a spin, it comes in straight and true. Very easy for batters to hit. I'd spent so much time worrying about putting the ball over the plate that I'd lost the touch for releasing a knuckler with no rotation.

The Hawks teed off on my 60-mph batting practice deliveries—that is in effect what knuckleballs that don't knuckle are. Even their number-nine guy, a .210 hitter, nearly took my head off with a drive up the middle. As the leadoff hitter prepared to bat for the second time in the first inning, Bismarck led 4-0 and had the bases loaded. Two men were out, but only because a couple scorching line drives had found their way into my fielders' gloves. Curtis had seen enough.

"I suppose you want the ball," I said, after he arrived at the mound.

"Nah, you hang onto it for a minute. That thing's still got smoke coming off it. Don't want to burn my fingers." He snickered in amusement with himself.

"Funny."

"Hey Fish, you remember *The Dukes of Hazzard*?"

I stared at him for a second, before glancing at Snowman's confused face. "Yeah, sure."

"You know that Daisy girl?"

"Yes Curtis, I remember Daisy Duke."

"The gal who played her, that's not Ringo's wife is it?"

I studied his face, wondering where this was going with this. "No, Catherine Bach was Daisy. Barbara Bach is Ringo's wife."

"Yeah, that's it. I always get them two confused." He smiled and nodded. "Both fine lookin' women though. Am I right?" He backhanded Snowman's chest protector.

The catcher nodded with a nervous chuckle. "Yeah, sure Skip."

"Uh, Curtis," I said. "Did you really come out here to talk about Daisy Duke?"

His smile vanished. "Of course not, Fischer. I'm just giving McGrady time to finish warming up."

"So I'm not going to be pitching to this guy?"

"Oh, hell no! You *are* done. Don't even need to stick a toothpick in you to see that."

"Right." I examined the rosin bag in the dirt.

Curtis motioned to the bullpen for a right-hander. "Hey Fish," he said, turning to me. "You remember when those boys who played Bo and Luke wanted more money? The network didn't give it to them, so they sat out. The show had to hire a couple new guys to fill their parts."

I nodded.

"It just wasn't the same with them fake Duke boys." He shook his head. "Some things just can't be replaced, you know. Probably shouldn't have even done that season at all."

My eyes met his. I wondered if he was trying to tell me something. If so, I'd have a few things to tell him. *But maybe he's right.* With that thought, all I could say was, "Here's the ball." And I started the long walk back to the dugout.

A drink sounded great. Could start things off with a few beers and then move on to some Scotch. How good would that taste sliding down my throat? The law firm of McCormick, Rodgers, and Davis added to the temptation by presenting an effective case for how much fun it would be to throw back a few brews. Recalling my history with the bottle, I found enough precedent to overrule their arguments. So all I did after the game was hit Arby's with Snowman and a couple other guys, then I went back to the motel to hang out with Harry Potter and his pals Ron and Hermione.

Truth is, as I had time to think about things, I was more dumbfounded than depressed about my shellacking. In the bullpen sessions I threw on off days, my knuckleball danced like a showgirl. Madam Knucklina I called her. And she stayed around the plate too. That left me with the obvious question: *What is different when I get into an actual game?*

It was kinda weird. After my first loss, I wanted to quit this comeback. After my second loss—an even worse performance—I couldn't wait to get out there and try it again. Over the years, I've heard people say that pitchers, especially lefthanders, aren't right in the head. That assessment is absolutely correct. You want proof? Just look at what I was doing later that night. I wasn't getting any sleep, so at 2:30 I grabbed an old baseball and went out to the motel parking lot. I stood about sixty feet away from the building and started throwing knucklers against the brick wall. Even though most of the pitches didn't bounce back to me, I followed the ball wherever it rolled, resumed my grip, and kept tossing out there under the stars. Probably for a half hour or more. Dumb as it sounds, it made me feel better.

After dropping three of four to Bismarck, we headed south to face the Pierre Cavaliers. By this time, I'd found out that Larry the Geek chose the movies we watched on the bus. For this trip he rewarded us with *Ishtar*. See what a jerk this guy was?

After the Giants split the first two with Pierre, it was my turn to pitch. Before the game, Curtis and Larry met with me to go over the opposing team's lineup. A pointless exercise. I threw knuckleballs, so it didn't matter who was at the plate. If the pitch danced, the batter would struggle to hit it. If the pitch didn't dance, the batter would improve his slugging average. I wanted to tell them they were wasting their time, but I said nothing. After two disastrous starts, I was on thin ice. No need to give them any more reason to cut me.

A chilly wind swept through the ballpark that night. Some mist swirled in the air too. Not the best conditions for a knuckleball. Nonetheless, the show went on. I felt good warming up in the bullpen. Madam Knucklina danced through the strike zone with that wicked shimmy of hers. But as I knew all too well, the good madam was a fickle vixen whose mind could change on a whim. What would be her mood this time?

In the top of the first, the Giants put two on the board with a walk and back to back doubles. Then it was time for the Fish to do his thing. I sent my knucklers over the plate, or within the vicinity. The Cavalier batters may have helped me out a little with some overly aggressive swings. I rang up two strikeouts and kept them from scoring in the inning.

In the second we pushed our lead to 3-0. Unfortunately, I gave one back in the bottom of the frame with a couple walks, a bunt, and a wild pitch. Still, I liked the action I was getting on my tosses. And I liked even more that they usually went close to where I was aiming them. Things got even better in the third when the Cavs went down in order. On the way back to the dugout, I drew in a deep breath of cool Dakota air. Good stuff. My eyes roamed the ballpark. I felt like a pitcher again. It had been a long time since I'd had that feeling.

Then the bitch turned on me. Madam Knucklina decided she would dance for the Fish no more. She left me to go cavort with those Pierre boys. And let me tell you, she gave them exactly what they wanted—nice easy pitches that put up no resistance to their advances. I got plenty of exercise backing up third base as the Cavs plated four runs in the fourth. I finally got the last out of the inning by slipping a couple sliders past their weakest hitter.

Curtis went to his bullpen for the fifth, so my night was done. Five runs through four innings. The Giants never regained the lead—that meant another loss for the Fish. In my quest to return to professional baseball I had burst out of the gate with a 0-3 record. The phone in the Giants front office was no doubt ringing off the hook with calls from big league GMs clamoring to get the first shot at signing me.

It was a typical scene in the locker room after the game. Players showered and dressed. Curtis said something about getting back on track tomorrow. Somebody cranked up some rap music on a boom box. A mouthy little reserve infielder named Chris started making stupid wise cracks about how much we sucked, so some of the bigger guys wrapped him in duct tape and tossed him (fully clothed) into the shower. Based on the victim's shrieks, the water by this time was ice cold.

Afterwards, the boys decided to take in the glittering wonders of Pierre's night life. With the crummy mood I was in, there was only one right move to make. I needed to go back to the motel and call Tim. So of course I went out with the gang. Truth is, I was tired of fighting. I'd been working for more than a year on this comeback. Rehabbing the shoulder. Getting back in shape. Learning a new pitch. Staying sober. And the results? I was just making a fool of myself. As I shuffled into some nameless bar in Pierre, South Dakota, one thought dominated my mind: *I don't want to do this anymore.*

Even if I wanted to give you the details of what went on that night, I really couldn't do it with any accuracy. I know it started with a few Miller Lites. Then a fan recognized me and started buying me shots. He was some travelling businessman on a hot streak, so his cash bought a river of booze. Scotch and bourbon mostly.

I woke up a little before noon the next day face down on the floor in Hank Nordeman's room. Big Hank was our starting right fielder. He hailed from the commonwealth of Virginia, so we had yet another son of the Confederacy on our team. And this guy looked the part, even more so than Rodgers and McCormick. Just picture one of those young southern officers in the Civil War. You know, with the long beard and steely eyes. Well, add another hundred pounds and a wad of chew bulging from his cheek and you've got Hank Nordeman.

As two invisible hammers pounded my temples, the big Hank man recounted my misdeeds from the previous evening. His roommate, a reserve infielder named Chavo Berroa, sat on the edge of his bed listening eagerly. I really hoped that Hank was exaggerating, but even if half of what he said was true, the Fish had been a bad, bad boy. Hitting on a table of college girls (surprisingly, I struck out). Knocking over a waitress carrying a tray of drinks. Climbing up on the bar to belt out Abba's greatest hits (Hank said I really nailed "Dancing Queen"). Pissing in the bed of a pickup. Ripping loose a downspout while trying to shimmy up to the roof of the tavern. Puking into a curb sewer. That's apparently how I passed out, lying on my belly with my face planted in a sewer grate. There were a few other alleged antics that, embellished or not, I'd rather not repeat.

I hoped that Curtis and Larry the Geek somehow hadn't gotten wind of what had happened. Those hopes were dashed when I showed up at Cavalier Park and found a note inside my locker instructing me to report to Curtis's office. Oddly enough, my old teammate did not have a smile on his face when I entered the broom closet reserved for the visiting manager.

"I gotta admit, Fischer, you pulled it off."

I could barely hear him over the hammers still pounding away at my skull. "Oh."

"I mean you had everybody convinced you'd changed. Wright and Mendenhall, they especially ate it up. I even started believing you myself by the end of spring training." His eyes remained fixed on me.

I wished he were working on a crossword puzzle. "Curtis, I know I screwed up, but ..."

"Yeah, that was brilliant." The corners of his mouth curled into a smile—not a happy one. "That whole song and dance about how you're working hard on getting back to the big leagues. And how you're sober now. Not gonna mess around like you did in your younger days. Bravo, Fischer. You convinced us all."

"That wasn't an act. I was sober a whole year." My tongue felt like it had been injected with Novocaine, so the words came out in a mumble. "I have changed."

"Oh no, you have NOT changed. What happened last night is the same kind of crap you been doin' for years." His expression smoldered for a few seconds before turning contemplative. "Well now, wait a minute. Come to think of it, you *have* changed. Back in those days, you used to win. You sure ain't doing that no more."

I should've gotten mad, but the hammering pain made it hard to offer much of a response. "Just one mistake, Curtis. Won't do it again."

"No, the mistake was signing you in the first place."

"So cut me."

"Wish I could. There's this kid down in Santa Fe throws ninety-seven miles per hour. I got a cousin down there told me about him. Man, I'd love to see what that boy could do for us." Curtis shook his head, disdain dripping from each movement. "But the honchos won't let me drop you. They still think people want to come out and watch your sorry ass get knocked around the park. So not only do you get to keep taking up roster space, but also a spot in my rotation. Wright won't even let me move your dead weight to the bullpen."

"I am not dead weight." I wasn't sure I believed my own words.

"You're right. At least dead weight don't do no damage. You on the other hand are a destructive influence. There are some talented kids on this team. A couple of them may have a shot at the majors someday. But they are kids, so they're already inclined to do stupid things. They don't need any encouragement from a washed-up has-been."

My first thought was to tell him that it was some of those talented kids who convinced me to go out last night. But that fact didn't make me look any better. So I just stood there steadying myself against the back of the wooden chair in front of his desk.

"Fischer, you might see the Giants as a playground. One more chance for you to pretend you're a big star. Tell the young guys stories about how great you once were. Go out drinking and partying like in the old days." His tone softened. "But for some of us, this is our career. We take what happens with this team very seriously. See, I didn't get any other managing offers. And the Giants only took me because their first choice got hired somewhere else. If I'm gonna make it as a skipper, I need to win now. This season. So I'd appreciate it if you didn't make things any harder for me."

"I'm sorry Curtis." My eyes remained on the grungy tile floor.

"Do the right thing, Fischer. This affects more than just you."

The hammering continued as I left his office.

That night the Giants won 4-3 behind eight strong innings from Luis Batiste. Following the game, I called Buddy before the all-night bus ride back to Lincoln.

"When are you coming back?" she asked.

"Tonight. This was the last game of the road trip. You mean you haven't been following the Giants in the paper?"

"Yeah. I was just makin' sure."

"Everything good there?"

"Oh sure. Life in Lincoln is one gleeful trip to the Mardi Gras right after another."

"Great. Get any beads? Wait a minute, I don't want you getting any beads."

"Don't worry. I wouldn't get any beads even if I took *everything* off."

"You better not be doing that."

"Relax, Dad. You do realize that I'm not actually in New Orleans?"

"Yes. It's just … never mind." It isn't easy being a father with a day-long hangover still pounding away at your brain.

"Goofball." She snickered. "Hey, can we hang out tomorrow? There's this ice cream place I want to show you."

"Of course."

"Coolness. Talk to you tomorrow, Dad."

She hung up and I boarded the bus.

Chapter 6

We made it back to Lincoln around 7:00 AM. I got about two hours of sleep on the rolling junk heap that carted us south through the night. We didn't have a game or a practice that day, but the front office geniuses had scheduled a team promo appearance at a department store in town. The event started at 1:00 PM. Since my days with the Giants were likely numbered, I decided to skip that opportunity to meet our adoring fans. Earlier in the week I'd heard that the store manager was counting on me appearing with the team. Guess he figured that getting your picture taken with Zane Fischer was something of a drawing card. I kinda felt bad for him and the fans that were hoping to see me. Actually, that's not really true. I was asleep at the time, so I didn't feel much of anything. But I feel bad now, if that means anything. So let me pause to formally apologize to all those who showed up at Shopko in Lincoln, Nebraska, on June 2, 1998, hoping to see the Fish. Nothing personal. I just didn't feel like being around people that day.

Later that afternoon, after school got out, I drove to Toni's to pick up my daughter. I pulled up to find her sitting on the front stoop next to a beanpole of a kid with a dark buzz cut.

"Hey, Dad, this is Stick. He was hangin' with me till you showed up."

The boy stood and extended a hand. "Hello, Mr. Fischer." His palm was wet and kinda gross.

"So you're the Stick? Heard a lot about you."

"Ha. Hopefully all good." His eyes moved from mine to the ground. The boy was only a couple inches shorter than me, so he had to be about six feet all.

"Nope. Not really. But I know Buddy likes to exaggerate, so I'll give you a pass for now."

He stuttered out a chuckle. "Oh, ha, thanks. I mean, for the pass. Giving me a pass."

"The phone's ringing inside," Buddy said. "Be back in a sec."

She disappeared into the house leaving me with Stick, who was now examining a nearby tree. As he stood there slouching with his hands shoved into his pockets, I felt something for him. Ninth grade was an awkward time for me too. Well, not *that* awkward, but still, I could relate. Sort of.

He cleared his throat and turned to me. "Uh, Mister Fischer?"

"Yeah, Stick." The acne pattern on his face reminded me of a connect-the-dots activity in a children's book.

"I was actually hoping to get the chance to talk to you one on one." He glanced at the house. "She'll be out soon, so I'll get right to the point." He took a deep breath and summoned something from deep within. "Sir, I really like your daughter ... Buddy. And, uh, I want to be her boyfriend." Another deep breath. "So I'd like to ask your permission to date her."

It took everything I had to keep from cracking up. I know, laughing at him would've made me the biggest jerk in the world. The poor kid was really putting it out there and he deserved a serious response. So, stifling any hint of a snicker, I said, "You two are pretty young, you know. Just finishing your freshman year, right? Maybe you could keep hanging out as friends this summer and see how you feel next fall."

"Um, we've been friends since fifth grade, sir. I think I'm pretty sure about my feelings for Buddy." His eyes seemed so hopeful.

"Okay. But I gotta say, Stick, whenever she mentions you to me, she describes you as a friend." His eyes dimmed. "A good friend though. Sounds like you two have a good time together. I'd hate to see this end. You know things could get weird if you moved too soon."

"Too soon?"

"Yeah, fifteen is strange age for girls." I didn't really know if that was true, but it sounded plausible. "Buddy might need some time to sort out her feelings for you. I mean, she—"

Buddy threw open the front door, bringing an abrupt end to my statement. "Okay, I'm ready to go," she said, marching toward my pickup. "Catch ya later, Stick."

I nodded at the boy and turned to go.

"Thanks, Mr. Fischer. I think I get it. Maybe we can, um, talk about things again sometime."

"Sure, Stick. Take care."

Great. Boys wanting to date my daughter. I knew this day was inevitable, but it always seemed like something way down the road. Like when people would be flying around in jetpacks and robots would be our servants. As I drove down the road though, the idea of Stick dating Buddy didn't seem so bad. He was a helluva lot better than the tattooed ex-con with the nose ring that typically haunts the nightmares of every teenage girl's father. And Stick was way better than most of the troublemakers I'd shared a locker room with over the years. I didn't think Buddy would go for him though, not in that way. I hoped he'd take my advice and postpone making any bold moves.

Buddy directed me to an ice cream place not too far away called Zesto's. We grabbed our cones and leaned against the side of my truck to watch the traffic pass by on South Street. The afternoon sun felt good on my face. Since it was early June, temperatures were still civilized. I'd pitched quite a few games in St. Louis and Kansas City in July and August, so I knew what type of unholy Midwestern heat to expect in the coming months.

"How's it going?" I asked.

"Fine."

"You gonna pass Algebra?"

"I may squeak by with a C-minus." She gazed at a large brick building across the street and licked her fudge nut ice cream.

I pointed at her cone. "Is that good?"

"Yeah. How about yours?"

"Yep, good stuff. You were right about this place."

"Why'd you get strawberry?"

"Because, my dear girl, it reminds me of when I faced Darryl Strawberry in September of '88. He was one of the most feared hitters in the league back then. And your old man struck him out three times in one game. Whaddya think of that?" I nudged my elbow into her arm.

"Wow, Dad, that's amazing." Sarcasm oozed from every word.

"Yes, it really was amazing." I thrust out my chest like Superman.

She stifled a smile. "You are such a nerd."

"Ohh." I clutched my heart as if I'd just been shot. "Out of the mouths of babes."

"Truth hurts, huh?"

"Alright young lady, for Christmas this year I'm getting you an official Zane Fischer baseball jersey. Then you can properly appreciate my awesomeness and proudly declare your love for your dear old Dad."

"Great. We could use something to replace the old shammy in the garage."

"What a wise guy, we got here. You know you should respect your elders. Didn't they teach you that in school?"

"Must've been sick that day." She bit off a piece of cone and crunched it in her teeth.

"Figures." A Mustang filled with a coven of teenagers pulled into the parking lot. That reminded me of something. "Hey, you still reading that Harry Potter book?"

She shook her head. "Finished it last week. Turned in the report today."

"You finished it already?"

"Had to. School ends in three days."

Drat! There went my surprise. With all the stuff that had happened on the road trip, I spaced off that her report was due by the end of the semester. I'd made a lot of progress, but still had maybe a third of the book left to read. Oh well, no point in telling her that now. "You excited about school getting out?"

"Not really."

"What? Finishing ninth grade is a big deal. Got a year of high school under your belt. And the whole summer is ahead of you now."

"Yippee." Indifference coated her voice.

"You're not excited about three months of freedom? Are you really my kid?"

"That just means I'll be around the house more."

"Is that so bad?"

"It is when *he's* there." Her words came with a sharper edge.

"Cole?"

She nodded and started fiddling with the heart-shaped charm on her necklace.

"He doesn't come around till evening, right? When he goes out with your mom?"

"Sometimes he's there in the day now too."

"Cole hangs around your house during the day?"

"Sometimes."

"Does he stay over?"

"No, Mom doesn't let him do that." She crunched the final remnants of her cone. "Yet."

"So you're thinking he'll be around the house this summer? When you're there."

"She lets him hang out there now. By himself in our house during the day." She wiped her hands on her pants. "When he feels like taking time off from work."

"What's his job?"

"Contractor."

"Like construction work?"

"Yeah. He also does remodeling stuff inside. Like he put in a new kitchen counter for Mom."

I lost interest in finishing my ice cream. "Does he do anything to you or your mom that you don't like?"

She shrugged.

"Buddy."

"He drinks … all the time. And when he's drunk, he yells. Then he gets bossy and swears at her."

"Has he ever hit her?"

She shrugged again.

"What's that supposed to mean?" I stepped in front of her, so she had to look at my face. "Buddy, has Cole hit your mom?"

"No. I mean, I think he pushed her once. I was in my room and heard this noise in the living room. When I came out, she was getting up. She said they were goofing around and she tripped. An accident." She shook her head. "He looked mad."

My fist closed around my cone. What was left of the pink ice cream oozed through my fingers. "Has he ever done anything to you?"

"Not really."

"Not really?"

She waited a few seconds before speaking. "One time he couldn't find his wallet, so he barged into my room. Just opened the door without knocking. Said, 'Is it in here? Did you take it?'"

"He barged in? Were you dressing or anything?"

"No. I was at my desk doing homework."

"Then what happened?"

"Nothing. Mom said she found it in the couch, so he left."

I scanned the neighborhood sorting through my thoughts. After some time had passed Buddy asked, "Dad, can you help me get a summer job?"

"Where do you want to work?"

"I dunno. Since I'm fifteen, not too many places will hire me. Detasseling doesn't start for another month, and I don't know if I'd like that anyway. So I was thinking, maybe you could get me on at Sherman Field. Concessions or something."

My daughter obviously wasn't aware of my waning popularity within the Giants organization. "Yeah, I'll talk to somebody. See what I can find out."

I asked what she was doing that evening. She said that she and Stick were going to a movie—*Godzilla*. So she was going to be out of the house. That gave me an idea.

I dropped Buddy off at Toni's and then drove to a diner that wasn't too far away. There, I waited.

Later, after the movie had started, I headed back. Toni probably wasn't going to be happy to see me, but so what? This was about my daughter.

After I rang the doorbell, my ex-wife opened the door. We stared at each other through the torn screen. I don't know what she was thinking, but I had a moving van of emotions rolling through my head. One time up in Seattle, Tom Paciorek lined a ball off my noggin. The lights went out for few seconds and after I came to, the Kingdome spun around and around. Seeing Toni after so many years had a similar effect.

"Zane, what are you doing here?"

"We need to talk."

"You couldn't have called?"

"No, can I come in?"

"I don't think that's such a good idea."

"Fine. It's about Buddy."

Her expression softened from granite to oak. "What's wrong?"

"That's what I'm hoping to find out. Seems that our daughter doesn't feel safe in her own house anymore."

"What? That's crazy."

So I told her what Buddy had told me. Toni looked stunned, like I'd just slapped her. Then her face clouded with concern. She opened the screen, stepped out and sat down on the stoop. I didn't know what to do so I sat next to her, just like Stick and Buddy earlier in the day. Reminded me of high school when Toni and I used to sit on her parents' front porch all the time. Her old man didn't think too highly of me at first (or ever), so we usually stayed outside when I went over to her place.

Toni sighed. "I knew Buddy wasn't too crazy about me seeing Cole. But I thought she'd come around after a while."

"The yelling and swearing might have something to do with it."

"And I've talked to Cole about that," she replied tersely. "He's a good guy. He would never hurt me or Buddy. Yes, he drinks. And when he drinks too much, he can do dumb things. You of all people should understand that."

Me of all people? Nice. "I never hit you or threatened our children."

"Well, Cole hasn't either. You're just getting one side of the story. And that's from an emotional teenage girl. He treats me good. Buddy too, if she'd let him."

"Fine."

"It *is* fine. Buddy will be okay. You know I wouldn't let anybody hurt her, Zane."

"Yeah." I spotted a little girl riding her tricycle on the sidewalk across the street. "Guess I should get going."

"How's the shoulder?"

"Feels alright." I massaged my left deltoid. "No pain so far this season."

"Well, that's good."

"Can't get anybody out though."

"You'll figure it out."

"Nah, it's just not happening for me this year. I think it's time to pull the plug."

Some time passed before she spoke. "You're relying on your knuckleball too much. Should work in your other pitches early on. Mix things up."

"Yeah, but I've got to get this knuckler down if I'm gonna get back to the bigs." *Hey, wait a minute! How does she know what I've been throwing? Has she been listening to the games?*

"Yes, but the hitters are ready for it. You should snap off a few benders in the first couple innings. Go up and in with some cheese too. Give 'em something to think about. Right now they know you're going to start off with nothing but knuckleballs, so they just sit back and let you fall behind in the count."

She had a point. That shouldn't have surprised me. Toni always had a sharp mind for sports, especially baseball. "Maybe I could work a little more on the curve." *Assuming I ever pitch again.* I glanced over and a caught a tiny smile. Always loved that. For the first time in this conversation, I lingered on the features of her face. She always looked so pretty, even when she wasn't trying. Especially when she wasn't trying. When she turned away, my eyes drifted to the light brown ponytail that flowed nearly halfway down the back of her maroon spaghetti-strap top. I sprang to my feet. I had to get out of there before I did something stupid, like put my arm around her.

"I'm glad we had this talk," I said. "Just wanted to make sure our girl is getting along okay."

Toni stood. "I understand. She'll be fine."

And then a black GMC pickup pulled into the driveway, right behind my truck.

"Oh," she said in a tone that people use when reviewing their credit card bills after Christmas. "I didn't think he'd be here for another hour."

"Cole?"

"Yes." Then she whispered. "You be cool."

He slammed the door and strutted around the front of his truck with a big grin. "Well, what a treat." He looked over at Toni. "You know he was coming here?"

"Zane just came over to pick up Buddy. But he missed her, so he was just leaving."

Cole marched up to me like Earl Weaver approaching an ump. "That's right, you get to be a father now that you're in town. Little bit, anyway." He was few inches shorter than me and stocky. Big shoulders, thick arms, and pecs bulging under a tight black T-shirt. Could've been one of those fireplug running backs in high school. He had short dark hair with a little goatee arrangement around his mouth. His eyes reminded me of how the sky looked an hour or so before a thunderstorm.

"Well, it's good to finally meet the great Zane Fischer," he said, extending a hand.

I returned his firm, calloused grip. "Nice to meet you too, Cole." As we eyed each other, I noticed the pockmarks on his cheeks and a cross tattoo on his leathery neck.

"Rough start this year, huh?" A leer flickered through his smile. "Well we're rootin' for ya, pal. You oughta be able win a few games against the bums in this league. Go out with some dignity, right?"

Some less-than-warm sentiments wanted to exit my mouth, but I restrained myself. I just took a breath and said, "Yeah well, I should be on my way."

"Right," said Toni, now standing almost between us. "Zane has to get to the ballpark. So if you'll move your truck and let him out, Cole." She gestured at the driveway.

"Oh right," he said. "I'll do that. But I gotta piss first." He brushed past me toward the front door of the house.

Toni exhaled in exasperation. "Cole, just back out. It'll take five seconds."

"Sorry, babe. Nature calls." He went inside.

She stomped after him and slammed the door behind her. I could hear their faint voices inside the house. "Cole, what is wrong with you? Give me the keys so I can let him out."

"*You* are not driving my truck."

"You're being a jerk."

"Oh yeah. You're the one getting together with your ex behind my back. How long's that been goin' on?"

"I told you … forget it. Just hurry up."

"You don't tell me what to do." Only muffled words after that.

I went over and leaned against the side of my pickup. While glancing at Cole's truck, I wondered how it would look with a big Z keyed into the driver's side door. Seemed to me that would be an improvement.

After five minutes, maybe a little longer, Cole emerged from the house and sauntered to his vehicle. His puffed out chest swayed with every step. He didn't say anything. I didn't either. Just got behind the wheel of my Chevy and waited until I could back out. Surprisingly, neither of us waved goodbye.

The next afternoon, I showed up at Sherman Field for practice. A day earlier, I was pretty sure I'd be quitting. But now I wanted to stay on the team a while longer to see if I could help Buddy get a job. Unfortunately, I still had to account for my past behavior.

When I entered the locker room, Javon Tate and Sylvester Larson were consoling a teammate seated at his locker. "This don't mean nothing, Jerome," said Sylvester, our lean left fielder. Nicknamed "the Cat," Sylvester liked to think of himself as the next Ricky Henderson. He was fast like Ricky, but he hit the ball in the air too much and made too many errors. The Cat knew how to dress though. "You'll catch another gig by the end of summer."

"Nah man, it's over for me," Jerome replied. "This was my last shot at baseball."

"Don't talk like that," Javon said, resting a beefy hand on his friend's shoulder. A man of average height, Javon was bulky with a capital B. Could hit the ball a long way, but he had little plate discipline and no wheels.

All three of them looked over at me as I approached my stall, which was only two down from Jerome's. "Gentlemen," I said with a nod.

"Hey, maybe the Fish can help you out," said Sylvester. "He's been everywhere in the bigs. He got connections."

"They get one of us today?" I asked. "That sucks, man." I really did feel bad, even though Jerome and I hadn't said two words to each other all season. Aside from Snowman, Dirk, Gale, and the rednecks I roomed with on the road, I hadn't socialized much with my teammates. But it was never easy seeing a guy get cut. The downcast face, the crushed dream.

"Yeah, they got Jerome," Sylvester said. "So you think you can help him catch on somewhere else? You know, make a phone call."

"I can try. Not sure I'd be much help though. I had a helluva time getting GMs to return my calls last off-season. Just don't have much clout anymore."

"Looks like Fischer's got his own problems anyway," Javon said, gesturing at my locker.

My eyes shifted to a green Post-it note stuck right in the middle of my stall. "Report to the General Manager's office" was all it said. The Fish had to go see the principal.

As I headed over to the Giants front office building, I tried to remember if Wright or Mendenhall was the GM. It wasn't easy to keep straight, because they usually referred to themselves as the team president and vice-president. But they also served as the GM and assistant GM. And, for some reason, I think it was the VP who was the GM and the president was the assistant GM. A minor league front office shouldn't be this confusing.

Turned out, it didn't really matter. Both Wright and Mendenhall awaited my arrival. They opened by assuring me that I still had their full support. And they were confident that things were soon going to turn around for me on the field. But there were some things that concerned them: 1) my breaking curfew and the unfortunate events that followed in Pierre; 2) my no-show at the promotional event; 3) my continuing refusal to do a pregame interview with Chip Sandquist, the Giants radioman; 4) my ongoing reluctance to sign autographs for fans; and 5) my refusal to have my picture taken for the team's baseball card set.

I'd forgotten about that last one. Who knew that minor league teams issued their own sets of baseball cards? I didn't. Hey, at least I'd showed up for the team photo at the start of the season. I sure didn't want to do that.

Wright (or maybe it was Mendenhall, whichever one had the salt-and-pepper hair) then not-so-subtly hinted that the manager no longer wanted me in his starting rotation. I already knew that. Curtis had told me himself. I didn't say anything though. Didn't want to break Wright/Mendenhall's momentum. Salt and pepper continued by assuring me that my roster spot was secure, but they were troubled by the direction I seemed to be heading. He asked if there was anything they could do to help me succeed as a Giant.

This is the point when Zane Fischer the star pitcher would make some smartass comment mocking them and their concerns. But Zane Fischer the whipping boy for mediocre bush league hitters knew he skated on thin ice. I was still on the team, not because they thought I had something left on the mound, but because they thought I could put butts in the stands and money in their pockets. Embarrassing as my performances had been, people still wanted to see a former star. Even so, there were limits as to how far I could push it. One more bad outing, off-field screw up, or insubordinate wisecrack, and the patience of my self-interested guardian angels could evaporate.

At that moment I had to ask myself, *Do I still want to do this?* The answer was no and yes. I was sick of putting in all the work and not getting one damn thing to go my way on the field. But my daughter wanted a summer job, and my staying on the team might help with that. And, truth be told, I really didn't want my career in baseball to end with a 0-3 record in an independent league.

So I thanked them for their support and apologized for my transgressions. I promised to be a better teammate and representative of the Giants organization. I added that my pitching would improve as well. That last statement didn't seem too likely to me, but I figured they'd be happy to hear it.

Wright and Mendenhall erupted in smiles. We all stood and shook hands. They patted my back and proclaimed their confidence that I would soon be mowing down hitters again. Before our lovefest ended, I mentioned my daughter's interest in working concessions or some other job at the ballpark. The blond one said he'd look into it. He then mentioned that it would sure be great if I could find time to join Chip Sandquist for a pregame interview before my start tomorrow night. I said I'd be delighted. Salt-and-pepper casually added how wonderful it would be if I could sign a few baseballs for an upcoming giveaway. I told him it would be my pleasure.

Batting practice had already begun by the time I'd reached the field. Larry the Geek told me I could skip shagging flies and throw a few knuckleballs in the bullpen if I wanted. *If I wanted?* That had to be another directive from above. If Curtis had his way, I'd be running wind sprints from foul pole to foul pole until the game started. Since I never much cared for standing around the outfield during BP, I decided to take the offer.

Our backup catcher Cy Yamato awaited my arrival in the bullpen. We had never talked much. Actually, Cy didn't say much to anybody. But I managed to work in some conversation with him between throws. Found out he was from California. His parents were born in Japan. They wanted him to be a chemist like his father, but he loved baseball. So here he was in Nebraska, dreaming of playing for the Dodgers, like his hero Hideo Nomo. Cy didn't possess a whole lot of talent—more than half my knucklers bounced past him—but you had to admire his heart and determination. I enjoyed our conversation. I also enjoyed watching Madam Knucklina dance in all her unhittable beauty. This however was just another rehearsal. What would she do on stage in front of an audience?

The Giants won that evening behind six effective innings from Lee Rodgers. Though I'd kept Cole out of my head while watching the game, thoughts of him were multiplying by the time I got home. Gale could tell something had me riled. Not wanting to discuss my ex's boyfriend, I told him I was focusing on my upcoming start. Helpful as always, my roommate put on some classical music and demonstrated a few of the breathing exercises that made Gale Force so dominant on the mound. Never mind the two runs he'd given up in relief of General Lee. "Those tallies were just an unfortunate happenstance of fate," Gale explained, "not a true indicator of my superior abilities." I actually appreciated what he was doing. Gale's attempts to "mentor" me as a pitcher provided an amusing distraction from all the crap that was bothering me.

When I showed up for practice the next afternoon, a box of baseballs sat in front of my locker. This presented a dilemma: I wanted to keep my promise to Wright and Mendenhall, but I didn't want to cramp my pitching hand signing a bunch of balls. Weed the mascot entered the clubhouse. I waved a ten-dollar bill under his red nose and twenty minutes later my problem had been solved. Hey, don't judge me. I signed at least a quarter of those balls. Besides, using "ghost autographers" is a tradition in our sport. Haven't you ever heard about the clubhouse boy who signed for Mantle? Recruiting Weed (a former pitcher I might add) was the perfect solution. Well, almost perfect. The idiot misspelled my name a few times, but who's going to notice?

Curtis still wasn't talking to me, so it was just Larry the Geek who went over the opposing team's lineup before the game. Though his egghead voice grated my ears, I actually paid attention (sort of) to his exhaustive statistical analysis of the St. Cloud Trappers' strengths and weaknesses. Then I talked to Snowman about calling different pitches to complement my knuckler. He welcomed that suggestion with great enthusiasm—anything to reduce the number of passed balls he had to chase to the backstop. After finishing with my catcher, I went to the announcer's booth for my pregame interview with Chip Sandquist. It wasn't so bad. I actually had a little fun recounting some favorite moments from seasons gone by.

Finally, it was showtime. In my previous starts for Lincoln, I began by throwing almost all knuckleballs. Against St. Cloud that night, I mixed it up more early on. About half my tosses in the first were knucklers. For the other pitches, I gave them fastballs and sliders, with an occasional curve. The visitors went down in order. Not knowing what to expect was apparently messing up their timing, so I kept it up in the innings that followed. It really helped that my stuff was sharp that night. The knuckleball fluttered and the sliders broke. I even snapped off a few sharp benders. Kinda like old times.

I struck out eight in my seven innings of work, while giving up five hits, three walks, and only one run. Lincoln came out on top 4-2. My first win as a Giant.

Guess the ex knew what she was talking about.

Chapter 7

The boys whooped it up in the locker room celebrating my "big" win. During the postgame interview, Chip Sandquist pointed out that it was my first victory in the minor leagues since 1977, a span of 21 years. Had to be some kind of record, he said. I remembered that night back in '77. It was my last game in the minors (until this year). I tossed a complete game for Utica. The next day Toronto called me up to the Show. Good times.

Unfortunately, I had to pass on my teammates' plan to hit the bars after the game. I'd fallen off the wagon once big time this season, and I couldn't let that happen again. Not if I wanted to make it back to the majors. I thought about joining the boys for a soda, but the risk still would have been too great. Red flag moods weren't limited to defeats. The high after a win could lead me into temptation just as easily as the foul mood that followed a bad outing.

When I got home, I remembered that I hadn't talked to Tim about Pierre. This seemed like a good time, especially since Gale went out with a "special lady friend" after the game (probably to some art gallery or violin concert) and wouldn't be back for a while. So I flopped onto the couch and dialed.

"Hello," a familiar voice answered.

"Captain Underwear!" That joke just never gets old. Well, not to me anyway.

"If it isn't the aquatic one. What's going on, my friend?"

"Oh, not much. Just basking in the glow of my big win over the St. Cloud Trappers."

"Congratulations. I knew you'd get back on track if you stuck with it. Must have baffled 'em with your knucklers, huh?"

"Yep. Worked in some curves and sliders too."

"Great. Oh, wait. Looks like ESPN is showing highlights from your game right now."

"Really?" I looked around for the TV remote.

"Yes, Zane. ESPN is now covering the scintillating baseball action of the Central States League. Looks like you've put on some weight."

"What? Not that much … oh." I realized I'd been had. "The game's not on TV, is it?"

"Nope."

"Aren't you the wiseass? I'd forgotten about the rapier wit of Tim Haines."

"Can't believe you fell for it."

"You know us starting pitchers, looking for attention wherever we can get it. Vain as the day is long, I tell ya."

"Good point."

"Hey, I gotta tell you something. I ran into a problem."

"Too much celebrating?"

"No, tonight was good. It was the game before, up in Pierre. I took the loss, my third in a row. Went out with the boys afterwards."

"How bad?"

"Bad. Downed a lot of poison that night. Our right fielder had to drag me back to the motel. The way he tells it, I made quite the ass of myself before passing out."

"I see."

"Yeah … and so the streak ends. Just missed getting a year."

Tim didn't say anything for few seconds. "Well, guess it's time to start a new streak. You say you didn't have any drinks tonight, right?"

"Right. Just grabbed a burger at Hardees and came home."

"Your new streak is off to a good start then?"

"I guess."

"Do you know what went wrong in Pierre?"

I wandered over to the sliding door and went out on the deck. The stars took turns winking at me from the clear dark sky. "Yeah, I do. It was stupid to go to a bar the way I was feeling that night."

"And?"

"I was tired, Tim. I'd gotten knocked around, yet again. Nothing worked. It wasn't that long ago I was on top in the majors. And this season I'm struggling to last three innings in a bush league I hadn't even heard of a few months ago. It's been frustrating, man. Bustin' my butt for so long and not getting any results. You wouldn't understand something like that."

I've said a lot of moronic things in my life, but those last words may have been the dumbest I'd ever spoken.

"You're right about that, Fish. It's been nothing smooth sailing for Captain Underwear the past couple years."

"Tim, I didn't mean that. I'm sorry." I hadn't felt like that big of an idiot for quite some time. The adversity Tim Haines had faced made my issues look like nothing. In the summer of '96, he was heading home after a game in Pittsburgh when a drunk driver sped through a stoplight and broadsided his SUV. Tim Haines would never pitch again. Tim Haines would never walk again. So there I was telling a man sitting in a wheelchair, his career cut short, that he wouldn't understand my stupid little frustrations.

"Don't worry about it, Zane. I know it's been a challenging year for you. But you've made great progress. A year of sobriety is huge."

"Thanks. I wouldn't have made it a week without your help." It's true. He carried me through some dark times when I was struggling to clean up my act. And he'd just been through it all himself. He got really depressed in the weeks after the accident. Drank more and started snorting the powder. I remember visiting him that fall thinking his days were numbered. In his condition, the end could've come on purpose or through an accidental overdose. One day his wife came home from Christmas shopping with their three kids and found him messed up bad. Having his young children—the oldest was five maybe—see him like that was a wake-up call for Tim. He recommitted his life to Christ and kicked the alcohol and drugs. In a matter of weeks, he became a whole new person. A rock, really. So when I was looking for a sponsor a few months later, Tim Haines was the name at the top of my list.

"You're gonna be all right," he said. "Sounds like tonight you found reasons to be encouraged about your pitching."

"Those hitters weren't exactly the '27 Yankees, so encouraged isn't quite the word I'd use. But it's a start."

"Well, I'm encouraged. Tonight will be the start of a big winning streak for you. The Fish is back."

"Let's hope."

He asked what else was going on in Lincoln, so I told him about Buddy, Toni, and my meeting with the delightful Cole. After we'd talked for a while, Tim wanted to make sure I didn't end up passed out in the gutter again. "You'll call me next time you're facing that type of situation, right?"

"Right."

"Promise?"

"Yes."

"Alright. Mind if I close with a word of prayer."

"Nah, that's okay. Thanks anyway."

"Great, I'll pray." And he did.

For my next start a few days later, I faced the Columbia Patriots at Sherman Field. In the first few innings, the ball jumped and the batters chased. The Giants held a 4-0 lead heading into the fifth. Then the Patriot hitters starting showing some patience. And the ump stopped giving me the corners. A knuckleball pitcher—actually every pitcher—needs the corners to be effective. After walking my second batter in a row, I yelled in at him, "C'mon Andy, that was a strike two innings ago." He just shook his head. Thinking I might be close to getting tossed, Snowman hurried out to the mound to defuse the situation. He didn't need to. I'd been dealing with umpires for longer than he'd been alive. I knew what I could and couldn't say. And I wasn't close to unleashing the magic word. Yet.

The Patriots pushed a couple runs across with another walk and a single. Our shortstop and second baseman—Ricky Garcia and

Julio Juarez—then turned a nifty double play to get me out of the jam. We still held a 4-2 lead in the sixth when my pitches stopped dancing. Madam Knucklina just glided in flat and easy right where the batters wanted her. The whore. Columbia knocked home three more to take the lead. My evening was over. Fortunately the Giants rallied in the late innings, so at least I didn't get pinned with another loss.

We didn't have a game the next day, so Buddy and I hiked the forest trails at Wilderness Park in the morning. After lunch she gave me my Father's Day present early, because the team was going to be out of town on the actual day. The wrapped package had a label that read, "To my favorite pitcher in the whole world." I tore off the purple paper to find a framed picture of me on the mound at Sherman. It was a good action shot, taken by a newspaper photographer during my first win as a Giant. I loved it. What a cool thing for Buddy to do.

That afternoon I was looking forward to golfing with Gale, General Lee, and Hank. But the clowns in the front office had scheduled me to shoot a TV promo with Weed in his mascot costume. For the commercial, I would be standing in front of the dugout in my uniform tossing a ball up in the air. Yeah, that would look natural. Because in my free time I often hang around the ballpark doing just that. After the stoner walked up to me on his stilts, our crisp dialogue would commence.

Me, looking up: "Hey, Big Abe. How's the weather up there?"

Pothead Abe: "Splendid, if I do say so myself. And the forecast is looking even better for the Fourth of July." That was three weeks away, so nobody had any idea if that was true.

Me: "Really? Is there anything fun to do in Lincoln that day?"

Pothead Abe: "There sure is, Fish. I'm counting on you to lead the Giants into battle against the St. Joseph Bandits at Sherman Field."

Me: "Yes sir, Mr. President. Those rebels won't have a chance."

Pothead Abe, turning to the camera: "Huzzah! And this is a great opportunity for you fans to save some greenbacks. Listen now to my Sherman Field Address. [dramatic pause] I proclaim that on Independence Day all baseball fans who venture forth to this ballpark may buy four tickets, four hot dogs, and four soft drinks for only thirty dollars."

Me: "All that for only thirty bucks? Is that really true?"

Pothead Abe: "They don't call me Honest Abe for nothing."

Me: "Sounds like you're emancipating Giants fans from high ticket prices." By this point, I was just trying not to crack up. Or throw up.

Pothead Abe: "That's right. And there will never be a better time to see Cy Young winner Zane Fischer pitch."

Me: "Well, I could sure use the support of a big home crowd."

Pothead Abe: "Indeed."

Me: "And you too, Mr. President. You'll be there at Sherman Field on the Fourth of July, won't you?"

Pothead Abe: "Of course. What else am I going to do that day? Go to the theater with Mary?"

I was then supposed to look into the camera with wide eyes and slap my cheeks like the kid in *Home Alone*. It would have been bad enough if we could've done it all in one take, but no, it took three hours to shoot the damn commercial. Weed kept forgetting his lines and wobbling on his stilts, so they had to find some braces (below the camera's view) that would hold him in place. He still flopped over and landed on his face a couple times. In case you're wondering, yes he was baked. Too bad I wasn't. If my pitching hadn't improved, I would've been tempted to smash the camera into the ground and quit the team right there.

The other reason I did the commercial was because Buddy had an interview that same day. Don't tell me Wright and Mendenhall didn't plan it that way. So I went along with the humiliation. At least the dark cloud had a silver lining. Buddy got a job working at a concessions stand at Sherman Field. The kid owes me. She'd better pick out a good nursing home for me when I'm old.

The next day, the team started a 10-day road trip that took us to Topeka, Columbia, and St. Joseph. I pitched the third game of the series against the Titans. The knuckleball jiggled like Santa's belly that night. My curve had a decent break too. I gave up only two runs (one unearned) in eight innings as Lincoln cruised 7-2. Afterwards, Curtis started talking to me again. This meant I no longer had to get his words of wisdom conveyed to me through Larry the Geek. More good news came when I called Buddy after the game. She said Cole wasn't coming over to the house during the day anymore. And he was being nicer to Toni. He seemed to be on his best behavior lately, she said. I was glad to hear it, but I still didn't trust the guy.

We swept Topeka and won the first game in Columbia, before dropping the second game the following night. It was an ugly loss, marred by seven walks from McCormick and several fielding errors and mental mistakes. Curtis at this time decided that we—the team—were getting lazy. And though he didn't come out and say it, he implied in one of his rants that some of us players were too fat (like he had room to talk). So we were going to run and burn off the flab. Make no mistake, we had always been running in practice. But now we would be running more, almost twice as much. Yay!

Even though I wasn't too keen on the extra exercise, I participated whole heartedly. After two months of fast food and Gale's late night cuisine, I'd put on some weight. I was still in pretty good shape though, only about fifteen pounds heavier than what I'd weighed a decade earlier. But my pants were getting tight around the waistline. And with what I was making, I sure didn't want to blow my meager earnings on a new wardrobe. So yeah, I was on board with a little extra running at the ballpark.

And, truth be told, we did have some lardasses on the team. Javon Tate, for example, was a fat, fat man. He looked kinda like a black Dusty Rhodes. Except Javon's gut was a bit larger than the American Dream's. Tate usually brought up the rear in our daily jogs, though sometimes Dirk would beat him out for that honor. And when it came to sweating, nobody could top Dirk Davis. We'd start at one foul line and not even halfway to other foul line, he looked like Irene Cara getting doused in *Flashdance*. You could fill a 30-gallon tub ringing out his shirt after practice. After watching

Javon and Dirk huff and puff their way across the outfield, I really hoped our trainer Jerry Hershberger was good at CPR.

We had some lean guys on the team too. Snowman was a toothpick. Still can't figure out why he wanted to be a catcher. I should mention though, he'd made progress catching my knuckler, but not without a growing collection of welts and bruises. It ain't easy tracking a knuckleball as it comes in at you. If you doubt me, just put on a catcher's mask, get in a crouch, and have a knuckleballer throw you a few. There's a reason why some teams keep guys on their rosters to do nothing else but catch their knuckleball pitcher. Early in his career Phil Neikro's personal catcher was Bob Uecker. Crazy guy, that Uecker. One time he and I were paired up at a charity golf event in Arizona. Maybe the funniest four hours of my life.

The fitness-conscious Giants took the next two in Columbia and then hit the road for St. Joseph. During the ride, I lost $10 to Sylvester "the Cat" Larson in a poker game. I should've known better than to get dragged into it, but Gale wanted to play and talked me into joining him. It was almost worth it, due to the Cat's tales about his many romantic conquests. The kid talked smooth and dressed sharp, but he was only 22 years old. He couldn't have done half the things he said he'd done with women of "all races, colors, and creeds." Still, the stories were entertaining. I also enjoyed watching Gale Force drop $55 to the Cat.

The other reason I joined the game at the back of the bus was because Dirk Davis was sitting near the front of the bus. Juarez and Garcia had taken him out for some authentic Mexican cuisine the night before. Yep, you know what happened next. Some of the guys near Dirk plugged their noses, while others crowded into the rear of the bus. The driver turned up his oscillating fan full blast. Larry the Geek gagged and puked a little on his charts. Even Curtis couldn't take it. He stood up and told Davis he had half a mind to stop the bus and make him walk the rest of the way. That remark brought a cheer from the boys. Dirk just sat there with his usual "what's the big deal" expression that followed one of his rancid outbursts.

I was scheduled to start the first game in St. Joseph. When we got to our motel, McCormick offered me a greenie. I declined. First off, I was trying to kick all outside stimulants. Secondly, getting jacked up wasn't all that helpful with my current style of pitching. Knuckleballs required a deft touch rather than power and energy. Yes, I'd downed about a million pep pills throughout my career. But Zane Fischer in 1998 wanted no part of them. McCormick and several of my other teammates more than made up for my abstinence. Our center fielder Shelby Turner had an old frat buddy with pharmaceutical connections. This guy kept the Giants well supplied with steroids, uppers, and other popular performance enhancers.

The St. Joseph Bandits concerned me. The team had no pitching, but their lineup bristled with heavy artillery. They led the league in home runs and batting average. Didn't matter that night though, because Madam Knucklina had never looked lovelier. She mesmerized the hitters with her naughty moves. The Bandits did plenty of looking, but they could not touch. And best of all, my flutterballs stayed in the zone. Yours truly pitched a complete game, surrendering only one run and striking out ten. The masterpiece evened my record at 3-3 and moved Lincoln into second place in the Western Division.

Chip Sandquist corralled me for a postgame interview, which mercifully lasted only about five minutes. After the interview, I went to the locker room where Jerry Hershberger saw me rubbing my arm and shoulder. He asked if I'd hurt something. I said no. He then asked if I wanted to use the diathermy machine when we got back to Lincoln. No again. Thing is, I was rubbing my arm and shoulder because they *didn't* hurt. No pain at all, a pleasant contrast from my last season in organized baseball. I'd just thrown 116 pitches and, since two-thirds of them were knuckleballs, felt like I could throw another 116. Good news, indeed. Not only had my injury healed, but I was getting my stuff back on the mound.

Lincoln split the next two games in St. Joseph. I should point out that the fans there gave me a healthy dose of boos and heckling throughout the series. Didn't matter if I was on the hill or not, they let me have it. See, in 1995, at the end of my second year with Kansas City (located just a half hour south of St. Joseph), I filed for free agency. In an interview with *Sports Illustrated* at the time, I made a comment that the organization seemed to be heading in the wrong direction. I didn't say it with any rancor, it's just that KC had finished 30 games out of first and that was my honest assessment. Not a big deal, so I thought. But Royals fans didn't like it at all. And they didn't forget what the Fish had said.

The Giants returned home in a happy mood. Even Curtis and Larry the Geek couldn't completely hide their delight with our 8-2 road trip. There was a noticeable improvement in the cinematic entertainment presented on the bus rides: *Major League*, *Caddyshack* (the first one), and *Rocky 3*. That's more like it.

I was really looking forward to seeing Buddy again. When I'd last talked to her on the phone a couple days earlier, she still sounded upbeat. She even seemed excited (or as excited as she gets) for the team to return so she could start her new job at Sherman Field. When the Giants got back to Lincoln, we had the evening off so I told Buddy I'd take her and Stick bowling. I pulled into the driveway expecting to see both of them on the front stoop, but she was sitting there alone. Stick had some family thing going on that night, so it was just the two of us who went to the alley.

I liked bowling. It's just dark enough inside to keep people from easily recognizing me. I'd been growing a beard the past few weeks and wore a red Husker cap to further improve my chances of remaining incognito. Yeah, I know, not much of a disguise. But it was better than Superman. All he did was put on a suit and wear a pair of glasses. And then he's suddenly unrecognizable as Clark Kent? The people in Metropolis must be morons. I probably shouldn't have said that. Now I'm gonna get booed next time I pitch there.

Buddy didn't say much on the drive to the alley. Her mood seemed darker than when we'd last talked on the phone. I didn't pry. I figured if something was wrong, she'd tell me on her own. We rented shoes and found our lane. I grabbed a 16-pound ball, which I planned to throw right-handed so as not to stress my pitching arm.

"They're all too heavy," Buddy said, examining the choices in the ball rack.

"Here's a 12-pounder." I held up a light green ball with speckles. "Wanna give this a try?"

She then busted out crying. I mean it was boom, like a flood.

"Hey, it's okay," I said, returning the ball to the rack. "We'll find you a lighter ball."

"It's not the ball, Dad!" She shot me a look that said, *you dumbass.*

"What is it, Buddy?"

She dropped into one of the plastic seats near the ball return. I sat next to her as she wiped her face with a Kleenex. "It's Mom."

A whole slew of bad thoughts entered my head. *Cole hit Toni. That has to be it.*

"She ..." A few more tears rolled off her round doll cheeks. "She's getting married."

"To Cole?"

"She told me this morning. How he popped the question. How surprised she was. Then she showed me her new ring. Made me want to puke."

"They haven't even been dating that long. Right?"

"Only a few weeks. It's so stupid." Buddy said that Cole had changed his act since that day I'd met him. Bringing Toni flowers. Buying little presents for Buddy. Not staying at the house during the day. Not drinking as much. Taking more jobs. Then last night he took her out to this nice steak place and a fancy musical. By the end of the evening, my ex was engaged.

I saw the weight of the world in Buddy's eyes. It was a look I'd never seen on her face before, and never wanted to see again.

"Dad ... I don't want to live in that house with him."

"I know, honey."

"He'll change back once they're married. I know he will."

My thoughts exactly. There was no doubt in my mind that Cole's Boy Scout routine was a sham. "Maybe your mother won't go through with it. Have they set a date?"

"No. But jerkhead says he wants to tie the knot as soon as possible." She sniffled. "Then my life is over."

"No it's not."

"I'm nervous when he's around. It's like being near a ticking bomb."

My arm slid around her shoulder. "I won't let him hurt you."

She was quiet for a while, and then said, "Dad, can I come live with you?" Her voice sounded so sad.

What could I say to that? Toni got full custody in the divorce settlement. To try and fight that would require a good lawyer—an expensive lawyer that I could not afford. And even if I could get a good lawyer, what kind of case could we make? Mom provided a stable home that would soon have two parents. Dad, on the other hand, traveled all the time, lived in a teammate's apartment, and brought home dirt for a paycheck.

Given my (lack of) financial status, you may be wondering about child support. Yes I still paid regularly. In fact, I'd never missed a payment. Nor would I. How did I manage that, you ask? After the divorce, when the Fish was making seven figures, my financial manager Kevin Yeager set up an untouchable account that would dispense the monthly payments until Buddy turned 18. It turned out to be a brilliant idea, protecting Buddy's child support fund from the thief I hired to manage my finances after Kevin retired.

So I had one factor in my favor, but the rest of them didn't look so good. "Honey, I wish you could, but I don't think the court would allow that." I felt so small and useless.

"Maybe I could hide out at your apartment," Buddy said. "They might stop looking for me after a while."

My heart broke. "You don't want to do that to your mom. She'd be worried sick."

"Yeah, right."

"Despite her questionable taste in men, your mother loves you. More than anything. She's not doing this to hurt you."

"Whatever."

"Don't give up hope, my Little Mermaid." I called her that when she was six, after the movie with that title came out. Buddy loved it—I was the Fish and she was the Little Mermaid. "We'll figure something out."

"Okay." She leaned into me.

I kissed the top of her bob. "Let's bowl. It'll take your mind off things."

Truth is, we both needed a distraction.

Chapter 8

The next day, Lincoln opened a series at Sherman against the Council Bluffs Black Squirrels. Early in the game, Curtis blew his stack over a bad call and got tossed. His burst of temper ignited the team, which came back and won 8-6 in 11 innings. Rain washed out the next evening's contest, setting up a double header the following day. The Giants won the afternoon game 3-2, and I took the hill in the nightcap to go for the sweep. Madam Knucklina wasn't her usual beguiling self, allowing the visitors to put up three early runs. I just couldn't prevent the spin. And since a spinning knuckleball is pretty much like setting a ball on a tee, I had to throw my other stuff. Emptied the old toolbox: fastballs, curves, sliders, and a changeup here and there. None of these pitches had much dazzle, but at least my command remained. Big league hitters would've feasted on what I served up. A lot of minor leaguers would've too. Fortunately, the Black Squirrels (who names these teams?) didn't have many thumpers in their lineup. Several of their drives ended up as warning track outs. Curtis pulled me after six with the Giants ahead 5-4. We held the lead until the ninth, when our closer Matt "Gatling Gun" Clooney lost it.

After the game, Gale, Dirk, Snowman, and I ended up at the apartment playing poker. They all grumbled about the loss, but I took it pretty well. Not that I like losing. That's never fun whatever level you're playing at. Especially if it comes at the hands (or paws) of a bunch of squirrels. But through the cloud of defeat I saw a silver lining: Despite losing my knuckleball, I got hitters out by mixing pitches and changing speeds. I even allowed myself the hope that my nasty curve of years past would soon be part of my arsenal again.

Dirk, ever the bright ray of sunshine, drew no positives from the defeat. He spent the first three hands griping about Clooney. I did not share his sentiments. Even though the Gatling Gun failed to hold what would've been a win for me, I still liked the kid. Yes, he was a bit wild on the mound, kinda like Charlie Sheen in *Major League.* But I could overlook the walks because his flakiness amused me. As the closer, he didn't have much to do during the first eight innings of a game. So he'd sit in the bullpen, chomping on sunflower seeds and checking out the girls in the stands. He wasn't alone in that, but the Gatling Gun was the only guy who brought a pair of binoculars. And he made no attempt to hide what he was doing. Sometimes after a game, he'd even climb into the stands to "get some digits." When he wasn't checking out the local talent, Clooney entertained himself with other antics. Say a teammate was engrossed in the action on the field, Matt would lean down with a Bic lighter and set the victim's shoelaces on fire. Other times he'd hide a fake tarantula or a rubber snake in a guy's locker. Clooney also did some great impressions, his best ones being of Curtis, Jay Leno, and our nation's president. "I did not have sexual relations with that woman …"

Not too many hands into the poker game the cards turned friendly for the Fish. It helped that I'd discovered some tells from my opponents. For example, the normally twitchy Snowman stopped vibrating his leg when he had a decent hand. And when Dirk had something good, his neck turned a little pink, like a medium rare steak. As for Gale, he was just bad at poker. Before I knew it, I'd turned the ten dollars I started with into $47.

The ten I'd brought to the table was actually a loan from Gale. Why did I have to borrow money from my roommate, you ask? Well, before the game, the Giant People's Court met in the clubhouse. The GPC was an informal judicial body formed by my esteemed teammates. Most teams I'd played on had some similar sort of kangaroo court that levied fines on the stupidity that ballplayers inevitably chose to engage in. According to court rules, a charge could be filed by anybody with at least two witnesses. A "jury" of five not so impartial peers then heard testimony from both sides and issued a verdict. The judge (Sylvester the Cat for this term) handed down the punishment. Team justice usually took the form of currency, which went into a fund for an end-of-season party. Sentences from this most recent session of the GPC included: $20 to Tommy Stickel for inviting a rather hideous-looking lady back to his motel room in Columbia, $25 to Dirk for making the bus smell like the inside of his rectum, $15 to Weed the mascot for his bizarre religious devotion to the TV actor Willie Aames, $5 each to Julio Juarez and Tracy Desjardins for being the only married guys on the roster, and $30 to yours truly for my "drunken jackassery" in Pierre. My status as a former big league star no doubt contributed to the severity of my fine. Jerks. So now you know why I was broke.

Broke at the *start* of the poker game, that is. After the final hand, my winnings had increased to $83.50. Since moving to Lincoln, I'd rarely had that much cash in my wallet. While finishing off his last beer, Snowman commented that I didn't seem too excited about my big windfall. Gale said the same thing. When they kept prying, I told them about Toni getting engaged to Cole, and the effect it was having on Buddy.

My three teammates surprised me. They actually listened to what I said and then sat in quiet contemplation, as if muted by their concern for my situation. And then came the advice. Dirk pounded the table, sending a few poker chips flipping into the air. "Best way to deal with this situation is to hit it head-on. I'll get Hank and us three will go pay Cole a visit. We'll tell him that he might want to reconsider this marriage thing." Dirk smacked a fist into his hand. "Let him know that staying a bachelor is a much safer lifestyle choice for his future."

The thought made me smile. "Gotta say I like the idea, Dirk. But Toni would flip out if we did that. It would just drive her closer to Cole. She might even marry him sooner just to spite me."

"How about this," Gale said, his fingertips steepled in front of him. "You could offer this Cole fellow a financial incentive to back

101

off. Whilst a teenager, my sister Julianne took up with a ne'er-do-well by the name of Niles. A true boar, that one. Daddy, as you can imagine, was not pleased. When it became clear that Jules's unfortunate association would not die of natural causes, Daddy had to intervene. He offered the lout fifty thousand dollars to disappear from our lives forever." Gale closed his eyes and sighed.

"Well, what happened?" Dirk asked.

"He accepted the offer. Broke up with Jules over the phone. Then took the money and ran. The fool. Had he feigned offense and refused, my father was willing to go as high as a hundred thousand."

"I like the results of your idea too," I said. "But I don't have fifty grand. What I won here tonight, that's what I've got. Think Cole would be willing to disappear for eighty bucks?"

"You could ask," Snowman said.

"Hmmm." Gale frowned. "Yes, I see your point. Perhaps I could call Daddy and discuss a loan. He would definitely sympathize with your predicament. And I could vouch for your potential return to the majors, thereby making his financial risk more palatable."

"I appreciate that, McGrady. But if Toni ever found out, she'd explode. Even worse than if we threatened Cole. I'd never see my daughter again."

"Did your sister ever find out about the payoff?" Dirk asked Gale.

"Sadly, she did. Niles's abrupt departure raised her suspicions. Jules snooped around and finally tricked our accountant into revealing the truth."

"Did she ever forgive your father?" Snowman asked.

"Actually, she did."

"Time heals all wounds, huh?"

Gale snickered. "Time, no. But a new Mercedes for her eighteenth birthday, yes. Amazing how that works. Plus, she found a new beau within the month."

"Did your dad like this guy?" Snowman asked.

"No. Hated him worse than Niles." Gale sucked down the remaining wine in his glass. "So of course Jules married the chap. They'll celebrate their fourth anniversary in August."

With curfew approaching, the party broke up. Before he left, Snowman offered his advice. "You could try talking to Toni. She might not realize how her engagement is affecting Buddy."

"Yeah? Think I should tell her?"

"No, not directly. But you might steer the conversation in that direction. Maybe say something like, 'I bet Buddy is excited about your engagement.' You know, force her to confront the issue without telling her your thoughts on the matter."

I liked the idea. Not as much as Dirk's, but at least this one wouldn't get Toni mad at me. I kept mulling it over that night. With no other solutions jumping out, Snowman's subtle approach seemed like the best approach.

A day passed. Then another. Whenever I'd get ready to call, something else came up. Truthfully, I didn't really want to talk to Toni. What she did, getting engaged to that idiot, ticked me off. Buddy, for her part, seemed a little better since the bowling alley. We'd gotten together a couple afternoons—she had a great time beating her old man at miniature golf. Laughed her ass off when I sent the ball and then my putter into a pond. And she liked her job at the ballpark. Met two new friends there named Lauren and Brooke. Sometimes I'd see Stick hanging out at Buddy's concession stand. Whenever he spotted me, he'd flash his goofy grin with a thumbs up sign. I still didn't like his chances.

My next start came on the Fourth of July. I'd been waiting for what seemed like an eternity for that day to arrive, so my commercial with Weed would finally stop airing. Every time I was near a TV set that infernal thing came on. And the guys in the clubhouse let me hear about it every day. Clooney had memorized all the lines and could recite the entire commercial verbatim. He especially loved imitating my Macaulay Culkin expression at the end.

A sellout crowd filled Sherman Field. I'd like to think that the chance to see yours truly was what drew them to the ballpark. But it could've been the hot dog-soft drink promotion. Or the sunny weather. Or the team's recent surge in the standings. Or the tradition of watching baseball on Independence Day. Who knows. In my head, it was because the masses wanted to see the great Zane Fischer do his thing. That's my story and I'm sticking to it.

I gotta say, a surge of energy ran through me during the national anthem. It felt good to be pitching on the Fourth of July. Sure it wasn't Riverfront Stadium, but there was a festive crowd on hand to watch baseball. And as Tim had told me, this game, like every game I pitched for the Giants, was an important stepping stone in my return to the majors. Further sharpening my focus was the clubhouse rumor that a couple big league scouts would be in attendance that day. *Knuckleball don't fail me now.*

My first pitch changed directions three times before gliding over the outside corner for strike one. It's a great feeling being able to throw such an unpredictable pitch for strikes. Actually being able to throw any pitch consistently for strikes is a great feeling. Think about it. The pitcher stands sixty feet, six inches away from a plate that is a mere seventeen inches wide. The average distance between a batter's waist and his knees is eighteen inches. So, to get a strike call, a pitcher has to throw a baseball sixty feet through an imaginary box measuring 18 by 17 inches. This box can increase or decrease in size based on the umpire's eyesight or disposition. Just throwing strikes, however, is not enough. A pitcher must make the baseball difficult to hit as it passes through the imaginary box. He tries to do this by delivering the ball at different speeds, or by making it drop, rise, or move to the side. Think it's easy? Look up sometime how many Americans make their living pitching a baseball. Not a large percentage of the national workforce. I guarantee you there are a lot more accountants, custodians, and lawyers out there than pitchers. That's probably a good thing. Truth be told, we really are flakes.

The Cavaliers went down one-two-three in the first. Same result in the second inning. With one down in the third, one of their speedy guys beat out a weak grounder for an infield hit. The runner promptly stole second and then third. Stopping the stolen base was a continuing weakness in my game. I still had a great pickoff move, mind you, but a knuckleball flutters slowly to the plate. And Snowman, bless his heart, seemed so happy just to stop the pitches, he usually hesitated before throwing to second base. So opposing runners enjoyed much success running on the Fish.

The inning ended with the runner stranded at third base. Pierre picked up another hit in the fourth, but nothing else that frame. Madam Knucklina was more seductive than ever. As she floated from my fingertips, you could almost hear the lies she whispered into the batters' ears. "Come on big guy, take a swing. You'll hit a home run for sure." Then as the hitter cut loose, she'd dart one way, and then another, eluding the heavy lumber swishing past. Adding to Pierre's woes was a relative of the Madam's who also showed up at the ballpark. See, Miss Knucklina had an uncle named Charlie who could be every bit as deceptive as the good madam. And Uncle Charlie told some nasty lies of his own to those Pierre boys. Years ago my curveball was among the best in baseball. Some even compared my bender to Koufax's. But after hurting my shoulder and sitting out a season, my curve had lost its mojo. Happily, the past couple weeks the bender started bending again. On Independence Day, my Uncle Charlie was once again the same sociopathic bastard I'd loved for so many years.

As the temperature rose that sunny afternoon, so did the Cavs' frustrations. Heading into the fifth they trailed 3-0 and looked helpless to make solid contact with my curves and knucklers. After I struck out the first batter that inning, a knuckleball got away from me and plunked a guy in the back. The pitch traveled no more than 65 mph and clearly wasn't thrown at him on purpose. But the hitter threw down his bat and shouted some words that can't be said on regular TV. Or basic cable, for that matter. Next thing I knew he was charging the mound. As he approached, I wondered if he was really mad or just trying to make a name for himself by taking on a former big league star. Either way, I'd have to do something fast.

I pulled off my glove and prepared to fling it at his face. But before I could let the leather fly, the batter hit the ground. Snowman had sprinted after him and tripped him up from behind, fifteen feet in front of the mound. Dirk then came flying into view from his position at first base. The big man flung himself through the air and dropped an elbow on the batter as he lay face down in the grass. It reminded me of watching Randy Savage in the WWF, except Dirk weighed considerably more than the Macho Man. The batter yelped in agony as Dirk's girth crashed down upon his back.

A typical baseball melee ensued. Both dugouts emptied. Pitchers from both bullpens raced toward the infield. I just stood there wondering how many of the batter's ribs Dirk had cracked. That was kind of a dumb thing for me to do considering that a bunch of Cavaliers were charging toward me. Yelling something in Spanish, our shortstop Ricky Garcia pulled me out of the path of a fist rocketing toward my face. Both teams then formed a scrum on the infield. A lot of pushing. A lot of yelling. One guy shoved me. I shoved another guy. Players then started pulling teammates away from the pile. Most guys wanted to avoid a season-ending injury in a stupid fight, so it didn't take long for cooler heads to break up the altercation. Nobody got hurt. Well, nobody except for the squished batter. He had to be helped off the field, spitting up blood with each step. Even if the umpire hadn't ejected him, he wouldn't be playing any more baseball that day. The ump also ejected Dirk and glared at me like I'd be next. Then Curtis got in his face. "You can't eject Fish. He didn't do nothin'."

"He plunked the batter," the ump replied.

"With what?" Curtis exclaimed. "Fischer throws fifty miles per hour, tops. His pitches couldn't break through a piece of cardboard."

After pondering that for a few seconds, the umpire let me off with a warning.

Fortunately, Madam Knucklina wasn't daunted by any of the preceding tomfoolery. She came back as if nothing had happened. When play resumed I gave up only a walk before retiring the side on a ground out and a pop up. I sent the Cavs down in order in the sixth and allowed a double, but nothing else, in the seventh. Heading into the seventh inning stretch, Lincoln led 5-0.

At this point, Wright and Mendenhall stopped the game to bring out their special Fourth of July entertainment. I'd thought that Giant Abe staggering around on stilts in a red, white, and blue top hat was plenty of special entertainment for this occasion, but I guess I was wrong. It was something of a tradition around here to bring in a special "act" during the July 4th game. A gate in the outfield wall opened and a horse-drawn cage entered the ballpark. Inside the cage sat two black bears. Yes, real live black bears. And they wore red, white, and blue capes. The horses pulled the cage all the way to the infield. The crowd gasped as two trainers wearing spandex body suits (guess which three colors) opened the door and beckoned the bears to come out. The trainers fed the animals treats and then led them through a series of tricks. Because what better way to celebrate our nation's independence than with circus bears prancing around on their hind legs?

After several minutes, the bears closed out their act by riding around on motorcycles. I could imagine the face of Stan the groundskeeper growing redder and redder watching his infield grass getting torn up. One of the bears slid off his bike and started ambling toward our dugout. I figured this was part of the act, but the frantic movements of the trainers quickly convinced me that Smokey had gone off script. The animal must have smelled something interesting in our vicinity. The buttered popcorn aroma wafting in from the stands did have an especially tangy appeal that afternoon. For whatever reason, the bear kept approaching. My teammates cleared out of the dugout. Some lady in the stands shrieked, "We're all gonna die!" A series of screams followed. Over the PA system, a panicked announcer yelled for everyone to "remain calm!" That of course stirred up the crowd even more, resulting in a near stampede for the exits. Surprisingly, the bear didn't get spooked by any of this. It's a good thing too, because this 500-pound beast now stood ten feet away from yours truly, still sitting on the dugout bench.

I'm not sure why I didn't run away with the rest of my teammates. I just didn't. Maybe it's because the lumbering animal didn't seem like much of a threat. His head bobbed around at the surrounding chaos, before pointing directly at me. His eyes conveyed sadness more than anything. I wanted to help him. I wanted to free him from his prison. Then we could hit the road together: The Fish and the Bear. Hmmm, that might not end so well. For the Fish, that is.

Within seconds, the trainers had hustled over, pressed a couple treats into the bear's mouth, and got him turned around. Soon both animals were back in their cage and being pulled off the field. Show over. Well almost. Both horses had defecated on the infield dirt, so we had to wait another five minutes for Stan and his crew to clean up the mess. During the delay, Curtis came over and sat next to me. "Bears," he said, shaking his head. "Not that long ago we were playing major league baseball. Now we got bears on the field. Man, what are we doing here?"

"Aw Skip, we just love the game so much, we can't stay away."

"Yeah, right." He chuckled. "You must really want it, huh?"

"Sometimes I wonder."

"Well, if you do make it back to the Show, do me a favor. Take me with you. *Please* take me with you."

"I'll see what I can do."

Lincoln plated another run in the bottom of the seventh to build the lead to 6-0. When I went out to pitch the eighth, I glanced up at the stands, something I rarely did. Wish I wouldn't have on this occasion, because five rows behind our dugout sat Toni and Cole. She was looking at the other people in the crowd, but he stared right at me. The smirk on his face was clear even at that distance. When my gaze lingered on him, he wrapped his arm around Toni. Then he started nodding, his smirk still in place.

Snowman yelled something, drawing my attention back to the field. Despite the parade of distractions, I had a great game going. Only six more outs and I'd have a complete game shutout. On the Fourth of July. With scouts in the stands. With Toni in the stands. Locking in on the catcher's mitt, I delivered a 12-6 curve that buckled the batter's knees. Strike one. I didn't win 290 games in the majors without being able to block out distractions.

As they did sometimes to fire up the Giants and unnerve our opponents, the crowd started stomping their feet and chanting, "FEE FI FO FUM." Aided by this ongoing thunderous commotion, I struck out five of the last six Cavalier batters to finish the shutout. It felt good. I even signed a few dozen autographs on my way to the clubhouse. Once inside, the guys showered me with beer and slaps on the back. Pretty much every one of them had to make some crack that "the old man's still got it." Some wiseass put a package of Depends in my locker in case all the excitement of winning got to be too much for me. Idiots.

After showering and changing, I headed over to the concession stand where Buddy worked. She sat at a picnic table, not looking happy.

"Hey why the long face," I said. "Didn't you hear? We won."

"I heard."

"And the old man did alright." I raised my fists and punched the air. "Beat up the other team. Fought off a ferocious bear. Pitched a shutout. Not a bad day at the office."

A smile flickered and disappeared. "Did you see them?"

My smile disappeared too. "Yeah, but not till the eighth inning."

"I bet he came here with Mom to try to mess with your head."

I took her hand and we walked toward the front gate. "You don't think he came out to see my amazing display of pitching excellence."

"No. He's a jerk. Even when he's pretending to be nice."

"Has he said anything mean to you?"

She shook her head. "Not really."

"Not really? So, in other words, yes."

Buddy kept quiet until we crossed the gravel lot to my truck. "He's a moron. Just forget it."

I didn't forget it and kept asking. Finally Buddy said, "He came up to me the other day and says, 'You know your dad's not doing too well financially. So he won't be able to afford to pay for your college. Or a nice wedding. I just want you to know, when the time comes, I'll cover everything. So you don't have to worry. I'll take care of you.'"

"Oh." My fingers squeezed the steering wheel.

"He's a snake."

"Yeah." My good mood from the game had evaporated.

"Dad?"

"You're still going to do something, right?" I could feel her eyes on the side of my face.

"Yeah."

That bastard Cole ate away at my brain the whole evening. I didn't provide much conversation for Buddy while we ate Mexican food downtown at a place called Tico's. She didn't have much to say either. We just sat there clanking our forks against our plates. My foul mood continued when we drove out to Holmes Lake to watch the fireworks show. There were some impressive displays, but every time I looked up in the sky, you-know-who's face was there. That was not right. I never let other guys occupy space in my head. Not even hitters who lit me up. George Brett batted close to .500 against me, but I still didn't let him get inside my brain. When he came up, I always went after him without thinking about what he'd done in the past.

This Cole thing was different. He really bugged me. I could handle Toni getting married again, but not to a guy like him. I thought about why she was with this jerk. When we were together, she was confident and cheerful. Always planning something fun for us and the kids. But after Luke died, it's like she couldn't let herself be happy again. I'd hoped that after so many years she would've gotten past this subconscious need to punish herself. But seeing her with Cole made me wonder if she'd let this ongoing guilt push her to be with someone who mistreated her. I had to call Toni and find out what she was thinking.

The next day I was supposed to be at Sherman by 4:00 PM for practice. That didn't work for me. I wanted to catch Toni around 5:00, after she got home from work and before the creep came over. Yeah, I'd catch flak for skipping practice, but I figured my shutout should have bought me enough goodwill to withstand the heat. And Wright and Mendenhall still owed me for that damn commercial.

So a little after five, I called. Figured I'd lead off with baseball. "Saw you at the game yesterday."

"Yeah," she said. "Cole decided at the last minute he wanted to go."

"Uh-huh."

"Great game."

"Thanks."

"It's weird seeing you throw all those knuckleballs."

"It's even weirder being the one throwing them."

"You've still got a nice bender."

"Thanks. You were right about mixing those in." She always liked it when I told her she was right about something.

She took a breath like she was about to speak, but no words followed. So I decided to change the subject. "I hear you have some news."

"Yeah." Another breath. "Quite a surprise."

"Uh-huh. Have you set a date?" No, I was not going to congratulate her.

"Not yet. We've been talking about sometime this fall. That's not too far off though."

"A lot to plan, huh?"

"Yes, but neither of us wants a big wedding. So we might be able to make October."

A memory of our wedding day popped into my head, before I pushed it away. I had to focus on the task at hand and throw one up and in. "What does Buddy think about all this?"

Silence. She was dusting herself off. "You talk to her. I'm sure she's told you her thoughts."

"It's a big change. A lot for her to take in."

"Yeah, well it's not the first time she's been forced to deal with big changes." Delivered with a nice accusatory tone.

"Buddy's a teenager. This can't be easy for her."

"What do you know about raising a teenager?" Such a delight, my ex. When she talked like that, it made me want to get divorced from her all over again.

"Did you ever ask her how she'd feel about you getting married again?"

"Uh, it's not her call, thank you very much. It's my decision. This is my life, Zane."

"A point you've made very clear to her."

"Don't start."

"I'm just trying to—"

"No, you're trying to use our daughter to butt into my life. Before you moved to Lincoln, how often did you see Buddy? Who's been raising her alone the past eight years? We were getting along fine without you. And if you weren't here now, it would be a lot easier for her to accept Cole."

"So it's all my fault?"

"Wouldn't be the first time." She hung up. From the sound of it, she may have needed to buy a new phone.

That didn't go so well. Let's see, what was Dirk's plan again?

Curtis wasn't pleased with my tardiness at practice, but I survived. Just had to do some extra running before the game. That was fine with me. Gave me a chance to blow off some steam. The Giants lost that night. I'm pretty sure they lost. I didn't really pay much attention to the action on the field. Afterwards I barely resisted the urge to go out and get hammered. I was pissed enough to do it. Fortunately, a couple logic circuits still functioned in my brain. They told me that trashing my comeback would not solve this problem. Making the majors was my only chance of getting the financial resources I'd need to help my daughter. Honestly, I wasn't sure if I had a chance at winning joint custody. But money would give me more options to deal with the situation. Like hiring a hit man to take out Cole.

Just kidding.

So I went home after the game and blew a couple hours playing Minesweeper on Gale's computer. The next day the team hit the road. Eight hours riding a bus through Iowa and Minnesota to St.

Cloud. About four of those hours, I shifted around trying to get comfortable in the lumpy vinyl seat. The rest of the time I spent digging my fingertips into a baseball and simmering about the thought of some jackass paying for my daughter's wedding. Yeah she was fifteen and probably wouldn't be getting hitched for another decade (assuming she could resist Stick's charms). But Cole's comments still got under my skin. I'm sure that's just what he wanted. And he was right, I didn't have any money. Up to this point, I'd accepted my financial status because I had a plan. But now, my lack of income bothered me. A lot of things did.

I pitched the third game against the Trappers. Believe it or not, I kept it together enough to toss a decent outing. Threw seven innings, scattering six hits and three walks. I left with Lincoln up 5-3. But Gale Force promptly let in two runs in the eighth, costing me another win. Fortunately, the Giants pulled it out in the 10th. So the evening still seemed like a step forward for the Fish, especially since the victory moved Lincoln into first place.

After taking three of four from St. Cloud, we traveled to Council Bluffs, where we won two out of three. Morale soared among the boys. Their youthful enthusiasm even provided a modest lift to my spirits. I tried to keep my focus on baseball as much as possible. And Harry Potter. The long road trip gave me the opportunity to finally finish the book. Then it was back to Lincoln to deal with my own Voldemort.

I called Buddy the night we got back to town. She didn't have much to say. Gloom still draped her voice. I couldn't help but think her old man was letting her down. She did share one bit of good news. The lovebirds hadn't set a date yet. Yippee.

The next day Curtis called me into his office. I was starting that night against Bismarck and figured he wanted to go over the lineup with me. But Larry the Geek wasn't there with his charts and stats. When Curtis asked me to shut the door, I realized something was up.

"Have a seat, Fischer," He didn't look happy. In fact, he seemed downright grave.

I feared it had to do with his health, like his diabetes had gotten worse. "Hey Skip. What's up, man? Did you trade me?"

"That would be good news compared to what I just found out." His head bowed, causing my concerns to multiply. "The league is in trouble, Fish. Big trouble."

"You mean like financial trouble?" I asked.

"Yeah. Bismarck and Cheyenne are facing bankruptcy. Can't meet operating expenses. Can't pay their players."

"So they're gonna fold after the season?"

"No, they're gonna fold after this week. When the next salary payment is due, they're finished."

"Then the league will have eight teams. The schedule will have to be adjusted."

"Actually there are three other clubs not much better off. Losing money. They're going under too."

I recalled the sparsely-filled stands in several of the ballparks where we'd played. "Attendance seems okay here. Heck, we sold the place out on the Fourth of July."

He nodded. "Lincoln's been doing alright. Especially when an ex-big league star pitches. But numbers are down for some of the other clubs. And there's been some mismanagement. In the case of Cheyenne, it was outright embezzlement." Curtis snorted. "It's a mess, Fischer. This league is a mess."

"So what does that mean? Our season is going to end?"

"That is a very real possibility."

My eyes fixed on his Texas Rangers coffee cup. "You going to tell the team tonight?"

He shook his head. "Nah, I'll wait till it's official. Let 'em hold onto their dreams for a few more days."

"Thanks for telling me, Curtis."

"I appreciate you keeping this quiet, alright?"

"Yeah, no problem."

I went into the locker room where a bunch of guys were playing a ballgame using a rolled up sock and an empty two-liter bottle wrapped in duct tape. They seemed so happy. It reminded me of when I first broke in with Toronto as a twenty-year-old.

Chapter 9

About two thousand showed up at Sherman that Monday night to see me face the Bismarck Hawks. Not a sellout, but still a decent crowd. As I finished my warm up tosses, troublesome thoughts kept stirring my head. Curtis's revelation being the latest. I had to focus. With the team's days likely numbered, I didn't have many more opportunities to show the big league clubs what I could do. Two scouts had watched me pitch on July 4th, but I hadn't heard anything from anybody. A frustrating situation.

Adding to my challenges were the twin aches that had taken up residence in my shoulder and elbow. These pains appeared after my start in St. Cloud. Perhaps too many curveballs. This theory was confirmed when I threw batting practice a couple days later. Since hitters don't like to face knucklers in BP, I stuck with heaters and breaking balls. Felt fine at the time, but afterwards the pain returned. A little worse even. I had to accept the facts of my baseball life—curves, sliders, and hard stuff stressed the arm. Especially an arm with as many miles on it as mine. At least I could still use the knuckler. The nice easy motion for a knuckleball didn't bring pain, but it made me uneasy relying almost exclusively on one pitch. No choice though. The Fish couldn't afford any kind of injury at this point.

So that night it was just me and Madam Knucklina. No Uncle Charlie. I tossed a couple of rotating knuckleballs in the first and gave up a run. Then in the second I found a groove and the wicked lady did her thing. The Hawks may have known what was coming, but that didn't help them much. The quivering baseballs eluded bat after bat. In eight innings I gave up six hits, three walks, and only two runs. The Gatling Gun nailed down the save to finish off the win, my fifth straight decision as a Giant. I threw 103 pitches, all but ten of them knuckleballs. An encouraging performance.

Didn't hear any more about the league's financial woes in the following days. No news is good news, I figured. Also didn't hear anything about my conversation with Toni. I hoped that meant she hadn't told Buddy about our spat. I had reason to believe that was the case, because Toni never did criticize me in front of Buddy or try to turn her against me. Even during the divorce. I was thankful for that, especially now, since I didn't want my daughter getting more stressed about things.

Tuesday night was a rainout and we split the doubleheader on Wednesday. Thursday night we faced the Hawks again with a chance to take three out of four in the series. That would preserve our one game lead over Pierre in the division. Unfortunately, ownership scheduled us for a youth baseball clinic at 9:00 that morning. This was normally the type of thing I'd blow off, but I felt bad for my teammates. Their whole world could get turned upside down any day now. I decided I should be there with them, especially since I'd skipped the Shopko event.

Amazingly, three-fourths of the Giants roster showed up at Sherman Field for the clinic. And most of us were on time. Or close to being on time. Hey, 9:07 ain't bad considering I had to pick up Buddy on the way. When I told her about this thing, she said she wanted to help out. That surprised me given that she didn't like baseball or mornings. Guess she wanted to spend time with her old man. Actually, it was probably the kids. Buddy didn't talk much about losing her little brother, but I know she missed him. Ever since Luke died, she'd had a soft spot for younger children.

About 200 urchins, ages six through eleven, awaited us on the field. Some of the youngsters were really jacked up, like they'd each downed a box of sugary cereal that morning. Who needs greenies when you can get a big league buzz from Sugar Smacks? I'm glad Weed wasn't there or he'd have been asking the kids about their suppliers.

The high school and youth league coaches running the clinic did a pretty good job maintaining order. After some calisthenics, they divided the herd into groups and set up stations to focus on different aspects of the game. After 45 minutes, the groups would rotate to another station. Five Giants hurlers, including myself, were assigned to the "pitching fundamentals" station in the bullpen. One of the staffers directed the kids to sit in the grass and gave some introductory remarks. He then turned it over to us, "the professionals." Unfortunately, none of us pros knew what to say. Before the silence grew too awkward, I pushed Gale forward and said, "Kids, this is Gale McGrady, one of the most feared relief pitchers in the league. He's known around here as Gale Force. Show 'em how it's done, Mr. Force."

I figured McGrady would be the perfect choice. He thought he knew everything about pitching and he loved to talk. To his credit, he took the ball and ran. "Yes, thank you, Mr. Fischer." He cleared his throat and placed his hands on his hips. "Listen closely, young people, for it is I, Gale McGrady, who will now impart to you the proper techniques necessary to succeed as a professional pitcher. Now do not expect to match my proficiency at what I am about to limn. Remember, you are but novices following the tutelage of a master. Think of this as a process. First off, you must assume a proper grip on the ball. Allow me to demonstrate ..."

As Gale bloviated (yet another word I learned from him) about his expertise, I glanced around at the other stations. Boys and girls were learning how to field grounders, catch pop ups, slide into bases, and keep their eyes on the ball while swinging. Some of the Giants, like Sylvester and Snowman, seemed to embrace their role as instructors. Others, like Dirk, stood by doing nothing but scratch themselves. In my own group, Will Jason (nicknamed "Slim" because he was kinda pudgy) stretched out on the bullpen bench and took a nap.

What about me, you ask? Alright, I admit it, I didn't do much either. Every so often when Gale made a point, I'd say "That's right" or "Yes" or "Mmm-hmm." These vital contributions helped reinforce the fine instruction being imparted (or limned) that day.

Actually the kids quickly got bored with Gale's monologue and started fidgeting and picking their noses. So we lined them up and let them throw some pitches. I showed a few of the more promising "prospects" how to throw a knuckleball. Clooney served as my catcher for this brief demo. Since he missed half the pitches, Buddy backed him up and tossed the balls back to me. She had a good arm. All told, she seemed to be having an okay time hanging out with the kids. Even smiled and laughed a couple times.

Before we'd dismiss a group, the coaches asked the kids if they had any questions for us. We got the standard stuff about what it's like to play pro ball, who could throw the fastest, and if we thought the Giants would win the championship. One youngster surprised me by asking if I thought Mark McGwire was on steroids. McGwire at this time was launching home runs at a record pace. If he kept it up, he'd easily pass Roger Maris for the single season record. And yes, I thought steroids contributed to this productivity. Didn't see how it could be any other way. I mean, half the guys on my own team juiced. But I didn't want to shatter any youthful illusions about the game's biggest hero. So I said McGwire got stronger from eating right, exercising regularly, and taking vitamins. Why let truth block an opportunity to give young people good advice?

When the Q & A session ended, the kids took off and another set came in. We pitching experts followed the same drill for each group. Gale led off with his brilliant instruction and then we did some throwing. The clinic ended just after noon, but I still had to sign about a million baseballs before we could leave the field.

"Where would you like to go for lunch?" I asked Buddy as we crossed the gravel lot.

"I don't care."

"How about the Broccoli Shack? It's this new place that serves nothing but broccoli."

"Fine."

"You never listen to me, do you?"

"Yes."

"Just not dignifying my stupidity with a response, huh?"

She shrugged. Her eyes remained on the ground as we walked.

"Sure you're up for this? I can take you home if you'd like?"

"No." She hooked her arm around mine and leaned into me. "I want to go with you. Wherever you want."

"Okay, just checking." We finally reached my pickup. After starting the engine, I asked, "You lettin' your hair grow out?"

"No, just haven't got it cut in a while."

"Oh, I thought you might be tiring of the flapper look."

"Still not funny, Dad." She put her feet up on the dash. "I thought about cutting it myself. Maybe I should get some clippers and shave it all off."

"Buddy, don't do that. I'll take you to a salon."

"Whatever."

As I pulled out of the lot onto South Street, I thought of something that might cheer her up. "You know I read that Harry Potter book? Want to discuss it sometime?"

"*You* read a book?"

"Hey now. Not only have I read books, I've even written one myself. Ever heard of *A Fish Story*?" That was my "autobiography" for young adults that came out a few years earlier.

A smirk appeared as she shook her head. "You had a ghostwriter for that. A real author did the writing."

"Still, my name's on the cover."

"You expect me to believe you read *Harry Potter* all the way through? I don't think so."

"But I did."

"When?"

"Took it with me on road trips. Cool story."

"Okay, so who are Harry's two best friends?"

"Ron and Hermione. Believe me now?"

She squinted skeptically. "Too easy. One of your literate teammates could've told you. How about the game they play at Hogwarts, what's it called? And who's the jerky kid Harry doesn't like?"

"Quidditch and Malfoy." I inhaled smugly.

Her eyes widened. "Wow. Maybe you did read the book."

"Of course I did. Contrary to rumor, most professional ballplayers know how to read and write."

"That's big news. I should contact the media."

"What a funny little sprite you are." I reached over and mussed her hair. "So, you want to get together to discuss Rowling? It'd be kinda like a book club."

Her face beamed for an instant. "Okay. How about tomorrow night. We could get some 'za at daVinci's and then talk about Hogwarts."

"Great. Let's see, tomorrow's Friday. Hey, there's no game. I could pick you up at 7:00. How's that sound?"

"Cool." A while later she said, "Thanks, Dad."

I slept late the next morning. Not the first time that had happened on a Friday. Woke up around 10:00 to the smell of Gale's raspberry pancakes. Ate five of them—delicious. If I lived with him all year long, I'd weigh 400 pounds. To drink, we had some of the best OJ I'd ever tasted. He'd squeezed the oranges himself that morning.

"Awesome breakfast," I said. "What's gotten into you?"

"What do you mean, old boy?"

I gestured at the table. "The pancakes. The freshly-squeezed orange juice. The humming."

"Humming?"

"Yes, humming. I pretty sure it's something from *Bye Bye Birdie*." My mom took me to that movie when I was a kid.

"Indeed it is."

"Well?"

"Let's just say, I've secured a date tonight with a most stunning lady. A daughter of one of Lincoln's finest families."

"Meet her at a cotillion?"

"Ha. Aren't you the jester?" He leaned back in his chair and clasped his hands behind his head. "I met the lass at Ted Kooser's poetry reading. Defenseless against my charms, she surrendered her number with nary a hint of reluctance."

"A poetry reading? Um, you might leave that detail out when you tell this story in the locker room."

"Ah Zane, don't be afraid of a little culture." He punched my arm. "I could let you borrow Kooser's latest collection of verse. You just might like it."

"Or not." I pushed out a belch in iambic pentameter.

Gale winced. "You're as bad as Dirk."

"Am not. So where you taking the lucky girl?"

"The Lincoln Symphony Orchestra. Tonight they perform at Kimball Hall."

The orchestra? Ugh. Gale and I lived on different planets, that's for sure.

That afternoon before practice, he went out to buy flowers for his date. I stayed at the apartment reviewing my baseball contacts. I made a list of a dozen managers and general managers I thought most likely to give me a shot. If and when the Central States League came crashing down, I wanted a place to land.

I arrived at the clubhouse a little earlier than usual. It wasn't on purpose, just happened that way. The only players there were Julio Juarez, Ricky Garcia, and Chavo Berroa. They spoke enthusiastically as they dressed for practice. Having been around Latino players for two decades, I'd picked up a few words in Español. And when I say "few words" I mean exactly that. So I couldn't follow much of what they were saying. Sounded like they were talking about a girl. Or girls. Apparently Gale wasn't the only one with big plans for the evening.

The other guy in the locker room was the clubhouse manager. Like usual, he diligently placed our freshly-washed uniforms in our lockers. After two months on the team, I still didn't know his name. Yeah I know, not cool. So I went up and introduced myself. Found out his name was Nicholas, but his friends called him Nicky. He had something of a speech impediment, probably the reason he rarely said much. Also found out he was a big Husker football fan. He loved baseball too. Told me he'd collected every complete set of Topps cards since 1977, his first year of Little League. He had all of my cards. Nicky may have been one of my biggest fans in town, and yet I had hardly noticed him. It didn't help that he was barely five feet tall and tried to stay out of sight as much as possible. Still, he did our laundry, organized our equipment, and cleaned up after us. He deserved our respect. I signed a couple baseballs for him and told him to bring in his Zane Fischer cards. I'd sign those too if he liked. He seemed pretty happy about that.

One by one the rest of the team filed in. That meant crude jokes, juvenile antics, and funny noises followed by foul odors. Or was it foul noises followed by funny odors? Either way, a typical day with the Giants. Weed shuffled by and asked if I'd accepted Willie Aames as my lord and personal savior. I said no, though I always thought Willie's TV sister Elizabeth was kinda cute. I asked if there were any religions based on her. Weed said he would check.

At some point Sylvester the Cat flung a pink bra at Tracy Desjardins. "Yo, Frenchy," the Cat announced, "your wife left this at my place last night. Thought she might want it back." Typical clubhouse humor, especially from the Cat. Such responses usually brought a few guffaws followed by a comeback. This time though, Tracy was in no mood for such nonsense. It could have been the two-week slump that had dropped his batting average below the Mendoza line. Or it may have been some real trouble between him and his old lady. Whatever the reason, he threw the brassiere back in Sylvester's face, adding a few choice words to underscore his lack of amusement. More words followed and tempers rose. Then a scuffle broke out.

The other players pulled Frenchy and the Cat apart before it went too far. Nobody got hurt. Nobody except yours truly that is. In trying to help break things up, I took an elbow to the forehead. That's what I get for being a good teammate. Not a big deal, though it opened a cut above my right eye. So I had to go visit Jerry in the training room. He cleaned it up and slapped on a large Band-Aid.

Trotting onto the field, I found Gale waiting for me with an anxious look. "It's alright," I said. "I'm fine."

"Whatever are you talking about?"

"The cut." I pointed to my forehead. "Thought you might be concerned."

"Oh, yes, yes. What a relief. Say, old boy, I need to ask you something." He placed a hand on my shoulder.

"I'm thinking I'll pass."

"What?" His eyes widened. "Oh Fischer, always the kidder aren't you. What would we do without your levity?"

"Who says I'm kidding?"

He chuckled dismissively. "See, it turns out that Beth—that's my date for tonight—well, she has a friend."

"And let me guess, for Beth to go out with you, you have to find somebody for her friend."

"That appears to be the precondition, yes." He shadowed me as I walked across the outfield grass to find a place to stretch. "So what do you say? Will you help a friend out?"

"No."

"Please, Zane. I very much fancy this girl. She's—"

"I'm sure Beth is delightful. And I'm sure her friend dines on Alpo."

"Ah, there you are wrong." He pulled a wallet-sized photo from his pocket. "Quite a comely lass, don't you agree?"

I did agree. "*That's* the friend?"

"Yes. Her name is Sydney. And she's heard of you."

On one hand, I had no interest in going on a double date with Gale. Not in this lifetime or the next. And I sure didn't want to sit through a symphony orchestra performance. On the other hand, Sydney was a knockout (assuming that was really her picture). Plus, I kinda owed Gale for letting me stay with him and for all the cooking he'd done for me. And, to be honest, the Fish hadn't been on a date for about six months. At first, it didn't bother me. Gave me the time I needed to focus on my comeback. But by this point, the idea of spending some time with a lady didn't sound too bad. So I told Gale I'd do it. I just hoped Sydney wasn't too much of a lady.

That evening, Gale wouldn't stop singing as we got ready for our outing. More show tunes. I slipped on the only sports coat and decent pair of slacks I still owned. And I must say, I looked good. McGrady looked alright too. He didn't wear a baseball uniform so well, but he could pull off a coat and tie ensemble. Had kind of a James Bond look going for him, just not quite as formidable as the real 007.

Off we went. Gale wanted us to each drive our own vehicles, so he could go off with Beth if the opportunity presented itself. Seemed to me a bit optimistic on his part, but I went along with the plan. While driving to meet the girls, I shut off my cell phone and tossed it in the glove compartment. Didn't want it going off during an electrifying cello solo or something.

So there I was on a Friday night listening to the Lincoln Symphony Orchestra. Not really my kind of music, but I'm sure they were great. Didn't really matter though because I was paying way more attention to Sydney Cruz, who was even prettier in person. She looked a little like the lead actress in that *Selena* movie that had come out a few months earlier. Sydney was in her mid-20s, but she didn't seem to mind the age difference. I sure didn't. She was a paralegal at a downtown law firm, and she loved baseball. Or at least she pretended to anyway. Worked for me.

After the performance (Gale told me not to call it a show), we all went to a somewhat fancy drinking establishment downtown. I had some wine. So did everyone else. Yeah I know I shouldn't have, but it happened. Some time later, the couples decided to part ways. More accurately, Sydney and I decided that this no longer needed to be a double date and we took off. Gotta say, that was a great idea Gale had for us to take two vehicles. He'd be getting his alone time with Beth after all. Not sure how she felt about the deal. Didn't really care at that point.

I woke up at Sydney's place around eleven the next morning. We had some Chinese food delivered, then I had to get going. I told her I'd call her, even though I knew I probably wouldn't. Don't get me wrong, I had a great time. There just wasn't much of a future for us. First, there was the age difference. It didn't seem like such a big deal the night before (actually it was kinda cool the night before), but over time it would become an issue. It didn't help matters when she cranked up her stereo and started singing along with the Backstreet Boys.

Second, I had to focus on my comeback, something that, if successful, would be taking me to another city. Possibly very soon. Third, I couldn't afford a girlfriend. Even though Gale had paid for the symphony tickets, the previous evening ate up nearly all my remaining poker winnings. Unless Sydney liked eating Doritos and watching movies on the USA network every weekend, I'm guessing the excitement of dating an older broke guy would soon fade.

No, I was not proud of myself. Since moving to Lincoln, I thought I'd become a different person. Yet there I was gallivanting again. Back in grade school the nuns used to call me "the incorrigible one." I didn't know what it meant until I looked it up years later. Driving home from Sydney's I had to admit, the sisters were on to something. If I'd had a ruler, I would have smacked my own knuckles.

Gale wasn't at the apartment, so I just flopped on the couch and took a nap. Since I didn't get much sleep the night before, my siesta lasted way longer than I'd intended. I arrived at practice a half hour late. Well aware that I'd been on a date the night before, the guys showed me no mercy. Of course, most of their comments focused on my advanced age. Hank called me "the geezer who tried to please her." Sylvester asked me how many of those little blue pills I needed to overcome my performance issues. McCormick asked which one of the Golden Girls I went out with. He guessed Blanche.

"Blanche would tear me up," I said. "Besides, my heart has always been with Rose." I figured I might as well play along. Otherwise their jabs would never end, great guys that they were. Thank you for being a friend.

Gale was noticeably silent. As we milled about the outfield during batting practice, I asked how things went with Beth. Even before he spoke, the look on his face told me he'd struck out. "Contrary to my expectations, the girl lacks culture," he said. "She wouldn't know class if it walked up and bit her on the buttocks."

"Is that what you tried to do?" I asked. "That's a no-no. You should always wait till the second date before biting a girl's butt."

"Very funny." He exhaled a heavy sigh. "Turned out to be a smashing evening for you, I see."

"Smashing? Well, we did knock a lamp off the nightstand."

"Charming. So you ended up with the fun one." He stepped to his left to field a grounder that had scooted into the outfield. "You're welcome."

"Yeah, Sydney was alright. Thanks for introducing us."

"Hmph. You going to see her again?"

"Nah, don't think so."

"Oh dear. You lure a young lady into her bedroom and never call her again. Tsk tsk. What's the word for men like you?"

"There are several." And I'd heard them all, unfortunately.

"You might be careful, old boy."

"Why's that?" I watched one of Javon's drives clear the right field wall.

"Beth told me that Sydney can be a bit, shall we say, volatile."

"No, she's a sweet girl."

"On the surface, yes. But if crossed, she can get ..."

"Crazy?"

Gale nodded. "I prefer the term unstable, but yes, crazy will do."

Great that's just what I need. "How about if you call her?" I said.

He raised an eyebrow. "You are no longer interested?"

"She's all yours. And she might even let you bite her butt."

"Sydney does have considerable assets ... but would I have a shot with her?"

"You're rich, McGrady. That gives you a shot with everybody."

He seemed pleased with that statement, and his bearing again brimmed with unfounded confidence.

Curtis, of course, was again not happy with my tardiness, especially since I was starting that night. He launched into a lecture, but, with larger issues looming, his heart wasn't in it. Felt like getting chewed on by a toothless dog.

That evening we faced the Colorado Springs Pikemen. They started out the season hot, but had faded over the past three weeks. As with my previous start, I delivered a heavy dose of knuckleballs. Not the best stuff I'd had this season, but I could put the ball in the strike zone more often than not. It also helped that the batters kept guessing wrong. They didn't swing at the spinning knucklers that loafed over the plate. Then they'd hack away at a flutterball that broke a foot out of the strike zone. I didn't mind.

In seven and a third innings, the Pikemen mustered just five hits and two runs (one of them unearned). Clooney gave up a run in the ninth and Lincoln won 6-3. That also turned out to be my record after the game. I was really glad to get the W, since it gave me twice as many wins as losses. Racking up six straight decisions had a nice ring to it too. My ERA after twelve starts stood at 4.03. Not bad, especially considering how horribly this season had begun for me.

The boys had fun celebrating in the clubhouse. Over halfway through the season, the Giants held a two game lead in the division. And we were heading in the right direction. Rock music blared, towels snapped, and cans of beer popped open. It energized me being around the young players. Hard not to get caught up in all the goofing around and stupid jokes. Then Curtis entered the room and stood among us like the Grim Reaper. The laughter came to a sudden end. "We got a team meeting tomorrow morning," he announced. "Be here at the clubhouse at 9:00. That means everybody."

A consuming silence fell over us as our manager exited the locker room. A few guys finally mumbled, "What's going on?" Shoulders shrugged and palms raised. Some of the boys looked to me for answers. The hope that had glowed in their eyes just a minute earlier now dimmed with uncertainty. I did know what was going on, but I couldn't tell them. I just shook my head and said, "Great game tonight." Then I left.

A fog blanketed my thoughts as I trudged toward Buddy's concession stand. I wanted to go back and talk to the team, but that wasn't my place. I had to let it go. Whatever announcement needed to be made should come from the manager, not me.

I looked behind the counter, but didn't see my daughter. Her friends Brooke and Lauren were cleaning the popcorn machine. I asked if they'd seen Buddy. They told me she didn't come in that night. Didn't call or anything. Then it hit me, a sharp nauseating ache. Like I'd been punched in the gut. I wished it were a punch in the gut, because the reality was worse: I'd forgotten about my plans to go out with Buddy the night before. I stood up my daughter.

"Hello, Mr. Fischer."

My head spun to the right. There stood Stick looking like Christmas had just been cancelled. "Stick. Do you know why Buddy didn't show up for work tonight? Is she sick?"

"She's not sick."

"Then where is she?"

His face tightened. "She went on a date."

"A date? What do you mean? With who?"

He looked down. "A guy called Dodger. His real name is Roger Bentley."

"She's never told me about this guy."

He shrugged. "Maybe she didn't want to upset you."

"Why would I be upset about Dodger?" I stepped closer to him.

"Because he's a senior. He has a car. And he's been after her for a while."

"She never went out with him before this?"

"No. He goes after a lot of girls and Buddy always thought he was a creep. Then today she called him and said she'd go out with him."

My fists clenched. I wanted to hit something, but poor Stick was the only thing nearby. *And he's just the messenger, I shouldn't kill him.* "So Buddy is out with Dodger, right now?"

Stick nodded.

"Where did they go?" My words escaped slow and pronounced through gritted teeth. "Where did that senior with a car take my fifteen-year-old daughter?"

His mouth quivered. "She wouldn't tell me where they were going."

I grabbed the bill of my Giants cap and flung it to the ground. Then I stomped on it. And again. Some time passed before I could speak. "Do you know if she was upset about last night?"

No response. The boy kept his eyes on his shoelaces.

"Stick?"

He nodded with a barely audible, "She wasn't too happy."

"Really upset?"

He nodded again with a pained expression. "She waited on the front step with her Harry Potter book in her lap. I sat with her for a while, but I had to go home when it got dark. She was still there waiting when I left."

I felt sick, worse than after any loss on the baseball diamond. "You need a ride home?" I mumbled.

"No. I rode my bike. My house is just a mile and a half from here." Stick shuffled away.

On the way to my truck, I realized that I hadn't checked my cell since before my date the night before. My stomach churned with dread as I pulled the phone out of the glove compartment and turned it on. Nine missed calls and nine messages. All them from Buddy. All of them from last night.

Chapter 10

As I drove away from the ballpark, two questions rattled through my head. *Where is Buddy, and how could I have been so stupid?* My mind replayed the events of the day before. I couldn't believe I'd forgotten about getting together with my daughter. She'd been so excited to discuss that book, and I stood her up. Just left her sitting there on the front step. That image remained burned in my head. I bet Cole loved every minute of it, especially when she went inside every fifteen minutes to call me.

I couldn't go home. I would've just paced back and forth staring at the walls. Or punching the walls. So I decided to drive around looking for Buddy and her date. No, I didn't know what Roger drove. Nor did I know where they were. I didn't even know the popular hangouts for Lincoln teenagers. But I drove around anyway. Aimlessly. Hoping desperately to spot my daughter standing in a crowd in front of a movie theater. Or in the parking lot at her favorite daVinci's. Or at the arcade she once mentioned.

If Buddy had a cell phone, I could've called her. But she didn't. I wanted to call Toni, but that didn't seem like a good idea. By midnight, my search had yielded nothing. I slumped in my idling pickup in an empty lot at Gateway Mall. I was out of ideas and almost out of gas. A few minutes later my phone rang. My heart jumped, hoping it was my daughter. It was Toni. She wanted to know if I'd heard from Buddy. I said no. She said it was past her curfew and she wasn't home yet. I said I'd come over and wait for her there. Though Toni's tone was softer than the last time we'd spoken, she discouraged me from doing that. I said fine and asked her to call me the minute Buddy got home.

After filling up my truck, I headed for Toni's anyway. I had to know that Buddy made it home. I had to see her. I had to tell her how sorry I was. My stomach throbbed from how crappy I felt about everything.

I parked in the street in front of Toni's house. She must have been looking out the window, because she came bounding out the door a moment later. I stepped out of my pickup as she marched down the driveway. From the glow of the porch light, I could see the displeased expression on her face. My eyes then lingered on her grey cotton shorts and killer legs. Told you those nuns were right about me.

"What are you doing here?"

I pushed the truck door shut. "I'm going to wait for Buddy."

"I told you not to come here." For some reason, she tried to keep her voice down. "I'll call you when she gets back."

"Sorry. Couldn't go home. I want to see her."

"After what you did, I doubt the feelings are mutual."

"I know, that was really bad." I looked down the street. "There was a fight in the locker room yesterday and some stuff is happening with the team. I got distracted and forgot."

"Your daughter isn't a good thing to forget."

"I know. I screwed up. That's why I'm here. I want to apologize."

From what I could make out in the dim lighting, her eyes seemed more concerned than angry. "Do you know anything about this guy she's with?"

"Just that he's a senior, and he's got a car. Do you know anything about him?"

She shook her head. "I didn't even know she had a date tonight. Around six this kid pulls in the driveway and lays on the horn. She comes flying out of her room. I asked her who was out there. She said Roger and then slammed the door behind her. I had to call Stick to find out what's going on with my own daughter."

"Yeah, he told me about Roger too." I stepped closer to her. "This is my fault."

Toni exhaled. "I didn't say that."

"Thanks. But it is. I really let her down."

Her demeanor relaxed a bit. "It's a lot of things with her, Zane. She's a teenage girl. She made a bigger deal out of it than it was."

"Forgetting about her like that wasn't right."

"Maybe not, but it doesn't give her an excuse to go out with an eighteen-year-old boy without permission. And break curfew and blow off work." Toni's eyes squinted. "She has responsibilities. She can't react like this at every little disappointment that comes into her life."

My gaze shifted to the corner intersection. "I'll feel a lot better once she's home."

"Me too."

The front door opened, drawing my eyes to the house. Cole flung aside the screen and stomped outside. "Well, look who's here," he announced.

A quick groan escaped Toni's throat. "Cole, I'm handling this. Go back inside."

He snorted and stepped down from the front stoop. Based on the totter in his gait, I guessed he'd been drinking something other than soda pop this evening. "Just being polite. Got to greet our guest and all that."

"Zane is just worried about Buddy. That's why he stopped by."

"Worried, huh? Didn't seem too concerned about her last night. Poor girl sittin' out here all alone waiting for her papa." He stopped his unsteady advance and threw out his hands. "But Papa never showed up. Reminds me of my old man. Took off when I was five and we never saw his sorry ass again."

"Zane was just leaving," Tina said. "Go back inside, Cole."

He continued down the driveway. "Fathers shouldn't treat their kids that way, you know. We deserve better than that." His voice trailed off.

"I know," I said. "I made a mistake."

"One helluva mistake, I'd say." He stopped about five feet from me. "Now she's out with some older dude, and who knows what they're doing."

Toni clinched her fists. "Shut up, Cole."

Ignoring her, he kept his surly eyes on me. "Who knows what she'll do to get back at Daddy. Maybe make you a Grandpa." His lips curled into a sneer. "Whatever she does, it's all your fault."

When he resumed his advance, Toni blocked his path and tried to push him back. "Get off me," he yelled, flinging her away. She hit the driveway with a thud and skidded across the cement.

A switch flipped inside me. I stepped forward and smashed my fist into his face. It was a good solid shot, right on his mouth. He went down with an even harder thud. I knelt beside Toni. "Are you okay?"

After she regained her bearings, she whacked my chest. Quite hard, I might add. "Are you crazy?" she nearly screamed. "Get out of here."

I noticed blood trickling from the huge red mark on her skinned knee. "You're hurt. Here, let me help you up."

"You've done enough." She slapped away my hand and looked over at Cole, who lay on his back moaning and holding his jaw. "He's gonna freak."

"He ain't gonna do nothing."

Toni scrambled to her feet. "Go. Now!" She balled her fist like she was getting ready to slug me.

I backed away. "But he's the one who pushed you."

"Get out of here, Zane. I'll call you when Buddy gets home."

I retreated to my pickup. She limped over to Cole. I drove away.

An hour later my phone rang. It was Toni.

"Buddy just got home."

"Great. Is she okay?"

"She's fine."

"Are you okay?"

She hung up.

Needless to say, I didn't get to sleep right away. So Gale leaning over me the next morning was a most unwelcome sight. "Come on, Fish." He prodded me with his cane. Yes, he sometimes carried a cane, like the Monopoly guy. "It's after eight already. Up and at 'em."

"Errrr ... go away."

"You need to get up. Now, old boy."

"I'm tired. Wake me up at noon."

"Zane, we've got a team meeting at nine. Did you forget already?"

Crap. I did forget. And knowing the likely topic of the meeting didn't improve my mood any. Moving in slow motion, I ate a Pop Tart and got dressed. The knuckles on my pitching hand hurt a little. Then I remembered why. Replaying the left cross that dropped Cole brought a smile to my face. The good feeling didn't last though. All the bad stuff from the past two days pushed it away.

Gale drove us to Sherman Field, where Larry the Geek awaited in front of the clubhouse. He told us to go to the field. Several of the other players were already there lingering by the dugout. Looking as tired as I felt, they delivered fewer wisecracks than usual. Most of them weren't used to being up by nine o'clock on a Sunday morning. I sure wasn't. Curtis showed up with Wright and Mendenhall. They stood near home plate. Curtis directed us to take a knee.

"Alright men," he said. "we've got some news. League news. Over the past couple weeks, Mr. Wright and Mr. Mendenhall have been meeting with the other team owners. They had some big issues they were trying to work out, and uh ..." He dropped his head for a moment. "They considered a lot of alternatives, but none of them ended up being doable. So it's been decided that the league is gonna shut down."

That brought a few murmurs from the players. General Lee asked, "What does that mean for us? We're still going to play, right?"

"No. This means the season is over. The Lincoln Giants are done. This club doesn't exist anymore." His eyes passed from player to player. "I truly am sorry about this. You're the first pro team I ever managed and I'm proud of you all. What you accomplished. You came together and we made it into first place. None of us were expecting things to end like this, but there it is. We all have to deal with it."

After a few moments of silence, Hank shot to his feet. "This doesn't make sense," he said. "Leagues don't just end in the middle of the season. I've never heard of that."

"Yeah, how the hell does that happen?" Dirk added.

Curtis explained that four of the teams were facing bankruptcy. He covered a lot of the same stuff he'd told me earlier. Wright (or Mendenhall) then starting talking about the financial difficulties of the teams in question. He assured us that the Giants were doing okay, but several of the other clubs were buried in debt, a hole they just couldn't crawl out of with declining revenues and rising expenses.

The meeting lasted over an hour. The players had a lot of questions. Most of these queries related to our future in baseball. Such as, *what is our status now?* Answer: We are free agents.

Will we get paid the rest of our season salaries? Answer: We'll get paid for the games we already played, and that's it. With the league's dissolution, the Lincoln Giants were declaring bankruptcy like the rest of the teams and wouldn't be liable for player salaries beyond our last-played game.

Will the Giants help us get signed by teams in another league? Answer: Management will try to help, but remember there are players from nine other Central States teams flooding the market. Translation: Have you thought about a career in the fast food industry?

And so my career as a Lincoln Giant came to an end. Strangely enough, I didn't fret much about my future in baseball. My thoughts kept going back to Buddy. What happened on her date? Is she okay? Is she still mad at me? And then there was Toni. What happened after I left? Is she okay? Is she still mad at me? I wanted to call, but after the recent fireworks, figured maybe I should wait another day. Like usual, I didn't know what to do. Too bad Professor Dumbledore wasn't around to guide me. Or better yet, maybe he could cast a spell that would make things better: *LoveZaneAgainis.*

After the meeting, we trudged to the clubhouse to clean out our lockers. The mood reminded me of my grandpa's viewing when I was a teenager. At least nobody was crying this time. Well, Nicky had tears in his eyes, but none of the players did. A few guys asked if I'd put in a good word for them with the people I still knew in baseball. I said I'd do what I could. Truth is, I doubted that anybody in baseball would listen to me. The Giants were the only team to give me a shot last spring. Nobody else wanted the Fish. Sure, I'd had a decent run with Lincoln, but was it good enough to catch a scout's eye?

Gale drove us home. He seemed a bit down, but not as crushed as some of the other boys. Yes, being a ballplayer was a boyhood dream of his. But he had other options. More options than any of the other Giants, including myself. I thought about asking him what he planned to do next, but didn't really feel like talking.

"Well this sucks," he said while stopped at a red light.

"Yeah." That was about it for our commentary on the morning's events.

That afternoon, I napped and lay around the apartment doing nothing. That evening, Snowman and Dirk came over. We thought about playing poker, but with three of us now lacking income, decided to pass on cards. Instead, we watched a VHS movie that Gale had just bought. Appropriately enough, it was *Titanic.*

I tried to call Buddy the next morning, but no one answered the phone. Toni was at work and my daughter probably didn't want to talk to me. Or she was out with Dodger again. I tried not to think about that last scenario. While eating breakfast, I glanced at the paper. The sports section featured an article about the downfall of the Central States League. Another article described the history of the Lincoln Giants. Both were written by Brian Carter. From the history article I learned:

- The Lincoln Giants first started playing in 1971.
- The team was part of the San Francisco farm system until 1992; after that the team played as an independent.
- Don Angley managed the team from 1974 to 1994, winning the Giants only league title in his last season.
- Wright and Mendenhall planned to sell Sherman Field to the American Legion.
- Lincoln averaged 2,562 fans at home games this season when Zane Fischer pitched; 1,127 fans showed up when somebody other than Fischer pitched.

Alright, I admit it, I felt good about that last point. Made me think people still remembered the Fish and wanted to see him pitch. And I was happy that Wright and Mendenhall were somewhat rewarded for their confidence in me. Still, I felt bad for Lincoln. It seemed like an awfully big city not to have a minor league baseball team. I hoped they'd get another one before too long.

As the day dragged on, the urge to drink grew stronger and stronger. It was much easier resisting temptation when I'd been sober for several months in a row. But I'd had some drinks this summer. And now that I'd had that taste again, I wanted more. Reminded me of a vampire and his all-consuming thirst for fresh blood. Count Zane-ula wanted to drink and soon the sun would drop below the horizon. This is where they play that creepy organ music in those horror movies. Ooh, that's scary.

Surprisingly enough, I avoided the bottle that evening. After supper with Gale, (he grilled steaks!), I tried to call Buddy again. Toni answered and said she didn't want to talk to me. Before I could say anything else, she hung up. That really sucked. Getting shunned by both of them like that. I was just trying to help Toni, though I kind of understood her reaction. Buddy's rejection really stung. We'd had some good times hanging out this summer. For the first time in years, I felt like a dad again. Then I blew it. If only I could've gone back in time to that Friday night.

I spent the rest of the evening going over my list of baseball contacts. I'd picked up a *Baseball Weekly* to review the minor league teams in case I'd forgotten any. Then I jotted down a few notes, including my season stats, for my sales pitch. Short, simple, and direct was the plan. Have knuckleball, will travel.

Tuesday, I went to Sherman to pick up my last check. Gladys the team secretary was the only person in the office when I showed up. After we exchanged some flirty banter along the lines of James Bond and Moneypenny, she gave me my check and I headed out. Before driving away though, I wanted to take one last look at the diamond. Strangely enough, a wave of nostalgia came over me as I passed through the gate to the field. Sure I hadn't played there much. At the start of the season, I didn't really want to play there at all. But things turned around for me at Sherman Field. I became a pitcher again. I'll never forget how good that felt. Being able to succeed at something I wondered if I could ever do again.

I wandered across the infield and admired the empty bleachers as they reflected the morning sun. The ballpark seemed smaller with nobody in it. My imagination soon filled the stands with cheering fans. Before I knew it I was standing on the mound looking in to get the sign from Snowman. It was the Fourth of July and I was throwing a masterpiece.

"Hard to believe, isn't it?"

My head swiveled around. Someone approached from the home dugout. "No more Giants baseball," he said. "Just not right." It was Brian Carter from the newspaper.

"No, it ain't," I replied.

"This may not be Yankee Stadium, but there are a lot of memories here."

"Yeah. I learned about a few of them from your article yesterday."

"Thanks for reading. It's nice we had a Cy Young winner here for the last chapter of Giants baseball."

I finally figured out who he reminded me of—Robert Duvall. Duvall in his earlier days, like in *True Grit* or *The Godfather*. "That Cy Young was a long time ago. Don't think I'll be remembered as one of Lincoln's all-time greats. Now, Dick Stuart, he was a real legend around here."

"Yeah, sometimes I picture his blasts clearing that wall." Brian gestured to left field.

"Did he really hit sixty-six homers in one season?"

"He did."

"Glad I didn't have to face him."

"Me too." We both soaked in the melancholy atmosphere of the deserted ballpark. "So, what's next for the Fish?" he asked.

"Wish I knew."

"Got any leads?"

"No leads. Just phone numbers. I'll start calling today, once I get home."

"You had a solid season here. Six wins and three losses. That knuckleball was really moving your last few starts. Won't be long before you're in a uniform again."

My foot kicked the rubber on the mound. "Yeah, I don't know."

"You don't sound too optimistic. Having second thoughts about the comeback?"

I exhaled. "No. I'm still gonna try."

"But ..."

"But my daughter lives here in Lincoln. Hate to just take off and go to another city."

He nodded. "Well, baseball will be over in two months. Maybe you could live in Lincoln in the off-season. I could get you tickets to some Husker games."

"Yeah? That would be cool. This will be their first season without Osborne though. Think they'll be alright?"

"They'll be fine. Solich coached under Osborne for nineteen years. He knows the system. The Huskers should still win the Big Twelve."

My eyes drifted back to home plate, where they lingered. "Buddy's a teenager, you know. And something kinda came up between us recently. I hate to leave on a sour note like that. Especially since we'd been getting along so well this summer."

He nodded. "I bet you'll get things straightened out soon. You know how a teenager's mood can change from one hour to the next. She may have already forgotten about what came up between you."

"Wouldn't that be nice?" I scraped a line in the dirt with my toe. "You married?"

"Yep. Three years in October."

"Kids?"

"Expecting our first in November."

"Enjoy 'em. They grow up fast. Too fast … especially if you're not around."

"It'll work out, Zane. With your daughter and with baseball."

"Hope so." We stood in silence for a while before I said, "I should get going. Got some people to call."

"Yeah, I gotta get going too. Eileen will kill me if I'm late for our newborn parenting class."

We left the field. As we neared our vehicles, he turned to me and extended a hand. "Good luck, Zane."

I shook his hand. "Thanks. I need it."

On the drive home, my cell phone rang. I checked the caller ID. It was Sydney Cruz. I didn't answer.

That afternoon, I starting dialing—managers, general managers, farm system directors, scouts, personnel directors. Unfortunately nobody wanted what I was selling. Oh sure, some of them didn't mind reminiscing with the Fish. I shared some nice laughs, but didn't make any progress advancing my employment prospects. Nobody wanted to stick their neck out for a 41-year-old who hadn't pitched in the majors in two years. Even my 6-3 record in Lincoln didn't carry much clout, because I didn't do it with my old arsenal of pitches. No respect for Madam Knucklina.

I decided to make one more call. A year ago at the Hall of Fame induction ceremonies in Cooperstown I met the manager of the Pawtucket Red Sox, a guy named Les Burton. Turns out he went to high school with Dave King, the quarterback. King was one of my favorite NFL players in the '80s, so Burton and I talked football for a while after the speeches were over. I didn't know if he'd remember me, but I called anyway. To my surprise he did remember our conversation in Cooperstown. And in an even bigger surprise, he expressed interest in me pitching for Pawtucket. But he'd first have to talk to the powers that be within the Red Sox organization. So, no promises. I gave him my number, but wasn't too optimistic. The Boston front office had never shown much interest in the Fish, even in my prime.

Around 4:00, I'd had enough of trying to sell myself. I'd received thirteen rejections and one "maybe." Not the most auspicious start to my job search. I thought about calling Tim Haines, but didn't really want to get on the phone again. So I flipped on the TV and watched *Jeopardy*. Of course, I had no answer for most of the questions (or, to be more precise, no question for most of the answers). Well, I actually did okay in the "Potent Potables" category.

Gale returned from a golf outing at a country club. It dawned on me that our time together as roommates would soon be ending. Bummer. I was sure going to miss his cooking. Wanting to show my gratitude for all he'd done for me, I asked if I could buy him supper.

"Hmm. A tempting offer, old boy. What did you have in mind?"

"How about Misty's?"

"Ooh, isn't that a bit pricey?"

"Actually, it is." I remembered the small number on the check I'd just received. My *last* check from the Giants. "Could I borrow fifty bucks before we go?"

Gale rolled his eyes. "Mr. Fischer, you are hopeless."

"You know, I used to be rich."

"Correction, you used to have money. You were never rich."

"Well aren't you the snob? But I'll excuse your snootiness if you play a few hands of poker with me." My eyebrows bobbed up and down. "Then I'll have some money in no time."

He frowned. "You've been lucky at cards this summer. That's all." He lowered himself into the blue La-Z-Boy recliner in the corner of the living room. "We do have another dining option for this evening, you know."

"A better option than my generous offer to take you out to supper on your dime?"

"It just may be."

"Alright, let's hear about this *other* offer."

"It seems that our esteemed colleagues are throwing a soiree this evening." He checked his watch, a rare Swiss Roskopf from the 1930s. "Begins in a couple hours. One last bash to celebrate our truncated season with the Giants."

"Where at?"

"JK's in the Haymarket. The owner, as you may know, is a fan. He's allowing the team use of his banquet room and is even offering us a discount on spirits."

It sounded tempting. Count Zane-ula especially liked the discounted booze part. And a party with the boys would provide a nice distraction from all the crap that had gone down the past week. Tim would not approve. I could almost see him as a little angel standing on my shoulder urging me not to go. "You're in a red flag mood, Zane. Don't go. You'll regret it."

Tiny Tim angel had a point. Another setback with the bottle would not help my baseball career. Assuming I still had a baseball career. A little devil then appeared on my other shoulder and said my career was probably over anyway, so I might as well have some fun. He added that I wouldn't have to get drunk, I could stop whenever I wanted. Yes, the little devil looked liked me. Me wearing red and carrying a miniature pitchfork, of course.

The debate wore on with devil Zane eventually gaining the upper hand. When Gale grabbed his car keys and asked if I was going, I nodded and shut off the TV. Then my phone rang. It was Curtis. "You planning on going to that party tonight?" he asked.

"Thinking about it."

"Well, stop thinking about it."

"Why?"

"Because you don't want to get yourself into any trouble tonight. Last thing you need right now is your face in the paper for something stupid."

"What do you mean right now? What's so important about now?"

An annoyed exhale followed. "You need to get your sleep tonight, Fischer. Tomorrow you got a telephone meeting."

"With who?"

"The guy who just called me asking about you. That's who?"

"Does this guy have a name?"

"Walt Jocketty."

It took a second for that to register. "The Cardinals GM? Are you telling me …"

"Just get your butt in my office tomorrow morning at nine. Alright?"

I did not go to the party that night.

Chapter 11

Sleep did not come easily. I was like a kid tossing in bed the night before Christmas. Okay maybe not quite like that, but Curtis's phone call charged me up. There had been so many dark clouds hovering over me the past few days, it was nice to have some potential good news to think about. I scooted into the manager's office at a quarter to nine.

"You're early," Curtis said. His eyes didn't leave the newspaper.

"You're supposed to be impressed," I replied, settling into the wooden chair in front of his desk. The scene reminded me of our first meeting in his office back in April.

"Mm-hmm." He turned a page. "You keep yourself out of trouble last night?"

"I did. Watched a few innings of the Dodgers-Astros game and then hit the sack by eleven."

"Good."

I waited for more words of praise, but nothing came. "I gotta say, Curtis, I appreciate the interest you're showing in my career now. For a while there, I didn't think you liked me much."

"This ain't about me liking you."

"Then what is it."

He lowered his paper to cast eyes on me. "There's only four guys on the Giants who have a shot at landing anywhere this summer. Of the four, your name gives you the best chance. If I can deliver you sober and in one piece to a big league club, then at least

I'll have something to show for my time here. Make me look a little better when I go huntin' for another managing job this winter."

"Why Cruiser, I'm touched." I searched in vain for a hint of a smile on his face.

"Once you get signed on somewhere—assuming that happens—then you can go get loaded, stoned, or whatever the hell you want. As long as I can say Zane Fischer kept it together under my watch, we're good."

"You're gonna have to give me a moment here, Curtis." I fanned my face. "I've read about the special bond that can form between a player and his manager. And now, here I am experiencing it for myself. I think I'm gonna cry."

"Shut up, Fischer." He tossed a section of the paper to me. "Here, inform yourself about the world."

I glanced at a couple headlines. "Aren't you gonna tell me more about your conversation with Jocketty?"

"What about it?"

"Well, is he interested?"

Curtis furrowed his brow in annoyance. "He called, didn't he?"

"What did he say?"

"You're supposed to call the St. Louis Cardinals front office at nine-thirty. Then you'll find out everything you want to know."

I glanced at the humming clock on the wall. "Why'd you tell me to come in at nine then? Why did I have to come in at all? I could've called from home."

He snickered at a comic he'd just read, before directing a stern glare at me. "By making you come in at nine, I know you're up and alert for this meeting. If you think all you have to do is call Jocketty from home at 9:30, you're liable to go out partying and then set your alarm for 9:29. Then you'd be talkin' to him all hung over and groggy. Or you'd hit the snooze button and sleep till noon. Miss the whole damn thing."

He had a point. I didn't tell him that though. I just flashed an indignant look and skimmed the paper. Neither of us said anything until it was time to call St. Louis. I pulled out my cell phone and said I was going out to the stands to make the call.

"Don't do that," Curtis growled. "That cell thing of yours is filled with static half the time. And it could cut out on you. Here, use my phone. Might as well talk on the honchos' dime."

So I called from Curtis's office phone. Walt Jocketty wasn't available. The receptionist instead connected me with Jocketty's assistant, Jerry Walker, the Cardinals director of player personnel. The team's farm director and some other officials were with him. They put me on speakerphone.

Walker did most of the talking. He said they were impressed with the progress I'd made this season. He asked if I thought I could get big league hitters out with my knuckleball. I said I could. Like I'm going to say, "No way Jerry, I'm gonna get blasted off the mound like Charlie Brown." He then asked me if I'd been following the big home run race that summer. I said I had. Cardinals first baseman Mark McGwire was still on pace to shatter Roger Maris's single season home run record. Walker explained that the Cards had a great offense, but were looking for some pitching help. To bolster the rotation, they wanted to add a veteran arm—my veteran arm to be exact. I told him I looked forward to pitching at Busch Stadium.

They instead wanted me to report to their AAA team in Memphis. Log a few starts there and then, if things went well, I'd join the big league club. Though I hoped to be pitching for St. Louis right away, it made sense to send me to Memphis first. The hitters in their league would still be a step up from what I'd seen thus far this season. And I'd get a few more starts to hone my knuckleball skills before facing monsters like Sammy Sosa, Barry Bonds, and Jeff Bagwell.

We next talked numbers. My salary at Memphis would be triple what the Giants had paid me. Even though it was still a mere fraction of what I'd made during my heyday, I felt like I'd won the lottery. And if I got called up to St. Louis, I'd be guaranteed the league minimum—a number I hadn't sniffed in a long time. Amazing how one's perspective can change after a couple years of earning jack squat. At this point I realized that I didn't have representation, so I made a mental note to call some people. If this all worked out, I'd definitely want an agent to negotiate my contract for next season.

After we'd finished discussing business, I thanked them for this opportunity. I also made a comment about needing to buy a case of Jack Daniel's for the scout who recommended me. Walker said it was former Giants manager Don Angley who had told them about Zane Fischer. After he'd left the dugout in '94, Angley became the Cardinals scout for the Central States League. A local reporter, Brian Carter, also advanced my cause by sending some clippings and stats to someone he knew in the Cardinals front office. Walker said my current manager gave me a glowing recommendation as well. So the Fish had a lot of help making it onto the radar in St. Louis.

Throughout the call Curtis kept working on a crossword puzzle, seemingly oblivious to my conversation. After I hung up, I grinned at him. "You do like me."

"Do not."

"Do too."

"Go pack, Fischer." His eyes remained on his puzzle. "I got things to do."

I paused at his door and looked back. "Thanks, Skip. I won't forget this."

He nodded and waved me away.

Packing took less than an hour. Guess that's one benefit of not owning much of anything. I called Buddy, but she didn't answer. I thought about driving over there, but decided to wait a little longer before doing that. Sidney left me a couple more voice messages. Both her tone and word choices revealed a growing displeasure with me. I probably should've called her back, but I didn't.

Since my flight wasn't until the next morning, I had the afternoon free. Snowman and Dirk came over. Gale wanted to buy some groceries. None of us had anything else to do, so we went with him to the grocery store near our apartment.

"What's this crap?" Dirk asked as we meandered down the first aisle. His head pounding from a mighty hangover, he wore dark shades to shield his eyes from the florescent lights above.

"They're called vegetables," Gale replied. "You might want to try one sometime."

"Nah." Dirk poked a head of lettuce. "Too many bad memories of being force-fed beets as a kid. Besides, I put ketchup on my burgers. That counts as a vegetable, right?"

"Tell that to the paramedics after your inevitable first heart attack," Gale said. "I'm sure they'll be impressed."

Snowman grabbed an orange and spun it in his hand. "That is so cool you're going to the Cardinals." He tossed the fruit to me. "I knew you'd make it back to the Show. Even before the season started, I knew you'd make it."

"It's just Memphis," I said, placing a knuckler grip on the orange. "I'm not back yet."

"When did you find out?" Dirk asked.

I set the orange on top of some cantaloupes. "Curtis called me last night."

"That why you didn't go to the party?"

"Pretty much. Did I miss anything?"

"McCormick and General Lee brought in a couple of butt-ugly strippers," Dirk said. "When they showed up, I wondered what kennel they were from. Strange thing though, they were lookin' pretty good by the end of the night."

"Funny how that works," I said.

"A few guys climbed up on the bar and tried to imitate their act," Snowman said. "The Cat has some pretty good moves, I gotta say. So does Cy."

"Clooney on the other hand, does not," Gale added. "Poor chap fell off a table and broke his arm. Good thing the season's over."

"See what a blast you missed, Fischer," Dirk said, trying to burrow his thick fingers into a honeydew melon. "You should've come."

I shook my head. "What I've heard so far confirms that I should *not* have gone to the party. Could've ended up just like Clooney."

"What are you doing to that fruit?" Snowman nervously asked Dirk.

"Relax, Snowflake. I'm just tryin' to make a bowling ball." It didn't work, so he smashed the melon against the edge of a counter. Dirk then wiped his juice-drenched fingers on Snowman's Rush T-shirt. The skinny catcher swatted away his arm.

We wandered down an aisle with a bunch of canned goods, and another aisle with pasta and cooking oils. Gale continued filling his cart. "So why you gettin' all this stuff, McGrady?" Dirk asked. "Ain't you takin' off soon like the rest of us?"

Gale examined the label on a jar of olives. "Actually, I'll be remaining in Lincoln for a while longer. I'd like to make another effort to woo a young lady who's caught my fancy."

"Is this the dame you took on your double date with Fischer?"

"One and the same."

"You told me Beth lacked culture," I said. "She wouldn't let you bite her butt, so you were done with her."

Gale rolled his eyes. "I decided to give her one more chance. Yesterday, I called and told her about the Giants recent misfortune. She seemed sympathetic. Even agreeable to another date. So I invited her over for a home-cooked dinner tomorrow evening. After sampling my culinary expertise, the lass will be powerless to resist the charms of Gale Force."

"Still calling yourself that, huh?" Dirk said. "You do realize that you suck as a pitcher?"

"I won't even dignify that with a response."

"Just sayin'." While trekking down the cereal aisle, Dirk ripped open a box of Lucky Charms and shoveled a handful into his mouth. In addition to that box, his trail of destruction thus far included the crushed melon, a package of spaghetti he'd snapped in half, three bags of sugar he'd punctured, and four hard rolls he'd winged at us in the bakery section. It probably wasn't such a good idea to take Dirk out in public so soon after losing his job.

"What are you going to do now without baseball?" I asked Snowman.

He shrugged. "Hang out in Lincoln for a while, I guess. Break out the guitar and see if I can get the old band back together."

"You were in a band?"

"In high school."

"Get a lot of gigs? Make some money?"

"Nah." He shook his head. "Nobody ever paid to hear us play."

"So what will you do for income?"

"My old man is making me apply at some places. Wal-Mart, Walgreens, Target."

"Good luck."

"We really were fortunate to be playing for the Giants," he said with a melancholy smile.

"Yeah." I felt bad for Snowman. More than anybody else on the team, he played for the love of the game. I asked Dirk about his post-Giants plans.

"Headin' to Tallahassee the day after tomorrow. Got a cousin who owns a bar down there. Said he needs a bouncer. Figure I'll do that while I'm waiting for the Yankees to call."

Gale collected the rest of the items he needed for his culinary masterpiece. Along the way, Dirk smashed a box of Ho Hos, ripped open a bag of barbeque chips, and crushed an untold number of eggs by sitting on the cartons stacked in the cooler. He of course had to fart on them for good measure. When we passed the beer display, he tore into a twelve pack, popped open a can, and downed it on the spot. More than a few shoppers flashed dirty looks at him (and us) during his rampage. An old lady told him he should know better than to engage in such childish behavior. He asked her what it was like to date George Washington.

"You'll have to excuse my bald friend," I said to her. "He was just released from the asylum and is still adjusting to life on the outside."

After Gale paid for his groceries, we headed for the exit. Blocking our path was the store manager, an assistant manager, a cop, and a surly-looking bag boy. Shockingly, the store employees had noticed Dirk's antics. I pulled my cap down further, hoping not to be recognized.

"You can't prove nothin'," Dirk said.

"Actually," the manager replied, "we've got video of everything you did. You do realize there are cameras throughout the store?"

Dirk did not realize that. And now he faced a choice. Pay for everything he destroyed or accompany the police officer to jail. For an instant, I thought he was going to make a run for it. But he knew he couldn't run very far before hacking up a lung. So big Dirk emptied his wallet. Since that covered only about half the bill, he had to borrow the rest from Gale.

Even though there was only one culprit, the manager proclaimed that we were all banned from entering his store again. So I had to add the Russ's Market on 70th Street in Lincoln, Nebraska, to the list of establishments in this country where the Fish wasn't welcome. And this time it wasn't even my fault. So unfair.

After we got back to the apartment, Les Burton called to tell me that, despite his best efforts, the Red Sox weren't interested in me. I thanked him for trying. So much for starting a bidding war for my talents. While Gale practiced his cello, Snowman and Dirk decided to go see *Saving Private Ryan* that evening. They asked me to join them, but I had to pass. With just one more night in town, I had to try to make things right with my daughter before I left.

I called around five. It came as something of a surprise when Buddy answered. I told her about the Giants disbanding. She already knew. I'd forgotten they were her employer too. I told her I'd be leaving town tomorrow and asked if we could get together that night. She said yes. Thank God.

After she climbed into the passenger seat of my truck, I asked where she wanted to go. She picked the mall. On the way over, we traded small talk about movies, traffic, and the weather. I said I liked her longer hair. She said she was trying to grow it out like Rachel from *Friends*. We ended up at Amigos in the Gateway Mall food court.

"I'm sorry," I said.

She looked down at her soft taco and nodded.

"I feel horrible, Buddy. Some stuff happened in the locker room that day and then Gale kept pestering me about going out with him that evening. I know that's not an excuse, but …"

"I'm sorry too." Her voice was barely audible over the mall noise. "I shouldn't have reacted like I did."

"I was really looking forward to discussing Harry Potter with you. I don't know how I forgot."

Her mouth formed a faint smile. "Well, you are getting old. And memory loss is common among the elderly."

"Very funny, Betty. I mean Brandy. No wait, it's Bunny, right?"

Her smile grew before fading away. She shifted her food around with a plastic fork.

"Your mother and I were really worried about you that night."

"Nothing happened. I don't even like Roger. I'm not going to see him again."

"He didn't pressure you to do anything?"

"Oh, he did. But I didn't let him get anywhere. So we ended up hanging out with a bunch of his friends in some guy's basement."

"Some guy's basement?" My brows rose.

She set her fork down. "Yes, I had a beer. Just one. It tasted like crap, so that's all I had."

I swallowed a bite of burrito. "You should have called. I hated not knowing where you were. Wondering if you were okay."

"Yeah, that sucks not knowing where someone is. It's like you're calling over and over, but they don't answer. So you're sitting there in the dark, wondering what's going on."

I sighed. "I know I screwed up, Buddy. It will never happen again. I promise. But what you did was dangerous. Something could've happened and we wouldn't have known where to find you."

"I know, Dad. Mom already gave me a long lecture about it. You don't need to add anything."

"I just—"

"She grounded me for two weeks. That should make you happy."

Actually it did make me happy that Toni had laid down the law. Even though Buddy had a right to be mad at me, she was still a fifteen-year-old girl and shouldn't have disappeared with an older boy.

Some time passed. Then I asked, "You hear about what happened that night?"

"You mean how you decked Cole?" She grinned. "That was so awesome."

"Your mom still mad at me?"

"She shouldn't be. That creep had it coming, the way he treats her."

"Has it gotten worse since that night?"

She thought for a second. "I don't know if it's any worse. He was always a jerk, and he still is."

"He hasn't hit her?"

"No. But he talks about hitting you. He stomps around saying, 'This ain't over. You tell your deadbeat father that payback's gonna be a bitch.'" Buddy shook her head. "He thinks he's so tough. Says you sucker punched him and that he'd destroy you in a fair fight."

I snorted. "The way he threw your mother down, I don't think he cares much about fair fights."

"I know. He's such a poseur. He'll brag about how strong he is, like he can bench press 300 pounds, and then he talks about his gun. I feel like saying, 'If you're so tough, why do you need a gun?'"

"What? Cole has a gun?" Something cold ran down my spine.

"He says he does. I've never seen it."

"A handgun?"

"I guess so. Like I'm trying to watch TV and he'll start going on about his Smith and Wesson. He must think he's Jesse James or something."

"That's disturbing."

"What?"

"Cole having a gun."

"He probably doesn't even know how to use it. He's an idiot."

An ill feeling expanded in my gut. "Yeah."

"What's wrong?"

"I don't like leaving town with things so stirred up in your house."

"That douche bag won't do anything." She smirked. "And if he gets out of line, you'll put him in his place again. Right?"

I nodded. "Absolutely." *But does he really have a gun?*

When we were about finished with our food, Buddy's expression dimmed, like she just remembered something unpleasant. "When are you leaving?"

"Tomorrow morning. Plane takes off at 9:23."

"Memphis, huh?"

"Yeah."

"So you're gonna get back to the majors?"

"If I pitch well for Memphis, I might."

"Then when you're in the majors, maybe you could get custody of me."

I knew that was a long shot. "I'll sure try."

"If I told the judge I wanted to live with you, would that help?"

"I don't know. Maybe. But I don't think the courts let kids your age decide who they get to live with. They base their decision on a bunch of other stuff."

Her face drooped. "I wish I could go to Memphis with you."

"Me too, Sweetheart."

"Really?"

"Yes. I hate leaving you now."

She didn't say anything for a while. I was about to ask if she wanted to go, when she looked up and said, "When you and Mom got divorced, did you still want me?"

Her question almost choked me up. "Buddy, of course I did. I never stopped loving you. It's just, your mom got custody."

"Did you try to get me for part of the time?"

"Well, your mom wanted what would be best for you."

"You didn't fight for me?" The hurt look in her eyes tore my heart out.

"The divorce was really hard on your mother. She was still hurting bad from losing Luke, and me being around seemed to make things worse for her. I thought that a long custody battle would be too much for both of you to go through. So I let her have you."

A single tear crawled down Buddy's doll cheek. "Did you miss me?"

"Yes, I missed you terribly. I felt horrible not being around you." I took a breath to keep my composure. "I made sure I could still see you every year."

"That wasn't much."

"I know."

Her eyes flicked on me and then drifted elsewhere. "When you left and I didn't see you anymore, I felt like you didn't care about me. Like baseball mattered more."

"Buddy, I always—"

"When I got older and we talked more, that helped. I thought maybe you did care. Then you moved out here this summer and that was so much fun. It's like I had a dad again." She dabbed her eyes with a napkin. "But when I was waiting for you on the porch that night, the old feelings came back. And now you're going away again. And with Mom getting married to that jerk, it feels like I'm losing her too."

"Buddy, you're not losing me. Right after the season's over, I'll be back." I reached across the table to hold her hands. "Don't ever think I don't care about you. You mean everything to me. Getting you back in my life has been the best thing that's happened to me since the four of us were together. There is nothing more important than you."

She examined me with misty eyes. "Really?"

"I remember when I first held you in the hospital after you were born. You were pink and wrinkly, like a little alien baby from outer space. Then you opened your tiny blue eyes and looked up at me. You stole my heart that moment and you've still got it today."

She let go of my hands and grabbed another napkin. "Even when I've got snot running out of my nose?"

"Well, let me think about that…. Yeah, I guess so."

That brought a fragment of a smile. We sat there in the food court watching the people walk by. Later we went to some stores where she checked out the clothes, music, and novelty items. I bought her a bracelet. It was purple—Buddy said it reminded her of the Giants. We stayed until the mall closed. When I pulled into her driveway, she sat in my truck not saying anything. Then she gave me a long hug and said, "Bye, Dad. I love you."

My thoughts shuffled like a Rolodex on the drive back to the apartment. I convinced myself that I was doing the right thing. That this was all part of the plan. Things had to be this way, for now. My phone rang. It was Gale.

"Hey, old boy. Thought I should give you a heads up."

"About what?"

"A young lady showed up tonight looking for you."

A sigh escaped from my deflating lungs. "Sidney?"

"Yes. And she displayed a most unpleasant demeanor. Pounding on the door. Breathing threats and invectives. All the while taking your name in vain. You know how some women are beautiful when they're angry? Well this one is just scary. I must ask, Fischer, what did you do to her?"

"Nothing. That's the problem."

"You must have done something. She was swearing like a soccer hooligan in both English and Spanish."

"After that night we were together, I told her I'd call her. But I never did. You know what it's like."

"Sadly, I don't. But that's neither here nor there. There is a more pressing matter at hand."

"What? She still there?"

"Yes. Your angry paramour prowls outside, pacing like a lioness in the parking lot. Hence the reason for this call."

"She's outside the apartment right now?"

"I'm watching her through a crack in the blinds even as we speak. I felt compelled to turn out the lights so she wouldn't see me. Don't want her coming up here again."

"How long has she been there?"

"Nearly three hours. I told her you were out for the evening, but I don't think she's going away anytime soon."

"Damn it!" I slapped the dash. "I'd rather not deal with her right now."

"Obviously. But your suitcase is still here. You'll need that before tomorrow morning."

I pulled into the empty lot of an insurance agency to figure out what to do. With no back entrance to Gale's apartment, I couldn't slip in without Sidney spotting me. I thought about just going home and confronting the situation, but images of Glenn Close in *Fatal Attraction* kept playing in my head. *I'm not going to be IGNORED, Dan.*

So I drove to another apartment complex a mile away and found a spot in a dark section of the parking lot. There, I spent the night, sleeping in the cab of my pickup. Not very honorable, I know. But I just couldn't face the wrath of Sidney Cruz.

The next morning around 8:00, I called Gale. He said the coast was clear. Sidney apparently went home sometime during the night. "Unless she's waiting on a nearby rooftop with a sniper rifle," he said. I did not find any humor in that comment.

I picked up my suitcase and thanked Gale for all that he had done for me that summer. "Not a problem," he said. "I actually enjoyed our little adventures and misadventures as roommates."

"Me too."

"Good luck in Memphis, old boy. And please don't scorn any more women."

"Yeah, I'll try to remember that."

I drove to the Lincoln airport and steered my pickup into the long-term parking lot. Then I raced inside and made my flight with only minutes to spare. When the jet ascended above the city, I pressed my face to the small window next to my seat. As the buildings got smaller and smaller, I imagined Buddy looking up watching the plane fly away.

Chapter 12

After landing in Memphis, I took a cab from the airport to Tim McCarver Stadium. The ballpark wasn't all that visually appealing truth be told, but that didn't matter to me. As the home of a Triple-A affiliate, it represented the final rung in my climb back to the majors. So that made the stadium just lovely in my estimation.

I eventually found myself sitting in a small conference room with a couple front office suits, the pitching coach, and Gaylen Pitts, manager of the Memphis Redbirds. With his good-old-boy mustache, Pitts reminded me of one of those tough southern sheriffs. "So what er you doin' in these here parts, boy?" He didn't actually say that, but I could imagine the words coming from his mouth. At least he wasn't working on a crossword puzzle.

One of the suits, the general manager as it turned out, welcomed me to Memphis and asked if I'd ever been there before. I had not, which kind of surprised me given all the U.S. cities I'd frequented during my career. Just after we were married, Toni and I had talked about driving to Memphis for a quick vacation, but some other destination always won out. After a few more pleasantries, Pitts asked if I was ready to start. I said yes, anytime he wanted to pencil me in. He had me slated to go the following night against New Orleans. Sounded good to me. Then he asked if I knew that pitchers batted in the Pacific Coast League (yes, Memphis was in the PCL even though it is 2,000 miles from the Pacific Coast). I said I did not know that, but I'd do my best not to embarrass myself at the plate. I then reminded everyone of my sparkling .139 batting average from my days in the National League. That brought a chuckle from the gathering.

Actually, I did have one slight reservation about my start, and it had nothing to do with the prospect of picking up a bat. The next day was a Saturday, a full week since my last outing for Lincoln. Normally, a couple extra days between starts isn't a big deal. But I hadn't thrown any bullpen sessions. Since the knuckleball can get fickle, it's a good idea to throw it regularly. Back in Lincoln, I'd been tossing with Snowman or Cy nearly every day between starts. That really helped. Hopefully this little break hadn't soured my relationship with Madam Knucklina. In a perfect world, I could have thrown three practice sessions before facing live hitters again. But I didn't verbalize this concern. Didn't want to come off as difficult or give them any reason to change their mind about me. So I just said I was looking forward to getting in some work that afternoon.

After the meeting concluded, the GM's assistant led me to an accountant's office. There, I filled out the paperwork making me an official member of the 1998 Memphis Redbirds. If all went well, I wouldn't be on the team for very long.

By the time I'd finished with the forms, practice had already started. I walked into an empty clubhouse and changed into my practice uniform. Pitts had a catcher waiting for me in the bullpen. My first dozen tosses were either flat or wild. Then my fingers gradually regained the feel of the knuckler. The good madam came back. Unfortunately, I'd developed a painful kink in my neck, a product of sleeping in my pickup the night before. Nonetheless, I threw a longer session than usual. Afterwards, I felt confident I'd be good to go the next night.

One of the Redbird pitchers who'd recently lost his roommate to a trade had agreed to let me share his apartment. I hoped he could cook. That evening before the game I met the guy, a reliever known as Fender. He looked, walked, and talked like a cowboy. His real name was Dallas Bender, and he'd played for the Lincoln Giants a few years earlier. Small world. After the game, he and some of the other pitchers planned to hit a club on Beale Street. They invited me to join them. Catching some blues and downing some brews sounded great, but I knew that wasn't my wisest course of action. Especially my first night in town. So I told Fender I was beat and asked him to drop me off at my new home on his way to the bar.

Fender's apartment complex was a brick structure nestled in a neighborhood that could best be described as "not terrible." I don't know if Gale would've approved, but I'd seen worse. Guys in AAA ball weren't getting rich, but they made enough to avoid living in squalor. At least that's what I thought before pushing the door open. Picture the fraternity in *Animal House*. Now imagine what it would've looked like if John Belushi had detonated a dozen hand grenades in the living room. That was my first impression of Casa Fender. As I stepped inside, the stench of recent debauchery overwhelmed my nostrils. I guessed that at least nine of the Ten Commandments had been broken in there over the past 48 hours. My eyes scanned the floor for a chalk outline, but all I saw were empty pizza boxes, crushed Lone Star cans, tobacco juice stains, and a few roaches scurrying for cover. I had to use the bathroom, where another unspeakable horror greeted me as I lifted the toilet seat. The brown pattern resembled one of Jackson Pollack's creations. Returning to the living room, I brushed some pizza crusts off a nasty old sofa and sat amid the destruction. When the last guy found out he was traded, it was likely the happiest day of his life.

The urge to drink intensified. I thought about checking what liquid delights the refrigerator offered, but instead decided to call Tim. It had been a while.

"Hello." He sounded a bit groggy.

"Captain Underwear! Hey, you weren't in bed yet, were you?"

"Uh ... not anymore." I heard him hoist himself off a mattress and into his wheelchair.

"Sorry, man. I keep forgetting to check the time before I call. Sara probably hates me."

"No, she doesn't. She'll get back to sleep." He shut a door. "How you been?"

"Doin' alright. Just thought I'd get caught up with the Captain."

"Did you know that someone just wrote a children's book about a superhero called Captain Underpants?"

"What? Someone stole your gig?"

"I'm meeting with my attorneys in the morning."

"Good. I knew we should've trademarked that name…. Hey, you'll never guess where I am."

"Hmmm. Well if it's not Lincoln maybe I'll guess Memphis as a shot in the dark."

"How'd you know?"

"Read an article on the Internet that you signed with the Cards. Congratulations."

"Thanks. Just got here today. You should see this apartment they stuck me in."

"You there now?"

"Yeah. The guys went out after the game. I wanted to join them, but figured I should take it easy my first night in town."

"Wanting a drink?"

"Yep."

"How's that been going?"

I gave him the highlights and lowlights of my life since our last conversation. That included my evening with Sidney Cruz, forgetting my plans with Buddy, and the ensuing fallout with Toni and Cole. I also covered the details of the Central States League collapse.

"You've had an eventful month," he said.

"Yeah."

"I'm glad you called me. You didn't have to wait so long, you know."

"Yeah, sorry. Things got crazy there with the team folding and my misunderstanding with Buddy. I really hated leaving her."

"That would be tough. But it's good you got to smooth things over with her before you left. Sounds like overall things went well with your daughter this summer. You established a foundation and hopefully you'll make it back to Lincoln after the season is over."

"Yes, definitely."

Tim continued by pointing out the other positives that had occurred in my life over the past few weeks. He encouraged me to avoid future distractions and to stay focused on pitching. "You're close to achieving your goals, Fish. All your discipline and hard work over the past year is paying off. Stay with the program, my friend."

"Yeah, I will."

"And if anything comes up, you call me. Alright?"

"Thanks, Tim."

"You bet. How about if I pray for you now?"

"Nah, that's really not necessary."

"Great. Heavenly Father, I lift up my brother Zane tonight and ask that you watch over him during his time in Memphis …"

I found a surprisingly untarnished twin-sized mattress in an otherwise empty bedroom. I figured that one had to be my room, since the other bedroom was littered with spit cups, dirty laundry, and other vile debris. The Dallas Cowboy cheerleader posters above Fender's bed were a nice touch, though I'm pretty sure the girls didn't approve of the carnage they overlooked.

At some point around nine the next morning, I got up and wandered down the hall.

"Yer up early." Fender slouched on the sofa playing a shoot-em-up game on the PlayStation. A wad of dip bulged below his bottom lip and he wore a black Stetson and dark socks. That's all he had on.

"You too."

"Yeah … woke up at seven and couldn't get back to sleep." He turned and lowered his head to spit into a red plastic cup wedged between two of the sofa cushions. "Hate when that happens."

"Me too. You eaten yet?" I recalled the flavor of Gale's crepes.

"Just a peanut butter and banana sandwich. There ain't nothin' else in the cupboards here." His eyes remained on the screen. "Eat lead you zombie son of a bitch!" Gunfire and explosions roared from the television. Fender twisted his hairy white body and tilted the controller, feverishly pushing buttons with his thumbs. "Oh hell no! ... Great, I'm dead." He tossed the controller aside, fully exposing body parts that can't be shown on television.

"Stupid zombies."

"I know, right?" He deposited more dip juice into the red cup. "Hey, ya wanna get some grub?"

He slid into some Wranglers and cowboy boots, and drove us to a nearby IHOP. After we devoured our pancakes, he asked if I'd ever been to Graceland. I said no. Next thing I knew, we were touring the mansion where Elvis once lived.

"I love this place," he drawled. "Something spiritual about being in the presence of the King. When things ain't goin' so well on the mound, I come here. Gets my head right again."

"Good thing you ended up in Memphis," I said.

"I know it. After pitching here, I don't wanna go nowhere else. Unless it's the bigs, of course."

"So where all have you been?"

As we sauntered through a living room with a stained glass peacock and the longest couch I'd ever seen, Fender recounted his career in baseball. After helping his high school team win the Texas state championship, he played college ball at SMU and then pitched professionally for Bristol, Lincoln, Pawtucket, and Oklahoma City. This was his first season with Memphis. "I figured I'd make it to the Show by now," he said. "But that labrum rip messed up my motion. Took over a year to get to feelin' good again. Still don't have the velocity I had in Pawtucket."

"I know how that goes." My eyes lingered on a 1970s RCA console television that reminded me of the set my mother still watched. "That's why I'm tossing the knuckler."

Fender asked if any of his former teammates were still in Lincoln. "I hear Weed's the mascot now. That true?"

"Yeah ... well he was before the team folded."

Fender shook his head. "Was he any good on those stilts?"

"Not really. Oddly enough, marijuana doesn't do much to improve a person's balance."

"I told that boy to cut back. But after the Giants dropped him, he didn't have much goin' on, ya know. Got baked all the time after that." We entered Elvis's Jungle Room, an interesting space filled with fur-upholstered furniture, Polynesian-themed carvings, and green shag carpet. "Don't get me wrong," Fender continued. "I like to light up as much as the next guy. Takes the edge off. But Weed, after baseball that's about all he did anymore."

"He still has that Willie Aames thing."

Fender snorted. "That boy needs help. I oughta call him when we get home."

"Was Brian Carter on the Giants when you were there?" I asked.

"You mean Boo?"

"Boo?"

"Yeah, that's what we called Carter. One of the boys named him that on account of how much he resembled Boo Radley from that mockingbird movie."

I pictured Brian's face. "I can see that."

"Yeah, I was there the same time as Boo. He was one of the starters. I was the closer. We won the championship that year. Ninety-four." He nodded reflectively. "How's ole Boo doin' nowadays?"

"Good. Writing for the paper."

"Still married?" Fender paused to admire the King's white rhinestone-studded jumpsuits.

"Yeah. His wife is pregnant."

The cowboy chucked. "So Boo knocked up Eileen. How about that? Ya know, she was Sam's girl before she got with Boo?"

"Sam Judge?" He was a star pitcher for the Giants who got into trouble with some gamblers a few years ago. After winning a game he wasn't supposed to win, the mobsters got him. That's one version of the story anyway.

"Yes sir. Man, you wanna see a pitcher." His arm cut through the air in a throwing motion. "The Judge had it goin' on."

After examining a display of framed gold records, I recalled a past conversation with Nicky, the Giants clubhouse manager. "I heard a rumor that Judge is still alive. Maybe in Mexico. Think there's anything to that?"

Fender ambled toward a pink Cadillac. "Might could be." His eyes remained locked on the car. "Don't know."

"If Judge is still alive, why doesn't he come back to the states? If he was as good as everybody says, big league teams would be lining up to sign him."

His eyes fixed on me. "Probably on account of those mob guys. Judge sure did a number on them. If he returns, there could be some payback against him or his family. As long as they think he's dead, nobody gets hurt."

We went outside to Meditation Garden where we ended up at Elvis's gravesite. Fender removed his hat and bowed his head. I did the same, noting that Elvis was forty-two when he died, just one year older than me. "This puts things in perspective," I said.

"You got that right, partner. Too much perspective."

The opening lines of "Heartbreak Hotel" played in my head as we stood in quiet contemplation.

After paying our respects to the King, we headed for Fender's beat-up Ford F-150. He checked his watch. "You ready for some beef?"

"Nah, I'm still full from all those pancakes."

"Not food. I'm talkin' about meetin' some of the local talent."

"Oh, girls."

"You know it." A toothy grin beamed beneath his Stetson. "Got a couple fillies meetin' up with us at the Long Branch in fifteen minutes."

The plan did have some appeal. But then Sidney Cruz's face flashed before my eyes. And I remembered that I'd be pitching that evening. *Eyes on the prize, Fish.*

"Can't do it. Too much going on today."

"Aaw, c'mon now. No time for tail?" He fired up his truck. "You are the same Zane Fischer who used to raise all kinds of hell, aren't you?"

I sighed. "I am. Just a little bit older and a little bit wiser."

"Well, I ain't neither. So I'm gonna squeeze in some afternoon delight before practice." His brow furrowed. "They'll be an extra girl though."

165

"Is that a problem?"

His grin widened. "No sir, it sure ain't."

The facilities at Tim McCarver Stadium were by no means top of the line. But they still represented a significant upgrade from the clubhouses I'd frequented earlier in the season. I especially appreciated the larger locker room—it was nice to be able to change without getting elbowed by the guys next to me. The abundance of clean towels and free Gatorade were nice too. Best of all was the food. On this day, the Memphis clubbie had set out a spread that included little smokies, hard-boiled eggs, carrots, oranges, Twinkies, and three varieties of Doritos. In Lincoln we were lucky if there was a bag of generic potato chips for the entire team to share. Wasn't Nicky's fault; Wright and Mendenhall were too cheap and the players were too poor to kick in for such extravagances.

After practice I returned to my locker and found a Redbirds uniform hanging before me in all its glory. On the back it had my name and a red 33, the number I'd worn in the majors. I gotta say, that made me feel appreciated. Several of my new teammates regaled me with story after story along the lines of "I remember when I was a kid watching you pitch against Dodgers. Man, you were awesome that day." Then I had to sign a few dozen baseballs. That was nice and all, but my mind remained locked in on upcoming events. *Gotta get that knuckler over the plate ... don't let it spin ... work in a curve from time to time ...*

The ballpark appeared to have a capacity of around 10,000. Looked to me that at least three-quarters of the seats were full—the largest crowd I'd pitched in front of in two years. I want to say that most of them were there to see the Fish, but that might not have been the case. The Cardinals had just promoted to Memphis a can't-miss prospect named J.D. Drew. Like me, Drew was hoping he'd soon be playing in St. Louis. Unlike me, Drew was just starting his career and brought unlimited potential to the field. So it seemed more likely the fans that night wanted to see a rising star just starting to shine rather than an aging one trying to keep from fading away. Didn't bother me. I had a job to do and I intended to do it.

My catcher Keith McDonald could handle the mitt, so I didn't have to worry about my erratic pitches bounding to the backstop. Going over the signs beforehand, I told him I wanted to go with at least 75 percent knuckleballs. The other stuff we'd work in as needed to keep hitters off balance. A decent breeze blew in from the west to help counter the oppressive heat and humidity. The roar of the crowd charged me up. Standing on the mound, I felt good …

Until my first pitch flew over the batter's head. *No problem, must've slipped.* The second knuckler died five feet in front of the plate. After walking the first two New Orleans Zephyrs, I had to send in some fastballs. Unfortunately, hitters at the AAA level are quite able to crush straight pitches coming in at 80 miles per hour. Three visitors had crossed the plate by the time our shortstop Adam Kennedy speared a line drive for the third out.

In the home half of the first Drew ripped a double to give our fans something to cheer about, but the Redbirds didn't plate any runs. My second inning on the mound went a lot like the first. I'd planned on taking Madam Knucklina out for a dazzling night out on the town this evening, but she stood me up. The bitch. I walked two and gave up several hard hits. Fortunately the gloves behind me made some nice plays to limit the damage to just one run that inning.

I retired the first hitter in the third, but then walked the next two. My knuckler was getting closer to the strike zone, but not close enough. Gaylen Pitts came out to the mound. "The knuckleball's not working so well tonight," he said.

"Doesn't look that way."

"Inky's next. Think you can get him with sliders?"

He was talking about Pete Incaviglia, a former big league slugger. He'd first broke in with Texas in '86, a year after I'd left the Rangers. Inky could launch balls into orbit, but his powerful swing missed more often than it connected, causing him to strikeout with much frequency. When we were both in the National League in the early '90s, I owned him with sliders low and in and fastballs up and away. Couldn't recall him ever getting an extra base hit off me.

"Yeah," I told Pitts, "I can get him. I'll strike out Inky and then get the next guy."

Pitts nodded his approval of that plan and departed for the dugout. Incaviglia settled into the batter's box. The crowd hummed in anticipation. McDonald put down three fingers for a slider. I gave him one a little low and just off the inside corner. Ball one. The Zephyr manager must have flashed the take sign, because Inky normally would've hacked away at something that close. I tried to hit the outside corner with a curve, but missed high for ball two. Not the situation I was looking for. McDonald went through the signs. I shook him off until he gave me the knuckler. That was the pitch I was going to sink or swim with, and there was no way I was going to serve up a batting practice fastball to Incaviglia in this situation.

I pressed my fingertips into the cowhide and let the ball fly. The good news is the pitch headed right toward the middle of the strike zone. The bad news is it had a nice tight spin, so the baseball sailed in with no movement whatsoever. It sounded like thunder when bat crashed into ball. I think Elvis may have heard it. Inky has left the building. Fischer has left the mound.

I sulked in the trainer's room with my arm wrapped in ice. Normally I wouldn't have bothered after such a short outing, but I'd thrown a lot of pitches in practice the last couple days. Probably too many pitches. Definitely too many sliders and curves. And my neck still hurt. Adding to the physical pain were the old doubts about whether I could still pitch. After the game, Pitts and the pitching coach offered some words of encouragement. Couldn't tell how sincere they actually were. Given what management had said about the Cardinals needing pitching, I figured I'd get at least one more chance to prove myself in Memphis. The organization was paying me little more than the AAA minimum, so it's not like it was a high-risk investment to keep me around for a little while.

I wanted a drink. And Fender and some of the boys wanted me to hit the bars with them. I said I'd think about it. While the players showered after the game, I sat on a stool in the locker room with my head in my hands. Tim's words rang in my ears. He was right—I had to knock out the distractions and focus on my pitching. I was close to realizing my goal. And I might never get this opportunity again. Sure I could've gone out and had a Coke. But that would've been risky, and I had a lot to lose. So I went home and mowed down some zombies on Fender's PlayStation.

The next morning I called Buddy. She had already read on the Web about my first outing as a Redbird. "Sucky night, huh," she said.

"I've had worse. Get 'em next time."

"Yeah."

"How you been?"

"Okay."

"What's been going on?"

"Nothing."

"Is Lincoln devastated that the great Zane Fischer is no longer in town?"

"They're getting over it. Football season is only a month away."

"That's right. That means school is only a month away. You ready for tenth grade?"

"Wish it would start tomorrow."

"What? Still wishing away the summer so you can go to school? You sure we're related?"

"Well now that I don't have my job anymore, I'm home more often."

"That bad, huh?"

A sigh came through the receiver. "Same old crap."

"He bothering you?"

She didn't say anything, so I asked again. "They got home late last night," she said. "He was drunk again."

The hairs on my arms stood. "And?"

"I was in bed when I heard him yelling. There was a crash. I went in to see what happened. Mom was getting up off the floor. She looked pissed. The legs on the coffee table had collapsed. I told Cole to go home. He said, 'I didn't do nothing. And you don't tell me what to do.'"

"What did your mom say?"

"She said she tripped. It's like they think I'm retarded. But she kept making like it was no big deal. They were just playing around."

"What did Cole do?"

"He went to the kitchen to get a beer. Then he came out and started ripping on you. Said you left town 'cause you're afraid to face him. Said if you ever set foot in Lincoln again, he'll end you."

"He's still a charmer, huh?"

"Yeah … I hate him."

"I'm sorry you're going through this."

"Why won't Mom break up with him?"

"That could still happen. In spite of everything, your mom's a smart lady."

"Not anymore." Buddy pushed out a bitter chuckle. "Wish I could've gone with you to Memphis."

"Me too." I thought a change of subject might cheer her up. "Hey, we never got to discuss Harry Potter. I've got the book with me right here. Wanna talk about it?"

"You took the book with you to Memphis?"

"Sure. It reminds me of you."

"Yeah, right."

"I'm serious."

"Oh Dad." After a brief silence, she said, "I'll grab my copy."

I flipped to a page I had marked. "So what did you think when that troll had Hermione cornered in the bathroom? I thought she was a goner."

"It was too early in the book. I knew Harry and Ron would help her."

"How about Snape? I figured that guy was bad news. Reminded me of this coach I had in Toronto. Did you think he was the one trying to steal the stone?"

"At first, but then I thought that was too obvious. There had to be somebody else behind all that stuff that was happening."

We discussed Harry Potter for about a half hour. Spending time together at Hogwarts helped us forget about our real-life problems for a while. And it made the 650 miles between us seem not so distant.

Chapter 13

After finishing the series against New Orleans, we hit the road. As fate would have it, my first road trip as a Redbird took me back to Nebraska, where Memphis would play a four game series against the Omaha Royals. I'd been so busy getting adjusted to my new environment, I paid no attention to the team's upcoming schedule. I hoped I wouldn't be a Redbird for very long, maybe just one or two starts, so why worry about who we were going to be playing?

Once I found out I'd be pitching in Omaha, I called Buddy. Lincoln is less than an hour's drive from Omaha so I hoped her mother would take her to the game. Then we could hang out afterwards. Buddy loved the idea. She even seemed excited, a rare emotion for her of late. It was sure nice to hear some happiness in her voice. When I left Lincoln, I didn't think I'd see her again for at least two months. I couldn't believe how well things worked out for us to get together this soon. This is when you hear happy music start up.

And this is when you hear the needle scratching across the record. What happened next shouldn't have surprised me. Toni wouldn't take her to the game. At first she said she was too busy, but Buddy eventually got her to admit she didn't want to upset Cole again so soon after our "incident." I guess taking Buddy to see her father pitch in Omaha would be too much for Prince Charming to handle. Well okay, maybe I could give her the benefit of the doubt on that one. But what if Buddy went with Stick and his dad? Toni vetoed that idea too. Buddy was still grounded, and rules are rules.

From the sounds of it, this issue created quite an argument. Buddy started crying when recounting her futile attempts to persuade her mother. I still tried to think of a way this might work. Maybe she could serve her grounding sentence later, I suggested. Buddy said she'd already tried that idea. But Cole had convinced Toni that she would be showing weakness and encourage future misbehavior if she let Buddy go to the game.

I said I would talk to Toni myself to see if I could reason with her. Buddy told me not to, since it wouldn't do any good. I did it anyway. I called Toni at work during her lunch hour so she could talk without Mr. Wonderful being around. I figured she wouldn't be thrilled to hear from me at her place of business, but fortunately I caught her in a good mood. She'd sold a keyboard and two electric guitars that morning, and one of her students played "Piano Man" all the way through with no mistakes. Hearing her talk about music reminded me of when she'd play "Time in a Bottle" on our piano. That was a favorite of mine and one of the songs at our wedding.

Despite Toni's positive mood, she still didn't change her mind about taking Buddy to the game. "Zane, I can't. Not after what you did to Cole."

"He's still not a fan of the Fish, huh?"

"You punched him in the face."

"I did it for you. He knocked you down. Some women might even call what I did chivalry."

A few seconds ticked away. "Thanks, but I don't need you to protect me from anybody."

"I know that, but I still … I'm not going to stand by and watch somebody hurt you."

She sighed. "I know you meant well. But this thing with Buddy and the game would just make things more complicated. My life is stressed enough as it is. I'm trying to hold everything together—with Cole and planning the wedding and all this overtime at work. And I'm trying to be a good mother, but she keeps pushing me away. I can't keep up with everything. It's overwhelming."

A memory from the last year of our marriage flashed by. She always tried to do too much on her own. She should've gotten more help dealing with the loss of Luke. Me too. "Alright. I didn't mean to make things more difficult for you. I just thought that since Omaha is so close, Buddy could ... never mind, it's not a big deal."

"Zane, I appreciate what you did this summer. It's meant the world to Buddy to have her dad back in her life. But the timing of this game. I just can't." Her voice sounded so despondent.

"It's okay, Toni. Maybe it'll work out some other time."

So I'd be just 60 miles away from my daughter, but unable to see her. That was bad enough. Worse was how this had affected Buddy's relationship with Toni. Tensions in that house were already high. Now Buddy was saying things like she hated her mother and that she wanted to run away. I did my best to settle her down. Even though I was ticked at Toni myself, I told Buddy that her mother loved her and had her best interests at heart. One of these conversations with my daughter lasted nearly two hours, not ending till after midnight. I'd like to think that my words helped, but that girl was not a happy camper.

The trip to Omaha would be on a jet rather than a bus, another perk of life at the AAA level. The downside was that the team would be on a commercial flight that took off at the ungodly hour of 6:07 AM. Even though getting up before sunrise sucked, air travel was still way better than rotting in a bus for hour after endless hour. In a plane there were lovely stewardesses who brought us soda and little bags of peanuts. And the cabin was relatively cool, a welcome contrast from the convection oven that the Giants bus became when its AC stopped working. Even my teammates' farts weren't as smelly up in the sky. I at first attributed that to those little air jets we could direct at our face, but it was more likely the result of not having Dirk Davis onboard.

I pitched the second game of the series against the Royals. Rosenblatt Stadium in Omaha was a decent ballpark, best known as the home of the College World Series. I didn't go to college and was always busy pitching for a pro team in June, so I'd never been to a CWS game. I had pitched in Rosenblatt though. During my two years with Kansas City, we'd played a couple exhibition games against the AAA team in Omaha. So the surroundings weren't completely new to me. Not that it really mattered all that much. As long as the rubber was 60 feet, six inches away from the plate, I could pitch wherever.

A good-sized crowd showed up that night. I'd say at least five thousand, maybe close to six. Someone even held up a banner that read, "Welcome back to Nebraska, Fish." I liked that, even tipped my hat to them. Acknowledging specific fans was something I rarely did as a big leaguer. But this was the minors, a different atmosphere.

The knuckleball looked promising during warm-ups. I had control and the ball had movement. In the first inning, I needed only twelve pitches to get three outs. Ten of the twelve deliveries were knucklers and they all hovered in or near the strike zone. A welcome sight. After my last debacle I really needed a successful outing to keep the big league club's interest.

I struck out the first batter I faced in the second inning. The next guy scorched a line drive right back at me. In my younger days I never worried about something coming back through the box. I actually didn't mind it when drives came at me. Gave me a chance to make a play. Throughout my career, I prided myself on being able to stop, or at least deflect, most of the shots coming my way. Yes, sometimes I'd get stung, like that hit by Paciorek, but I held my own with the glove. At 41, however, I had to admit that my reflexes weren't the same as ten years ago. And this bullet in Omaha had the potential to do some damage. I jerked up my glove and ducked. The ball whistled past my leather shield and just missed clipping my ear. I felt the breeze as it rocketed by. Wow, those things move fast.

Having reached with a single, the batter yelled at me from first, "Sorry, Mr. Fischer." I'm not sure if he was mocking me with that "Mr. Fischer" business. He looked about eighteen, so who knows. Didn't matter. At the time, I was just happy to still be alive.

Even though my heart pounded, I kept my nerve. Two decades of big league experience came into play and my body locked in on what it had to do. My fingers found the grip and delivered a series of mystifying knuckleballs that ended the inning with no further damage.

Nate Dishington, our first baseman, doubled home a run in the third to give the Redbirds the lead. In the bottom of the inning, I walked a couple guys to put two on with two out when Jeremy Giambi stepped to the plate. I didn't know much about Jeremy, but his brother Jason had developed into a solid power-hitter for the Oakland A's. No need to get cute here, I thought. The knuckleball would again be my path to deliverance.

Giambi watched the first one flutter over for strike one. Then I missed high to even the count. A foul out of play put him in a 1-2 hole. Time for the good madam to send this young man to the bench. I went into the stretch and delivered a nasty one. The ball started off heading for the heart of the plate, then shuddered a bit to the left, before diving sharply to the right. Pretty much unhittable. So of course Giambi smashed it into the gap in right-center to plate both runners. That kind of thing didn't happen in the Central States League. When I threw a wicked knuckler in Lincoln, the batter couldn't do anything with it. At the AAA level, however, sometimes you'd make a great pitch and it would still get clobbered. Didn't happen often, but it did happen. Omaha led 2-1 heading to the fourth.

Neither team scored again until the fifth, when we put up three to reclaim the lead. Chip Hale drove in a couple with a timely hit and Joe McEwing added a solo shot. My pitches, meanwhile, kept dancing. I gave up a single in the bottom half of the inning, but otherwise the Royals did not make solid contact.

The score remained 4-2 when I took the mound in the sixth. After my warm-up tosses, I glanced into the stands. I knew Buddy wouldn't be there, but I looked anyway. Maybe Toni had changed her mind at the last minute. I didn't spot my daughter, but another young lady caught my eye. She sat about four rows behind the home team's on-deck circle. Yes, it was the lovely Sidney Cruz. Her fierce eyes zeroed in on me like lasers. I quickly turned away and focused on my catcher Keith behind the plate. Believe it or not,

I'd forgotten about Miss Cruz since moving to Memphis. It appeared that she still remembered me. Yay.

Okay, I admit it, seeing Sidney freaked me out a little. Sure, she wasn't the first lady I'd wronged. Usually they just cussed me out, told me what a jerk I was, and went on their way. Sometimes I'd get a drink in the face, but that would be the worst of it. This Sidney thing was different. Troubling questions popped up in my head. Just how far was she willing to go? Had she ever watched *The Natural*? If so, did it give her any ideas?

I walked the first batter that inning on four pitches that weren't close. The next guy went to a full count before also getting a base on balls. The third hitter laid down a bunt. I nearly threw it away, but Dishington stretched high to make the play. That put runners at second and third with one out. Pitts started warming up a reliever. I paced around the mound. The pitching coach strolled out to say hello. Keith and the rest of the infield joined us. We didn't talk about wedding presents like in *Bull Durham*, but we might as well have. One guy started quoting Chris Farley lines: "I live in a van, down by the river!" Then someone brought up *The Big Lebowski* and recounted a memorable scene involving The Dude. Two other guys then began listing all the movies John Goodman had been in. Dumb as it sounds, that nonsense helped me clear my head a little. When action resumed, I delivered some effective knucklers and got a chopper to short. The Royals scored a run but that gave us the second out. A fly to left ended the inning.

Pitts told me I'd done a good job to get out of that jam. He also told me my evening was over. The guys congratulated me on my performance. I'd pitched six innings and gave up three runs. Our bullpen held the lead, so I picked up my first win as a Redbird. Not dazzling, but definitely a step forward. Maybe the brass in St. Louis would be impressed.

And hopefully I wouldn't be murdered. My head swiveled back and forth as we made our way to the team bus after the game. Happily, I didn't see Sidney among the gaggle of fans lining the fence hoping for autographs. Ignoring their requests, I ducked into the bus, found a seat near the back, and anxiously eyed the people lingering in the lot.

Fender plopped down beside me. "What's up, Fischer? You lookin' for somebody out there?"

"You could say that."

"A girl?" His tone perked up.

"Yeah."

"Nice. Want me to help you spot her?"

"No. I'm actually hoping I never see her again." But I had a gnawing feeling that I hadn't seen the last of Sidney Cruz.

After splitting the four-game series in Omaha, we traveled to Des Moines to take on the Iowa Cubs. I scanned the stands for my favorite scorned woman. Des Moines is 200 miles from Lincoln, well within driving distance for an insane lady looking for revenge. Didn't see her the first two games, but I didn't pitch in either of them. My start would be in the third contest against the Cubs. If Crazy Cruz was going to show up, it would probably be then.

I went out with a few of the boys after the second game. While taking our seats in one of Des Moines' fine downtown drinking establishments, I made sure my back was to the wall. My action did not go unnoticed.

"Back against the wall, Fischer?" Fender said. "You think yer Wild Bill Hickok?"

"Yeah," an infielder named Shane added, "you've been gawkin' at the crowds a lot lately. Someone after you?"

"Maybe the mob put out a hit on him," a stocky reliever named Phillip said. "Is that it, Fish? Did you cross the Mafia?"

I tried to brush their comments aside, but they would not let it go. "Fine," I said. "It's a woman. I'm looking out for a woman."

"Well, we're all lookin' for that," Fender said. "Hey, you havin' trouble finding a cleat chaser? We can help ya out with that, right boys?" My other teammates chuckled and nodded.

"No, I'm not looking to find a woman. I'm trying to avoid a woman."

"Wait a minute, are you gay?" Phillip asked. "I never read that Zane Fischer was gay. That's okay if you are, but—"

"I'm not gay. I hooked up with this girl in Lincoln. Never called her again. She didn't take it too well. Been dogging me ever since."

"The Fish has got himself a stalker," Fender howled. "Maybe we should all be keepin' an eye on the door. Just how wacko is this lady?"

"It can't be good if she's from Lincoln," Shane said with a grave look in his eyes. "Those Nebraska chicks are craaazy."

"Really?" Phillip asked. "You ever been to Lincoln?"

"No. Just adding some flavor to the conversation."

"Is this gal the same one you were looking for on the bus in Omaha?" Fender asked me.

"Yeah. She was in the stands that night."

"No way."

"Yep, sitting about four rows back from the Royals on-deck circle."

"Ooh, I know the filly you're talking about," Fender said. "Smokin' Latina with shoulder-length black hair?"

I nodded. "How did you remember her in that crowd? That was three days ago and I just gave you a general area of where she sat."

A grin spread below his Stetson. "It's a gift," he drawled before downing some beer. "She was a honey, but yer right, she looked steamed. You're a dead man, Fischer."

And so the guys continued on that theme the rest of the evening. I just sipped my Roy Rogers and let them have their fun. Figured they'd get it out of their system and then they'd move on to something else. I was wrong.

In the middle of the night a light switched on in my hotel room, startling me from a deep sleep. I looked up to see my teammate Eduardo standing over me. He wore a long dark wig and held a big rubber knife above his head. Where he found those props on such short notice, I do not know. He contorted his face into a crazy expression and shrieked, "You said you loved me, you bastard! Now you die!" He then repeatedly stabbed me in the chest while imitating the score from the shower scene in *Psycho*. About a dozen other guys stood in the background giggling like schoolgirls.

I pushed Eduardo off the bed and bludgeoned him with my pillow. "Laugh it up, morons. If any of you ever gets good enough at baseball to attract an actual woman into your bed, I hope the same damn thing happens to you."

Idiots.

Despite the interruption to my slumber, I felt alert and ready to go by game time the next day. An enthusiastic crowd filled Sec Taylor Stadium in Des Moines. Once again I'd like to think they came out to see me, but who knows. There may have been a bobblehead giveaway that night. Or the fans could've been there to see the mighty Cubs, who were leading their division. The home team boasted a solid lineup loaded with power, so I had my work cut out for me.

I brought a decent knuckleball that night. Worked in some nice curves and sliders too. My command had sharpened since my last outing, so I stayed ahead in the count on most batters. J.D. Drew drove in a run for us in the first with a double. The lead held until the third, when Micah Franklin, who'd been tearing it up for the Cubs, ripped one of my flat knucklers over the right field wall with a man on. We plated a run in the fourth and again in the sixth to go on top again. In the bottom of the frame I gave up a walk and two hits to allow Iowa to tie it at three apiece. I got the first batter in the seventh but then walked a guy on a borderline pitch. I really would've liked that call because right after, Pitts came out to get the ball. I wanted to stay in and go for the win, but no dice. Still, it wasn't a bad line: three earned runs in six and a third innings. And the runner didn't score, so I got a no-decision. As far as I was concerned, the outing showed that Zane Fischer could get good hitters out with his knuckleball.

Didn't spot any nut-job stalkers in the stands, so that was another plus that evening. On the negative side, I had to bat. Since both the Cubs and Redbirds were NL affiliates, the teams did not use a DH in the game. When the time came, I stood in from the left side ready to rip into one like Lou Gehrig. Instead, I struck out in all three at-bats, even when trying to bunt. Probably couldn't have convinced anyone in the stands that night that I was a great hitter in high school. But I was. Really.

After the game I called Buddy. She told me that Stick had asked her out, like on a date. A real date. I had told that goofy kid to wait, but he made his move. My daughter didn't know what to make of it at first. Then when she did know what was going on, she rejected the poor guy like Bill Russell swatting away a layup. Sounded painful and awkward the way she described it. Buddy felt bad about how it went, but she really didn't think of Stick as a potential boyfriend. He slunk away and didn't want to be around her anymore. Can't blame him; getting rejected by someone you've pined after can be brutal. But now my daughter had lost her best friend. And the timing couldn't have been worse.

I tried my best to cheer her up. Even told her about the *Psycho* prank the guys pulled on me the night before. That got a little chuckle. I reminded her that school was less than a month away. And the baseball season would be over in less than two months. But nothing I said seemed to improve her mood much. Poor girl.

The next morning I called my mother in Indiana. For those of you who haven't read *A Fish Story*, I'll give you a quick recap about my parents. My father was a welder. He left us when I was three. I don't remember him much and never saw him again after he took off. Don't have any desire to now either, wherever he may be. Mom raised my sister and me by herself. Her parents had some money and she had a decent job as a manager at Montgomery Wards, so we did okay. Weren't rich, but we never lacked the essentials. My mother was a devout Catholic and tried to raise me as such. In return, I gave her a face full of winkles and a head full of grey hair. She especially didn't like it when I got divorced. And hearing about my lifestyle in the years that followed widened the gulf between us. Still, we remained on speaking terms and I visited her at least once a year.

My mother liked Buddy, but she didn't talk to her granddaughter much anymore. The divorce soured Mom on Toni too, so she didn't like to call their house in case my ex answered. I thought it might be nice for Buddy to hear from her nana. I didn't think my mother had any magic answers; I just figured a friendly voice and an experienced perspective might do some good. So, without revealing many details about what had gone down that summer, I suggested to Mom that she call her granddaughter to catch up. Maybe it would help, maybe it wouldn't.

The Redbirds returned home to Memphis and took the first two games of a series against the Nashville Sounds. Fender got the save in the second game. Since Pitts usually used him in middle relief, it was Fender's first save of the year. He was thrilled. Afterwards he invited me and a few other teammates to celebrate with him at Coletta's, an Italian restaurant that Elvis frequented back in the day. I can see why the King went there. That barbeque pizza was off the charts. Best food I'd tasted since moving out of Gale's apartment.

Fender went out lookin' for some action later that night, so I hitched a ride home with Shane. I wanted to hit the sack before midnight since I'd be starting the next day. Nice plan anyway. My cowboy roommate clamored in a little after 2:00 AM. He was not alone. Fender and his lady friend proceeded to enjoy each other's company in the living room for hour after endless hour. The cardboard wall between us did little to muffle the volume of their enthusiasm. I got maybe ninety minutes of sleep that night. More karmic payback for the antics of my younger days, I guess.

After dragging through most of the next day, including practice, my adrenaline kicked in right before game time. The two cans of Red Bull I'd downed in the clubhouse may have had something to do with my jolt of energy. Not that I needed to throw the ball very hard, it just helps to be awake when you're pitching. If anything, it's easier to dodge line drives if your eyes are open.

Knuckler after knuckler wobbled through the strike zone that night, eluding the vicious bats swinging at them. Try as they might, the visitors just couldn't make solid contact. They did get a run in the fourth when a dribbler snuck through the left side. They got another in the fifth when our shortstop threw away a routine grounder. Didn't matter though, because the Redbirds brought the thunder. When Pitts took me out after the eighth, we led 8-2. I remained in the dugout to watch our bullpen close out the win.

Strangely, my body felt really wired and really fatigued at the same time. The ice encasing my arm after the game injected some life back into me, but not for long. I crashed hard after I got home. It didn't matter what Fender had planned for later that night, I'd be sleeping through it.

The ringing phone ripped me back to consciousness around ten the next morning. It was Pitts. He wanted me to come in early that afternoon. Didn't say why. So I made it to the ballpark about a half hour before practice. He told me Dave Duncan had called him. That's Dave Duncan, the St. Louis Cardinals pitching coach.

"He asked what I thought about you," Pitts said, his face a blank slate

"Yeah? … What'd you tell him?"

His shoulders shrugged. "Told him you looked terrible. Just awful. Should be in Single A. Dunc said he knew we were wasting our time with you."

My mind turned to static. I said nothing.

"Looks like you seen a ghost, Fish." He walked over to the water cooler.

"So I'm … uh …"

Pitts snickered. "What are you, a rookie? You shouldn't be falling for crap like that."

"You mean I'm …"

"Yes, you're going to St. Louis." He grinned. "You made it back. Congratulations."

My lungs pushed out a gusty exhale. "Wow. You had me going."

"After what you did last night, why would we send you down?"

"Well, my ERA here is still north of five." I'd just checked my stats in the paper.

He snorted. "That's from that first bad start. You pitched great ever since."

"Thanks."

"Duncan wants to talk to you himself. You're supposed to call him this afternoon. And you fly out of here tonight. Go see Sandy about that."

I went outside to get some air. Had to clear my head before making the call. My body tingled. It was an eighteen-year-old kid who dialed Dave Duncan's number. He said he'd heard good things about my pitching and was looking forward to seeing the knuckleball first hand. I said I looked forward to pitching for St. Louis. Then we talked about the team. McGwire was still bashing home runs at a record pace. He had 46 already, barely a week into August. The Cardinals had won five in a row to put their record at 56-60, six games out of the Wild Card spot. Pitching, however, remained a concern.

"We need to keep winning," Duncan said.

"I'm ready to help."

"Good. We've got you starting Friday against Pittsburgh. See you tomorrow."

The rest of the afternoon went by in a blur. Not much time for tearful goodbyes with my teammates. Fender tried to get me to slip over to a nearby bar for a quick drink, but there was no way I was risking this opportunity. Since I didn't have much to pack, I joined him for one last video game session in the clubhouse. I kinda liked that cowboy, but I sure wasn't going to miss living in the pigsty he called home.

While sitting in the airport terminal that evening, I called Buddy and told her the big news.

"That's great, Dad." Her voice came through flat.

"Try to contain your enthusiasm, kid. You do realize that the St. Louis Cardinals are a major league team?"

"Yeah. Congrats."

"What's wrong?"

"Nothing."

"Same crap, different day?"

She was quiet. I wanted to ask if her grandmother had called, but didn't want her to know that I had suggested it. So I said, "Hey, you might be able to watch me on TV now that I'm in the bigs again. Maybe ESPN or Fox will broadcast one of the games I'm starting."

"Okay." Her response came out with a sob.

"Buddy, what's wrong? What are you not telling me?"

"It's …"

"It's what?"

"They've set a date."

"Oh, you mean …"

"November 7th. Mom wants me to stand up with her. I'm like, there's no way I'm doing that. She is so stupid."

A teenager came up to me wanting an autograph. I pointed to my phone and shoed him away. He gave me the finger. "When did she tell you?"

"Last night. She and assface told me together. They had me sit down like it was some great announcement. I'm surprised they didn't have Celine Deon playing, or something."

"I'm sorry, Buddy."

She blew her nose. "The dork said he wants to adopt me."

"Oh?"

"Yep. Like we're going to be one big happy [expletive] family."

As a ballplayer, I'd hear that word (or one of its many variations) about a hundred times a day. More if it was Little League night at the ballpark. But I'd never heard it spill out of my sweet daughter's mouth. Under different circumstances I'd have said something about her foul language, but I let it go. "What did you say to them?" I asked.

"Nothing. Just listened to their big news and then went to my room. Didn't even cry. I wasn't going to give him the satisfaction." She sniffled. "You should've seen the smug look on his face."

"Yeah … this sucks."

"But now that you're in the majors, you'll have more money for a lawyer. Maybe you can get custody, right? That's what you said when you left Lincoln."

"I'm sure going to try."

"Two more months left in the season?"

185

"Yeah, it ends the last week of September."

"Maybe I can move in with you before they get married."

I wasn't a legal expert, but I didn't think things could move that fast. I didn't want to tell her that, not when she seemed so fragile. "I'll try. Whatever happens, I'll be there for you."

"Promise?"

"Of course. I know this seems bad now, but it'll work out okay."

"I don't want him to adopt me. I don't want to live here after they get married. He'll be here all the time."

"I know."

"I can't do it, Dad." Her words rang with desperation. It was a scary thing for a father to hear.

Chapter 14

The Cardinals sent a car to pick me up at the airport in St. Louis. I signed a couple autographs while passing through the terminal, but otherwise no screaming throngs welcomed the Fish back to the majors. Go figure. The team had me booked into a downtown hotel not far from Busch Stadium. It had been years since I'd stayed at a place that nice. Compared to Fender's hovel, my hotel seemed like a castle with its uniformed bellhops, king-sized bed, Jacuzzi tub, 40-inch TV, complimentary *USA Today*, and mini-fridge stocked with all sorts of overpriced snacks and drinks. It was good to be back in the Show.

The next morning I strolled over to the stadium, a place where I'd pitched many a game. On my way to the ballpark, I admired the downtown sights—the old courthouse with the green dome, the modern high-rises, the giant Arch gleaming proudly in the sun. And finally, Busch Stadium. If you've ever seen an aerial view of that ballpark, you know that it's round, just like Riverfront in Cincinnati. To me, Busch always resembled a giant flying saucer. Especially at night when the lights were on. That perception, I should point out, came from the perspective of a visiting player. I'd always been the enemy on my previous trips to St. Louis. On this morning, Busch Stadium was my home—my home in the big leagues. And it looked majestic. For a moment, all seemed right with the world.

Once inside Busch, I headed to the office of Cardinals manager, Tony LaRussa. Though usually well-liked by his own guys, Tony was never too popular with opposing players. He was an intense competitor, always looking to gain any kind of an advantage. The man did not like to lose. He hated it, in fact. I respected that. But Tony's intensity often left him with a short wick and he'd sometimes rub other teams the wrong way with his on-field actions or comments to the press.

Tony managed the Chicago White Sox during my years with Toronto and Texas. I pitched quite a few games against his team, but nothing controversial or memorable came up between us in those days. I didn't like him all that much, but I didn't like many opposing managers. After I got traded to Cincinnati in '85 we were in different leagues and our paths didn't cross for five years. Then came the 1990 World Series. I pitched Game 3 and shut down the vaunted Oakland lineup. That put his team in an 0-3 hole and the frustrations started to mount. After the game LaRussa made a few comments about my pickoff move and my attitude that weren't too flattering. I responded with equally unflattering statements about his managerial decisions. Since there were so many other storylines going on at the time, our little tiff didn't go very far in the media. The next day Cincinnati completed the sweep and our comments were largely forgotten.

Fast forward eight years to 1998. Zane Fischer is now playing for LaRussa. What type of reception would the Fish receive from his former adversary? Hoping that Tony's professionalism would outweigh any problems he'd had with me in the past, I entered his office and said hello. He stood and extended a hand as something resembling a smile cracked through his flinty expression. "Zane, welcome to the Cardinals. Glad to have you here."

He asked about my flight, my accommodations, and my stay in Memphis. Then he moved on to some general baseball stuff. Our talk was brief, the typical banter between a manager and a new player. He didn't bring up the 1990 World Series and neither did I. We seemed to share an unspoken agreement that what had happened in the past between us was no longer relevant. He wanted his team to win ballgames, a goal I shared wholeheartedly. I came out of the meeting confident that I'd have no problems with my new manager.

Next I met Dave Duncan, the pitching coach. Duncan had been Tony's top lieutenant since the early '80s, so he too was there during the 1990 World Series. But Duncan was also a professional, and if he had any ill-feelings about the past, he didn't let it show. We talked about my knuckleball and how often I'd be throwing between starts. He said he wanted to watch me in a bullpen session that afternoon. Sounded good to me. I welcomed any opportunity to keep the knuckler sharp. As with my meeting with Tony, talking to Duncan left me feeling encouraged. He was one of the top pitching coaches in the game and had a reputation for helping veteran pitchers regain their effectiveness. I'd landed in a good place.

I later ended up in an office filling out paperwork. My new agent Murray Clement joined me for this formality. This was the first time I'd talked to him in person. Since it had already been established that I'd be making the league minimum for the rest of this season, I wondered if his presence was even necessary. But I was a big leaguer now, and big league ballplayers had agents. Tim had recommended Murray, so I signed with him without putting much thought into the matter. I figured anybody with Captain Underwear's endorsement had to be okay.

I next went to the clubhouse, where it fully sunk in that I was back in the majors. The room seemed gargantuan compared to what I'd gotten used to this season. It reminded me of my time back in Texas when I occasionally rode a moped around the Rangers clubhouse. I wasn't planning on doing that here, but at least the room was large enough for such mischief.

In my stall hung a gleaming white uniform with my name stitched in red on the back. Nobody on the team wore number 33, so the Fish got his old number. Seeing those familiar digits below my name gave me a charge. Rarely had a uniform looked so great. That vibrant white with the birds on the bat. I'd never really liked the Cardinal uniforms all that much in the past, but I sure did now.

The players started filing in. Some of the lesser-known guys came up and introduced themselves. The bigger stars waited for me to approach them. Didn't matter how many games I'd won in the past, I was the new guy. The Cards had some good players: Ray

Lankford, Brian Jordan, and Ron Gant formed one of the best outfields in the league. Todd Stottlemyre and Donovan Osborne anchored the rotation I'd be joining. Gary Gaetti, a former teammate in KC, and Willie McGee provided a veteran presence in the dugout. Since they were both pushing forty, I didn't feel quite so old.

Of course, the top star for the Cardinals in 1998 was Mark McGwire. With the team floundering around .500, his home runs kept fans filling the park. Many writers even credited his pursuit of Roger Maris's home run record with reviving baseball from the apathy and ill-will left over from the 1994 strike. In the St. Louis galaxy, McGwire was the sun around which the rest of the Cardinals orbited.

And wouldn't you know it, Big Mac played on that Oakland team that lost to my Reds in the 1990 World Series. In the game that I pitched, I retired him all four times, including two strikeouts. He did get some revenge years later by hitting a couple long home runs off me when I pitched for Kansas City. I don't think he liked me much. About all he said to me that first day was, "Hey man, how ya doing?" He then turned back to his locker and peeled off his shirt to reveal a Herculean torso. His cool reception didn't bother me. Sometimes it takes a while for former adversaries to warm up to each other. And if he hit a few monstrous home runs to help me pick up some Ws, I'd have no problem with him whatsoever.

Aside from Gaetti and a few of the younger pitchers, my new teammates didn't have much to say to me during practice. Guess it was hard for them to get too excited about an old pitcher most people had written off two years ago. The local press apparently felt the same way. A reporter from the *St. Louis Dispatch* asked me a few questions about how it felt to be back, but that was it for journalist attention. Instead of a media storm surrounding my return to the bigs, it was more like a media gentle breeze. I understood. The drama with Big Mac pushed my arrival under the radar. I actually preferred it that way.

It didn't take me long to get acclimated to my new home city. For housing I decided to remain in my hotel. With only six weeks left in the season, searching for an apartment seemed a bit silly. Plus, we'd be out of town half the time. Sure, the hotel room cost close to two hundred dollars a night. But with my major league minimum salary of $170,000, I could easily afford it. Nice to be getting some decent dough again. Gotta say, lounging in that hotel room made me feel like Donald Trump. Yes, I think I will have that six-dollar Reese's candy bar, thank you very much.

The big league exercise facilities were a major upgrade as well. I didn't pump all that much iron anymore, but I still liked to work out regularly. Mostly 30-minute jogs on the treadmill and some light strength training. The boost from the exercise room carried over to my bullpen sessions. The knuckler still wobbled and my command remained sharp. Duncan didn't say a whole lot other than advising me to get my hips more involved and to stay consistent with my release point.

St. Louis dropped two of three to the Mets, before Pittsburgh came to town. We needed a strong showing against the last-place Pirates to keep from falling out of the Wild Card race. My debut as a Cardinal would come in the first game of the series, Friday night. I was really glad that would be a night game, because Busch Stadium turns into an oven in mid-August. During the day it can hit 120 degrees on the field. Night games are no picnic either, especially when the humidity is high. But it's much worse with the unrelenting afternoon sun beating down on you inning after inning.

I wouldn't have believed it possible, but walking onto the field before my start gave me goose bumps. I took it all in, the vastness of the major league environment around me. There had to be close to 50,000 people there that night. And they roared when the PA boomed out my name as the starting pitcher. Everything took on a heightened significance as I absorbed my surroundings—the lights, the organ music, the mass of red-clad fans, the green grass, the smell of the hot dogs, McGwire's rippling muscles at first, and even the umpires in their dark uniforms. Wow, I missed playing at this level. I guess it's true what they say, you never truly appreciate something until it's gone. Standing on the mound there at Busch, I felt like a king who'd reclaimed his throne.

Over in the Pirates dugout, however, there were plenty of enemy knights ready to take my crown. I'd worn their uniform just two years earlier, but didn't see many familiar faces. My eyes returned to my catcher, Tom Lampkin. He was a veteran backstop who'd bounced between AAA and the majors the past decade. But he could handle the knuckleball—that was the important thing. Lampkin flashed through the signs and my brain locked in on the task at hand. Adrenaline coursed through my body as the Pirates leadoff hitter dug into the batter's box. I went into my windup and delivered a fastball right down the pike. Strike one. The crowd cheered. My heart thudded.

Unfortunately, things got rocky after that. The knuckleball went all over the place. Or it came in spinning straight down the middle. A walk, a deep fly out, a single, and another walk left the bases loaded with only one out. Duncan came out and told me to settle down and make quality pitches. Not wanting to walk anybody else, I abandoned my knuckler for the conventional stuff. A sac fly and a single plated two runs for the visitors, before a pop out finally ended the inning. Not the glorious return to the big leagues I was hoping for.

The Cards put a couple runners on base in the bottom of the first, but didn't score. In the dugout, I told Lampkin I wanted to go back to mostly knucklers again the next inning. The Pirates pitcher led off and grounded out on a mediocre curveball. But then the stupid knuckler couldn't find the strike zone. *Madam Knucklina, you ignorant slut!* Two walks gave the Pirates runners at first and second. So I had to go after the next guy, Al Martin, with benders and my not-so-fast fastball. I caught a break when the Martin lined a bullet that McGwire gloved over at first. Brian Jordan then corralled a fly ball at the fence to end the inning.

I took the hill in the third still down two runs. And my best pitch had again deserted me. Even though I'd feel it later, I was going to have to go with everything but the knuckleball. You've probably heard announcers talk about older pitchers who get guys out using finesse. You've probably also heard the term, *smoke and mirrors*. That's what I had to resort to that night. I fed the Pirates sliders and curves that nibbled the corners, lukewarm heaters that rode high and tight, and changeups that dropped a smidge just before reaching the plate. Surprisingly enough, the strategy seemed to be working. Although Jason Kendall rocketed a double down the line, the visitors failed to plate any runs in the third.

The Cardinal bats came alive in the bottom of the frame. A couple walks and a couple hits tied the game. Then with two out and two on, Lampkin blasted a pitch into the right field stands. Batting next, yours truly ended the fun by striking out. No matter, because the Cardinals now led 5-2.

The Pirates ripped the ball hard in the fourth putting men on second and third with one out. But like a magician, the Great Fishdini escaped by inducing a pop up and a sharply hit grounder to our second baseman, Delino Deshields. The fifth inning brought more of the same. I didn't have anything resembling velocity, but my breaking pitches moved just enough. Best of all, I could place the pitches were I wanted. Never underestimate the importance of command. The Pirates must have been getting tired swinging so hard at my junk balls, because they mustered only a single that inning.

I returned to the bench and slipped my arm into the sleeve of a jacket. Tony had seen enough. He told me I did a nice job battling out there. Lampkin congratulated me on my five "good" innings. My teammates then put up three more in the bottom of the fifth. St. Louis led 8-2 and cruised the rest of the night. And Zane Fischer picked up career win number 291.

The Fox network decided to cover the Cardinals' next game for its Saturday afternoon broadcast. Color man Tim McCarver (the same guy the Memphis stadium was named after) asked me to do a brief on-air interview with him before the game. I called Buddy to let her know her old man was going to be on TV. She sounded excited, or at least pretended to be anyway.

McCarver began by congratulating me on my win the previous night and remarked that it had been more than two years since my last major league victory. He then asked how I liked pitching in St. Louis. "It's great," I said. "The fans here have made me feel right at home. And it's an honor playing in front of the most knowledgeable fans in baseball." I didn't really know if the knowledgeable part was true, but I'd heard other players say that about St. Louis and thought it sounded good.

The next question addressed what I thought about McGwire's pursuit of Maris. "It's exciting to witness this home run chase first hand," I said. "The electricity reminds me of a playoff atmosphere. We're all rooting for Big Mac to break the record." I actually thought Sammy Sosa, the other guy chasing Maris, seemed like a nicer guy. But as a new Cardinal, there was no way I could show preference for a Chicago Cub over our exalted hero.

McCarver reminded me that I had been to the postseason only twice in my long career and asked what I thought of St. Louis's chances this year. "We've got some ground to make up," I said, "but don't count us out. The pieces are here for us to make a move in the stretch run." Truthfully, I would've felt a lot better about our prospects if we'd had a stronger bullpen.

The topic of 300 wins came up. McCarver asked me how important it was to me to reach that milestone. "Sure I'd love to get three hundred," I said. "But right now my priority is to do what I can to help my team reach the postseason. I haven't been there much, as you were kind enough to point out, so getting the Wild Card spot is more important than my career win total." That was the truth. Well, true-ish.

"Are you planning to come back next season?" McCarver asked.

"You bet."

"Which uniform would you like to be wearing?"

"Well, this Cardinal one fits pretty well. Hopefully I'll be here." Truthfully, I planned to go with the team that offered me the most money. Assuming any of them offered me a deal.

So to summarize, I kept my smartass tongue in check and towed the party line. Might as well butter up the good people who were signing my checks, and may possibly be signing my checks in the future. That's something younger Zane wouldn't have done. He would've unloaded whatever idiocy was on his mind. Older Zane had learned what it was like to have no money, so older Zane smiled at Tim McCarver and gave nice answers.

A few more of my teammates warmed up to me in the days that followed. Unfortunately, the Cardinals cut Gaetti. So that not only removed a friend, but one of the few guys close to my age. Such is life in baseball. Even in the majors, players come and go. Sometimes you miss the guy who goes away and sometimes you don't.

After finishing the series with Pittsburgh, we left town for a nine-game road trip. Our first stop was the Windy City for two games against the Cubs. I'd heard about the Cards-Cubs storied rivalry for years, now I got to experience it firsthand. I must admit, it lived up to the hype. The crowds at Wrigley surged with electricity. Even more so since the home run heroes McGwire and Sosa were in the house. They both had 47 home runs at that point. Chicago won Tuesday night 4-1 in a game with no homers. I would be pitching the next contest, Wednesday afternoon.

I couldn't have asked for a better baseball atmosphere. Roaring fans, heated rivals, blue skies, and baseball's biggest story—the home run race. Close to 40,000 fans crowded into the Friendly Confines. Since a lot of them wore red, we had plenty of people hollering for us. I hadn't pitched a game with this much national attention for a long, long time.

Because the ache had returned to my arm after my last start, I hoped to use a majority of knuckleballs. That would reduce stress on the old soupbone and save me from relying on "finesse" pitches that probably wouldn't cut it against Chicago. Besides Sosa, the Cubs had a terrific hitter in Mark Grace and a dangerous power threat in Henry Rodriguez. Actually, with the wind blowing out at Wrigley, pretty much everyone in their lineup was a power hitter.

The Cardinals put up two in the top of the first. It's always nice to take the hill with a lead. The crowd gave me a nice pop when my name was announced. That surprised me since Chicago fans never seemed to care much for me when I pitched for the Reds. Maybe it was "Be Nice to Old Guys" day at the ballpark. I hoped the Cub hitters got the memo. Happily, Madam Knucklina returned to me in the first inning. She danced and dazzled as if she'd never left. Sosa whiffed with a tremendous cut to end a 1-2-3 inning.

The Cubs got a couple hits off me in the second but didn't score. We still led 2-0 when Sosa came up with one on and two out in the third. Settling into his familiar stance, he looked like a disaster waiting to happen. A disaster for the guy on the mound that is. Pitching against Sosa in '98 was like playing Russian Roulette with two bullets in the chamber. Just like when McGwire batted, thousands of cameras flashed throughout the stadium. The fans wanted to see history, and ole Zane did not disappoint them. It wasn't the worst pitch I'd ever thrown, but it had just enough spin to keep it from fluttering the way a good knuckler is supposed to do. Sosa's eyes became silver dollars as he stepped forward and whipped his mighty war club around. The impact sounded like a gunshot and the ball took off like a comet. Sosa hopped out of the box as he had done so many times before. Cubs fans erupted and someone on Waveland Avenue got a souvenir he'd never forget.

It was bad enough that Sosa's blast had tied the game; what made it worse was that he now led McGwire in home runs, 48-47. The first time all year that had happened. So the Fish probably wasn't too popular with the fans in red at that moment. If McGwire ended up losing the home run race, I might be remembered as the guy who ruined the season for Cardinal Nation. I'm thinking my new teammates weren't too thrilled with me either, especially the big man at first. I didn't look over at him.

The game remained tied into the bottom of the fifth. Per LaRussa's instructions, I put Sosa on first with an unintentional intentional walk. Looked like it was going to work until the Cub third baseman Jose Hernandez launched a two-out shot over the ivy-covered wall in left-center. Tony left me in to get the third out, but my day was done after that. There were some positives from the outing—my knuckler showed life and I'd struck out five batters. But giving up four runs in five innings was not going to cut it. Slumped in the clubhouse with my arm on ice, I pondered all the negative comments being written about me at that very moment.

Fortunately, the Cardinals saved some fireworks for a late rally. In the eighth, McGwire blasted his 48th home run of the year to catch Sosa. St. Louis then tied the game at six in the ninth. In the tenth McGwire crushed another dinger and the Cards prevailed 8-6. More importantly for many of the Cardinal faithful, Big Mac had regained the lead in the home run race. Order had been restored. The big comeback win also transformed my shaky outing into a harmless no-decision. The Fish had wriggled off the hook.

I called Buddy from the hotel that evening. She had watched the game on WGN and told me I looked cool pitching on TV. She then informed me about the cuteness of Ron Gant and asked if he was single. I said it didn't matter, because she could never, ever date a ballplayer. No, no, no. Not even a nice guy like Snowman. Ballplayers equal trouble. I should know.

Even though the old issues at home remained unchanged for her, it sounded like Buddy and Toni were on speaking terms again. My daughter even seemed upbeat about the start of the school year, now just a week and a half away. The prospect of getting out of the house and meeting new friends gave her something positive to think about. Unfortunately, Stick still kept his distance. I told her he'd come around.

After we finished talking, I went down to the hotel gift shop and bought a postcard showing the Chicago skyline. I had decided to send Buddy a postcard from each of the cities I went to while in the majors. I'd write something goofy and sign it from one of the characters in the Harry Potter book. The first one was from Hagrid reminding her to feed Fluffy. My crude drawing of a three-headed dog accompanied the message. I hoped the cards would be a nice reminder for Buddy that her old man was thinking about her.

From Chicago we flew to New York, where we had to play back-to-back doubleheaders against the Mets. We split them both. Though I'd raised my share of hell in the Big Apple before, I stayed out of trouble. It had taken me too long to get back the majors to blow it all on a stupid bender. With my less than dominating pitching performances thus far, I couldn't afford to give management any other reasons to cut me.

After New York, we headed to Pittsburgh for three games. While there, I attended a meeting with my old AA group. Then I had dinner with Tim Haines and his family. Good people. Hanging out with him always picked me up in some way. Gave me extra encouragement to stay on the wagon. Timely support, since I now had more money and more opportunities to find trouble.

I pitched the last game of the series against the Pirates. LaRussa had decided McGwire could use a rest, so our biggest bat would sit in the dugout for that game. Not the news I wanted to hear, but there was nothing I could do about it. My job remained the same. The knuckleball came and went on that cloudy, misty day. It was enough of a threat though to keep the hitters from sitting on my fastballs and sliders. The Pirates got their share of hits, but another "finesse" performance kept them from pushing across many runs. If I kept this up, people might start calling me a "crafty lefthander." I'd been called worse. Tony pulled me after six with the Cards leading 5-3. The game ended with the score unchanged, so I picked up win number 292.

We returned to St. Louis for a six-game home stand. By this point I was starting to receive some fan mail at the ballpark. Okay, only about a half-dozen letters had arrived for me, but still it was something. My favorite was the crayon note from a six-year-old in Jefferson City who wanted to pitch "nuklers" like me someday. He even drew a stick-figure of me throwing a pitch that zig-zagged to the plate. My least-favorite letter came from S.C. in Lincoln, Nebraska. It started off calling me a "liar" and a "scum-sucking pig," and then it got insulting. Used a few word combinations I'd never even seen before. The note ended with, "This is not over Zane. Not by a long shot." Nice. Every time I'd forget about the lovely Ms. Cruz, she would pop up again to brighten my day.

I pitched against Atlanta on Saturday afternoon. Since the game was on national television, I had a great opportunity to show fans and GMs what Zane Fischer could do on the mound. Unfortunately, this would be my second consecutive start without the benefit of Mark McGwire's bat. In the first inning, Big Mac went down looking at a borderline pitch. He argued the call and got himself tossed. Umpire Sam Holbrook also ejected LaRussa and Duncan after they uttered a few words he didn't like. Not a great start to the ballgame.

Despite all the distractions, I kept my head together and continued dealing. The knuckler danced and shimmied near the plate. Atlanta couldn't get much wood on the ball the first few innings. Unfortunately, their pitcher Tom Glavine also brought his best stuff. We were tied 1-1 going into the sixth. Then the Braves started showing more patience. And Holbrook, perhaps still steamed over what had happened in the first, wouldn't give me the corners. Two guys walked on borderline pitchers and Andrew Jones later doubled them both in. When I got pulled in the seventh, St. Louis trailed 3-2. Glavine and the Braves bullpen made the lead hold up and I had my first loss as a Cardinal.

After the game I saw McGwire's ten-year-old son Matt moping around the dugout. He was the Cardinals bat boy. I gabbed with him about this and that, mostly sports and rock music. At the end of our chat, I grabbed a couple baseballs from a bag and signed them for him. Didn't think much about it until practice the next day. Mark approached me out on the field and struck up a conversation. First time that had happened. He smiled and told me I'd been looking good on the mound and that the knuckler had some wicked movement. We talked for a while about pitching and hitting and whatnot. Then he clapped my back and went off to get ready for batting practice. The Fish had gained acceptance with the big man. After that the other Cardinal stars started talking to me more too.

We left town for a three-game series against Florida. After the game on Tuesday, LaRussa called me into his office and asked if I could go the next day. That would be just three days rest since my last start, instead of the usual four. Tony was trying to plot out his rotation to get the best matchups over the coming week. He and Duncan figured that going on short rest would be least disruptive to a knuckleball pitcher. I said sure, he could use me on three days rest all through September if he wanted.

The decision to pitch me on short rest turned out great. First off, Madam Knucklina danced like a stripper. Her naughty moves transfixed the Marlin batters inning after inning. The second bit of good news came in the fourth when yours truly came to bat with the bases loaded. You may have noticed I haven't said much about my at bats with the Cards. That's because I hadn't done anything at the plate. Nothing but strikeouts, a weak ground out, and a can of corn to left. For this at-bat, the Marlin starter, a rookie named Jesus Sanchez, decided he was going to get ahead of me with a first pitch fastball. Unbeknownst to him, I decided I was going to take a rip at that first pitch, wherever it was. Our third base coach had flashed the take sign, but I figured since I was new to the team I'd have a good excuse for misinterpreting it. Fortunately for me Sanchez's pitch came right down the middle, waist high. I drilled it into the right field corner for a bases-clearing double. The guys in our dugout went nuts, yelling about how the old man can still hit. LaRussa didn't smile, but he also didn't say anything to me about swinging away with a take sign.

Florida pushed across two runs in the seventh (one of them unearned). Didn't matter. St. Louis pounded the ball all night, including two majestic home runs from Big Mac—numbers 58 and 59. The Florida crowd summoned him for curtain calls after each. We ended up winning 14-4 and Zane Fischer had notched career win number 293.

The team celebrated in the clubhouse. McGwire's home runs drew most of the attention, but my exploits did not escape notice. After returning from the shower, I found that someone had placed a walker in front of my locker. The attached note said if I used this, I might be able to make it to third next time. Very funny. Make fun of the old guy. I played along by grabbing the thing and clomping around the locker room like a geezer running the bases.

After five starts in the majors, I had a 3-1 record with a 3.68 ERA. I'd become a fixture in the Cardinals rotation and had reason to hope this season might not be my last. The only dark cloud to all this silver lining was that our postseason hopes had dwindled. Too many losses in late August had dropped us farther behind the Cubs in the Wild Card race. With less than a month to play, we didn't have much chance to make the playoffs.

Flying back home from Florida, I realized that I'd forgot to send Buddy a postcard from Miami. Felt bad about that. Since I'd been hanging out with my teammates more after the games, I hadn't talked to her on the phone as much either. When we did talk, she seemed distant. From what little she told me about school, tenth grade hadn't started like she'd hoped. I tried to cheer her up by recounting funny stories from the locker room and telling her some new jokes I'd heard from the guys. I also mentioned the improvement in her old man's baseball prospects. "That's great, Dad," was about all she'd say. Couldn't even get her to discuss Harry Potter anymore.

Back in St. Louis, McGwire continued hitting home runs. He blasted number 60 on September 5th against the Reds. Number 61 came on Labor Day against the Cubs. After 37 years, someone had finally tied Roger Maris's single season home run record. Sports fans across the nation were in a frenzy about the prospect of seeing number 62, which could come at any time.

The next game was Tuesday night. The crowd at sold out Busch Stadium would include a host of sports dignitaries, including Commissioner Bud Selig. And with the game broadcast on nationwide television, most of the baseball world, as well as many who didn't even like the sport, would be watching. And guess who was scheduled as the starting pitcher for the Cardinals? Sure, people wouldn't be tuning in to see me, but there I'd be on the mound dealing my wicked knuckleball. This was an opportunity beyond what I could've hoped for. An effective performance in this game would pretty much guarantee a contract with a big league team next year.

That evening I sat alone in the hotel bar sipping a Roy Rogers. As my left hand rotated an old baseball into different pitching grips, I pondered the possibilities. If I shut down the Cubs the next night, my salary could hit seven figures next season. Hoping to be well-rested for my start, I went to bed around 11:00. The next morning my phone jarred me awake. I checked the ID expecting it to be Buddy—I hadn't called her in three days. I meant to, but just kept forgetting. It wasn't my daughter who called though, it was Toni.

"Zane, I don't know what to do."

"What's wrong?"

"Buddy ran away."

"Maybe she's just over at a friend's today."

"It's a school day. The office just called. She's didn't show up for classes."

"When's the last time you saw her?"

"Last night when she went to bed. When I didn't see her this morning, I thought she had gotten up early to go to school. But she must have gone out in the middle of the night." I could tell Toni was struggling to keep it together.

"Maybe she's hanging out somewhere playing hooky."

"No Zane, she's …"

"She'll come back. Have you called Stick's parents?"

"She's not with Stick."

"How do you know?"

"I just found something in Buddy's room."

"Well, what is it?"

Several seconds passed before she could speak again. "I think it's a suicide note."

Chapter 15

Her words knocked me back like a heater thrown up and in. It took a few seconds before I regained my bearings. "Are you sure it's a suicide note? What does it say?"

Toni hesitated. "It said she's tired of fighting. That she can't take it anymore."

"That might not mean—"

"She wonders if anybody really loves her. If anybody would miss her if she was gone. She said she wants to disappear forever." Toni's voice choked with emotion. "Zane, I can't lose another child. She's all I have left."

"You're not going to lose her," I said. "We'll find Buddy."

"It's Leslie," she shouted through the phone. "Her name is Leslie. I never liked that stupid nickname you gave her. Call her Leslie."

"Okay, we're going to find Leslie." The name sounded strange coming out of my mouth. "What else did she say in the note?"

"A bunch of stuff about how terrible her life is."

"Did she say anything about hurting herself? Like something she's planning to do."

"No, not exactly. But she talks about going away where no one will ever find her."

"She could be venting. You know how teenagers get. We'll find her."

"She blames me for ruining her life. This is my fault."

"Don't think like that."

"But it's true. This is all my fault."

"What do you mean?"

Toni whimpered. "We got into an argument yesterday. It was over something stupid. She didn't clean up a mess in the kitchen. Then we started yelling about a bunch of other stuff. She said I loved Cole more than her. That he was the only person I cared about anymore."

"Kids say things, Toni. She didn't mean it."

Her breaths shuddered. "I hit her, Zane. I slapped our little girl across the face."

I felt like I was the one who'd been slapped. Picturing that scene left me speechless.

"I felt so horrible," she continued. "I said I was sorry over and over. She ran to her room and wouldn't let me in." Toni's sniffles ended with a clipped choking sound. "I can still see her face after I did it, how hurt she was."

"It'll be okay."

"If she does something to herself, I'll never ..."

"Blaming yourself isn't going to help anything. You've got to focus on finding our daughter."

"I should've listened to her. She tried to tell me about what was going on at school."

"What do you mean?"

"She hates it there. Nobody will be friends with her. Some of the older girls are making fun of her in gym class."

"You can't blame yourself for that."

"I wasn't there for her. Our girl's life is falling apart, and all I did is make things worse."

"Listen, you've got to stop beating yourself up and start looking for her. You know where she hangs out, you could start at one of those places."

Toni didn't say anything.

"You've got to start searching, Toni. Maybe you could start at one of her hangouts and Cole could look somewhere else."

"Cole isn't going to help."

"Why's that?"

"We broke up."

I wanted to ask what happened, but didn't. She made the question unnecessary.

"We got into an argument too. He said some mean stuff about Leslie. That she never liked him and that she was always trying to break us up."

"Oh." Not much else I could say given my feelings about Cole.

"He said I should've hit her a long time ago, that she had it coming. So we got in a fight about that. Then when I told him Leslie had run away, he said, 'Good.'" Toni's breaths became more forceful, as if describing the argument had rekindled her anger. "That was the last straw."

"I'm sorry."

"Last thing he said to me was, 'I hope that ungrateful brat of yours never comes back.'"

"Forget about Cole. You need to start looking for Bud— Leslie."

"Will you help me?"

"Of course."

"Thank you. I've been freaking out thinking about trying to do this alone."

"I'm pitching tonight. If she hasn't come back by then, I'll fly to Lincoln after the game."

"Zane, that's too late. Our daughter is out on the street right now. If she hasn't done something to herself already, then someone else might hurt her."

"I can't leave yet. This game tonight, I have to pitch." Thoughts of my unbelievable opportunity flashed through my head.

"Please come now. It hasn't been long enough for the police to get involved. So I don't have any help."

"I'll fly in right after the game."

"You haven't changed at all," she hissed.

Busch Stadium pulsed with energy. The fans buzzed like it was Game 7 of the World Series. The baseball bigwigs came out in force. Roger Maris's wife and kids were there. A sellout crowd packed the seats and millions more watched on TV. I kinda felt bad for the Cubs starter, Steve Trachsel. Everybody wanted to see him give up a long ball. A long ball to Mark McGwire, that is. Number 62, which would break one of baseball's most revered records. It was a magical night in St. Louis. I think it was one of those occasions that you just had to be there to truly appreciate the magnitude of what was happening.

The place exploded when McGwire stepped to the plate in the bottom of the first. At least that's how it sounded on the radio in my pickup. I had flown to Lincoln earlier that afternoon and was driving around the city when the game started. Despite what I'd told Toni on the phone, there was no way I could pitch or do anything with my daughter missing. It took me about two seconds to realize that after hanging up. I immediately booked the first flight I could get to Lincoln.

While waiting in the lobby at the St. Louis airport, I called the Cardinals office. Ended up talking to Duncan. I told him I had a family emergency and had to miss my start that night. He was not thrilled. Though he didn't say it, I got the sense I was burning a bridge in St. Louis. And maybe with the other big league teams, as well. If not lighting the fire, I was definitely pouring gasoline on the bridge. The radio announcers didn't dwell on my absence. All they said was "Tonight's scheduled starter for the Cardinals, Zane Fischer, had to leave the team for personal reasons."

Before leaving St. Louis, I called Toni and left a message that I was coming. She called back and told me to let her know when I landed. She had contacted the parents of all of Buddy's known friends, including Stick. Nobody had seen our daughter or knew where she might be. When I arrived in Lincoln, Toni was driving around downtown looking for a needle in a haystack. I called Tim and asked him to pray.

Toni didn't have any suggestions about where I should start looking, so I went to Buddy's favorite pizza and ice cream places. She wasn't there and none of the employees had seen her that day. Then I drove to her high school. After that chewed up more than an hour with no results, I decided to get more people involved. Most of my Giants teammates had seen Buddy when she worked concessions, so they'd be able to recognize her. I called Gale first since I knew he still lived in town. He said he'd start looking right away. I sent him to Gateway, Lincoln's largest mall. I next called Snowman. He lived with his parents in a small town a few miles outside Lincoln. He too dropped everything to join the search. I told him to check out the Haymarket and the warehouses nearby. That area struck me as a likely place where a runaway might go.

I asked Snowman about Dirk, but he had already moved to Florida. Curtis was next on my list. I got his answering machine and asked him to call me back whenever he got the message. I recalled a few other names from the Giants, but didn't know their numbers. Probably didn't matter since most of them weren't likely in Lincoln anymore.

While stopped at a light, I got to thinking about Stick. Toni had mentioned talking to his parents earlier, but not him. That made sense, because he would've been at school during the day. I wanted to talk to the boy myself. He was Buddy's best friend and if anybody would have an idea of where she was, it would be him. Worth a shot anyway. I called Toni and got Stick's phone number.

Nobody answered at their house so I called his mother's cell. Turns out Stick had left school early and he and his mom had started searching the different parks that Buddy frequented. They were currently at Pioneers Park. When she gave Stick the phone, I could tell he was really upset about Buddy's disappearance. He blamed himself, since he'd been ignoring her the past few weeks. I said it wasn't his fault and thanked him for helping. My conversation with the boy brought a flicker of hope. Buddy had always liked nature, so it made sense she might have gone to a park. She and I had gone to Pioneers Park a couple times during the summer. We'd also gone hiking at Wilderness Park, a vast forested area with miles of trails. I started heading there.

Then it hit me—Sherman Field. Buddy and I had spent a lot of time there this past summer. She even called it "our place," since that's where we both worked. The ballpark was little more than a mile from her house, so she easily could've made it there on foot. And with the Giants season long over, it would be a quiet place to think about happier times. My spirits jumped thinking about

Sherman. Something inside told me that it was the place. I called Toni and told her where I was going. She had the same thought I did—it was so obvious. Why didn't we think of it earlier? She told me to call her back whenever I got there.

Ignoring speed limits, I made it to Sherman Field in a matter of minutes. Not a single car occupied the gravel lot. The ballpark looked sad and lonely, an impression underscored by the fading light of the setting sun. I recalled my Fourth of July start in front of a packed house only two months earlier. It seemed like several years had passed since then. Funny how the memory works sometimes.

I ran toward the weathered ticket building with its peeling white paint. Glancing up at the "Sherman Field, Home of the Lincoln Giants" sign brought another memory to the surface. This one was from April when I'd first arrived there to meet Curtis. That too seemed like ages ago. I expected the front gate to be locked, but it wasn't. That meant Buddy could be inside. But if I did find her there, would she be okay? I wasn't much for praying, but I asked God right then to please deliver my little girl to me safe and sound. I pushed open the gate and entered.

When I was a kid, I watched a movie about a ghost town in the Old West. All the buildings were empty and nobody walked the dusty streets. The only thing that moved was a rolling tumbleweed. That and a wind-blown shutter banging against a building. *Thwack thwack thwack*. The sound still echoed in my head. I couldn't remember what happened in the movie, or who the main characters were for that matter, but I never forgot the emptiness of that ghost town. And now, more than three decades later, I found myself in an eerily similar scene as I advanced down the concourse at Sherman Field. No tumbleweeds of course, but an assortment of old scorecards, flattened Pepsi cups, and other debris stirred about in the evening breeze.

I first approached the boarded-up concession building where Buddy had worked. It appeared that no humans had been there for weeks. My fingers tested the padlock that secured the walk-in door in back. I called out Buddy's name, but heard nothing in response. It was a ghost ballpark.

I checked the team office, the storage shed, the Giants clubhouse, and the visiting clubhouse. Padlocks prevented entrance to each building. I thought about using a rock to break in, but that seemed pointless. If the doors were still locked, Buddy couldn't have gotten inside. There was only one place left to look, the field itself. My feet hesitated. I didn't want to check, because if Buddy wasn't there then she wasn't at Sherman Field at all. And just minutes ago, I'd been so sure that this was the place. The passage of time weighed down on me. How long had she been gone? Eighteen hours? Words from her note invaded my thoughts. I tried to push them away, but they bored through my skull. *What if that really was a suicide note? We could be too late.*

My body shuddered and then stood paralyzed. I had to clear the horrifying images out of my head. I had to think of something positive, some reason to have hope. Stick? He and his mom might find Buddy at the park. That's a possibility, right? The boy had been her friend for years. He knew her as well as anybody. And he was out there looking. If Buddy wasn't here at Sherman, Stick would find her at Pioneers Park. Yes, we were still going to find her.

Toni appeared in my head. She was single now. No attachments. Just like me. Could this experience bring us closer together? Losing a child had once torn us apart. Maybe finding a child would bring us together again. How crazy was that? Sure, we'd butted heads this past summer, but we were talking again. Seeing her had stirred up long-buried feelings inside me. Had the same thing happened with her? We'd have some issues to work out, but … you never know. The idea of her and me together again ignited something in my heart. And, crazy or not, the thoughts motivated me to move again.

I approached the gate near the home dugout and looked across the empty field. Nobody was out there in the growing dusk, only the ghosts of players long gone. I rounded the brick wall at the end of the dugout and stepped inside, expecting to see nothing but a long empty bench. I was wrong.

"I figured you'd come here." The man sat slouched with his hands burrowed into the front pockets of a threadbare grey hoodie. He didn't even turn his head.

"Cole." My brain struggled to catch up with what my eyes were seeing.

"I turned on the tube to watch the game tonight and the announcers said you'd left the team. They didn't know where you'd went ... but I did. I knew you'd come to Lincoln riding in on a white horse. And I figured you'd probably get the idea to check out your old stomping grounds to see if that girl was here. So I thought I might take a little walk here myself."

"Have you seen her? Is she here?"

"Nope. Not a soul around." He gestured out at the field. "Thought about leaving, then I heard you calling out for your precious little brat."

"Do you have any idea where she went?"

"Haven't the slightest clue, Fish-man." He kicked at one of the many crushed Budweiser cans lying near his feet. The flattened aluminum skidded across the concrete.

I stepped toward him. "Please, Cole. I know we've had our differences, but if you could help me find her ..."

"Our differences?" He turned his head to glare at me. "That's what you call everything you did to me? Our differences?"

"I'm sorry about what happened."

"Oh, you're sorry. About what?" He straightened up and leaned forward on the bench.

"About punching you. I'm sorry I did that." I actually wasn't sorry, but I needed to end this conversation and get back to searching for my daughter.

"Oh yeah." He slowly rose to his feet. "I'd forgotten about that, your little sucker punch." A snort escaped his nostrils. "See, I thought you were talking about that other thing you did to me. You know, ruining my life."

"I didn't ruin your life, Cole."

"No?" He took a step forward, closing the gap between us. "You come to Lincoln and spend all summer trying to get between Toni and me. You make sure that daughter of yours hates me, so she'll help you break us up. And after months of poisoning Toni's brain, you finally did it. Congratulations, you turned my woman against me."

"I wasn't trying to get between you and Toni. I'm sorry she broke up with you."

"The hell you are. That was your goal from the start. You come to town thinkin' you're still a big baseball star. Thinkin' you can snap your fingers and get your ex back. But guess what, Toni was with a real man. And you couldn't handle that. So you used a little girl to do your dirty work." A bitter chuckle escaped. "She was good though. The bitch kept whining and working her mother until she turned her against me."

"I didn't tell Buddy to do any of that."

"Toni and I had a good thing goin' before you showed up. The great Zane Fischer ... or should I say once-great. Now, you're just a broken-down has-been. Throwin' that girlie pitch. What do you hit on the radar now? Fifty? You should just throw it in underhand, Fish-man."

"Cole, my daughter is missing. She's out in the city somewhere and she could be hurt, or worse."

He shrugged. "Not my problem."

"I'm leaving now."

"No, you're not." He stepped closer.

My fists clinched and my body readied to spring toward him. But I had no time for that. I had to start searching again. "We can settle this later," I said.

"I think we'll settle it now." He pulled a pistol from the pocket of his hoodie and pointed it at me.

My eyes zeroed in on the barrel—it looked like a .38. Somehow I remained calm enough to speak. "C'mon man. Nothing good can come from bringing a gun into this."

"Oh, I don't know about that. The look on your face just now was priceless. Too bad I didn't bring my camera."

I raised my hands, palms out. "You made your point, Cole. I've been a jerk. I'm sorry." My cell phone started ringing.

"Sorry for what?" He ignored the sound.

"Hitting you."

"You mean sucker punching me?"

"Yes, I'm sorry for sucker punching you."

"Like a cowardly little bitch."

He moved one step closer. Seconds passed.

"Say it!" he yelled. "Say what you did."

"I'm sorry I sucker punched you like a cowardly little bitch."

"And for breaking up me and Toni." His rank alcohol breath abused my nostrils.

"I'm sorry for breaking up you and Toni."

His dark eyes narrowed into a squint. "I've had to deal with guys like you my whole life. The popular jocks in school. Thinking they're so high and mighty. Like they run the place. Tellin' everybody what to do. Then out in the real world, it's no different. Rich punks like you still trying to boss everybody around." He shook his head in disgust. "You see a guy like me, a working man, and you think you can step all over me. I've done plenty of work for rich guys, their snotty wives nitpicking every detail. Then when the job's done they try to screw me out of what they owe me. Threaten to sick their lawyers on me if I say anything."

"I'm not rich, Cole."

"Yeah, but you used to be. You've still got that rich man's attitude. Arrogant prick. You see me dating your ex and you can't stand it. Can't let a workin' man get a little happiness in his life. So you have to try to break us up."

"Cole, you're right. But maybe we can talk about this sometime without the gun. Shooting me is just gonna result in prison time." He was close enough that I could almost lunge for the weapon. Almost.

"Yeah, so? You took my lady away, so what do I got to live for now? At least by pulling this trigger, I'd get the joy of wasting your sorry ass."

"Oh my God!" The shriek behind me convulsed my body with a violent flinch. I turned to see Toni at the end of the dugout, her face like a ghost.

"Cole, no!" she shouted. "Put the gun down."

"You don't get to tell me what to do anymore," he sputtered. "You broke up with me, remember?"

"Get out of here, Toni," I hissed.

"Yeah, get out of here," Cole mocked. "Your bitch daughter ain't here. So you'd better go look somewhere else before she offs herself. If it ain't happened already."

Her fists clenching, Toni moved forward and stood beside me. "Cole, that's enough. Put the gun down before I call the cops and throw your ass in jail again."

Cole's face reddened. "You shut your mouth, woman, or I'll shut it for you." The gun now pointed at Toni.

"Put it down, Cole!"

"Sure," he said, nodding. "But first, I'm gonna waste him." With a sneer, he swung the barrel toward my chest.

Toni screamed and jumped in front of me. The gun went off with an earsplitting roar. Time slowed like a dream. Toni lurched backwards and fell. I tried to catch her, but couldn't. Through the smoke a furious face stared down at her. I lunged forward grasping at the weapon. Another explosion followed. It felt like someone hit me with a baseball bat, knocking me back. A searing pain ripped through my right shoulder. I didn't feel my body hit the cement below, but that's where I landed, flat on my back. The figure above stepped over me and hurried away.

I moved my hand to Toni lying beside me. I said her name, but she didn't respond. Though speaking brought stabs of pain, I said her name again. With a groan she rolled over onto me, her head cradled in my left shoulder and her arm draped across my chest. I felt her warm blood seeping through my shirt.

"Toni, I love you."

"I love you too." Her words came through weak, uneven breaths.

"I'm sorry we didn't stay together."

"Me too … I shouldn't have left you … shouldn't have blamed you."

"I should have been there for you." The dugout roof swirled above as my dizziness increased.

She slid her hand to my arm and squeezed. "Zane, find our daughter. Please save her …"

The final remnants of sunlight retreated below the horizon. I couldn't hear her shallow breathing anymore. "Toni?"

The strength in her grip ebbed away.

Chapter 16

A heavy weight pressed down on me. Movement seemed impossible. I listened for a sound from Toni, anything to tell me she was still breathing. My mind raced with memories of long ago. When we were married. When we were happy. The sky darkened and my spirit weakened. I let my eyelids fall and started to drift.

"Get up. You have to help them." My eyes opened, searching for the source of those words. The voice sounded like Luke's, but I saw nothing. Maybe it was in my head. A pain flared in my shoulder, shooting lightning bolts through my chest. I felt blood draining out of me. What had happened in this dugout? I was shot. Cole did it. He shot Toni and he shot me. An angry determination coursed through my veins.

Moving Toni's arm, I rolled onto my knees. The pain threatened to overwhelm me, so I stopped to draw in some air. Toni lay crumpled on her side. I stroked her long hair and listened. I may have heard a faint breath, or it may have been wishful thinking. Blood had darkened the entire front of her shirt. My hand reached down to where my phone had been clipped to my waist. It was still there, so I grabbed it and dialed 911. Unfortunately that put me in contact with a dispatcher in Ohio, where I had signed up for my phone service. After I explained where I was, my call had to be rerouted to Lincoln. During the wait, I grabbed my pocketknife to cut away part of my shirt to wad up and press against Toni's chest. I didn't know if that would help, but I had to do something.

An image of Buddy flooded my mind. *She's still out there. Missing. I've got to find her.* Reviewing the places where my daughter might be, I recalled again how she liked to wander through wooded areas. It made sense that she would go to a forest or somewhere secluded to get away from her problems. Stick and his mother were searching Pioneers Park. But what about Wilderness Park?

When an emergency dispatcher in Lincoln came on the line, I told her that a woman had been shot at Sherman Field and the man who did it had run off. She asked about the victim. I said she was lying in the home dugout and needed an ambulance right now. She was bleeding and didn't have much time. *If she isn't gone already.* The dispatcher asked me some other questions and wanted me to stay on the line. I said I had to go find my daughter.

Throughout the call I continued pressing against Toni's wound, trying to stop the bleeding. After hanging up, I whispered in her ear. "Help is on the way. Please hang on. You can do it."

I thought about how I could get to Wilderness Park. Even though I'd had plenty of experience driving under the influence, taking the wheel in my current condition seemed too risky. I needed help. Scrolling through the contacts list on my cell phone, I stopped on Gale McGrady and pressed the button. Listening to the succession of rings, I wondered what I would do if he didn't answer. Finally, he picked up.

"Have you found her?" he asked.

"No."

"No luck here either. I just finished sweeping all the shops at Gateway Mall. Quite a few you know. Now I'm going to head over to—"

"Gale, I need you to come get me."

A pause. "Okay. Are you all right?"

"I'm fine, but my pickup won't start." I didn't want to tell him I'd been shot, because he'd want to call an ambulance. Then I'd have to go to the hospital and would never find Buddy.

"You don't sound well. Something happen to you?"

"Just get here," I commanded. "I think I know where Buddy is, but I need a ride."

"All right. Where are you?"

"Sherman Field." The words came out as wheeze. "No wait. Pick me up across the street. You know, the softball field."

"Sawyer Snell? If you're still at Sherman, why do you want me to go there?"

"Just pick me up in the Sawyer parking lot. I'll explain later."

"Very well. I'm on my way."

When the approaching sirens grew louder, I leaned down and kissed Toni's cheek. I told her that I loved her. I always had and I always would. A couple tears dropped onto her. Just before releasing her hand, I felt a slight squeeze. My gaze fixed on her closed eyes. Wanting desperately to see them open again, I begged God not to take her.

My body had just enough strength to hoist itself onto the dugout bench. I leaned back against the brick wall. Each breath sent jagged nails rattling inside my right lung. The world around me shuddered and spun. I staggered out of the dugout toward the concourse. It came as something of a surprise that I could move without falling over. I made it to my truck in the gravel lot. There, I found an old T-shirt under the passenger seat to press against the leaking hole below my shoulder. With the ambulance and squad cars only a block away, I staggered across South Street to the softball complex parking lot and propped myself against the wooden Sawyer Snell sign. There, with a wadded-up shirt pressed to my chest, I watched the flashing lights at Sherman Field and waited for Gale.

Since I was still floating in and out, it didn't seem like much time had passed before a car pulled into the lot. I waved the T-shirt to flag it down. Once the blinding headlights moved past my eyes, I recognized Gale's Lexus. He got out and surveyed our dark surroundings.

"Well, I made it. You're lucky I have so little regard for speed limits. Got here in under ten minutes. Say, what's all that commotion over there at Sherman?" His eyes fell on me for the first time since his arrival. "Good God, man! What happened to you?"

I pushed off the sign and straightened up. "Don't worry about it." The spinning resumed, but then stopped long enough for me to focus on Gale.

"You've been shot! We need to get you to a hospital. Let me flag down the EMTs across the street."

"There's no time for that. I have to find Buddy ... now." Dark thoughts that it might already be too late invaded my head, but I fought them off.

"You could bleed to death."

"I'm fine." I removed the wadded T-shirt from my wound. "I think it's stopped for now."

"Who did this to you?"

"I'll tell you on the way. We need to get going." I took a shaky step toward his car and reached for the passenger door handle.

"You've gone completely mad," he said, circling around his car. He opened the passenger door and muttered something about his beautiful leather interior. Then he helped lower me into the seat. "This is insanity. I should drive you to the hospital right now."

"My daughter is out there alone," I barked. "She could be dying. We have to try to find her ... before it's too late."

"Well, first let me do this." He opened the glove compartment and retrieved a small first aid kit. "This isn't supposed to sting," he said, ripping open the wrapper of an antiseptic wipe. He was right, it didn't sting. But it did hurt like hell when he pushed up my shirt and rubbed the wipe over the afflicted area. His fingers probed the back of my shoulder. "Doesn't appear to be an exit wound, so the bullet is still in inside."

"Do me a favor and don't try to dig it out."

"But slug removal is the last badge I need to make Eagle Scout," he said. A smile broke through my pain as he affixed a large square bandage over the hole in my chest. "There, that should keep you from deflating too much further."

"Thanks."

He moved around the car and settled behind the wheel. "Where do you want to go?"

"Wilderness Park. It's not far."

"I know where it is. Took Beth there for a constitutional last month. Sadly, the afternoon didn't end well. I'll tell you about it sometime."

"Great," I moaned, before a painful cough sent a dark spray onto his dashboard. "Sorry."

He surveyed the mess with a heavy sigh. "Yes, you were about to tell me the source of your recent misfortune."

As he pulled out onto South Street, I heard more sirens in the distance. "I thought Buddy might have come to Sherman Field. She didn't … but Cole was waiting for me in the dugout."

"Cole? Your ex's beau?"

"Yes," I said through a labored breath. "He pulled a gun on me … then Toni showed up."

"Oh dear."

"Yeah. He shot her, then me."

"My God. So that ambulance is for her?"

"Yeah." My face tightened to hold back a wave of emotion. "If it's not too late."

"Zane, I'm sorry." He continued driving. "What did this man do next?"

"Don't know. He disappeared."

It didn't take long for Gale to reach the gravel entrance to Wilderness Park. That was the good news. The bad news was that the park consisted of more than a thousand acres of forest. And it was after dark. Even if my daughter had come here, the odds of finding her didn't look good. But I had no choice.

Gale helped pull me out of the car to a standing position. "You sure you're up for this?" he asked. "You could wait here while I search."

A slight dizziness remained, but there was no way I was waiting in the car. "I'm going. Do you have a flashlight?"

He actually had two—one in the glove compartment and one in the trunk. After shoving the first aid kit into the pocket of his Members Only jacket, he pulled a golf club out of the trunk. "What's that for?" I asked.

"In case you need a cane. I left my real cane back at the apartment."

He handed it to me. It was a 3-iron. "Thanks." I took a weak one-handed swing at an imaginary ball.

"Guess we can start calling you Bob Charles," he quipped.

"Who's that?"

"Only the greatest left-handed golfer in history. A southpaw like you should know that."

"Sorry, Nicklaus is my favorite."

"Well, I guess Bob can't match the Golden Bear, but he's the best you lefties have got for links heroes. He's from New Zealand, you know. I met him at our country club several years back. Daddy introduced us. I'll tell you about it sometime."

"Can't wait."

We set off down the trail into the woods. Not yet needing any walking assistance, I carried the club in my left hand. Though my shoulder throbbed, my right hand still had enough strength to grip the flashlight. Our two roving beams cut through the night, scanning the trees and brush that enveloped us.

I had no concept of time or distance as we trekked deeper into the woods. Gale led the way a few yards ahead of me. Every so often, he'd point out a root that crossed the dirt path below so I wouldn't trip. My pain continued to flare, but I kept up. The dizziness subsided, perhaps from adrenaline, but I didn't know how long it would take before my last vestiges of energy drained away.

When we'd first entered the woods, I called out Buddy's name every ten yards or so. But that took a lot out of me and after just three times my voice couldn't reach a normal conversational volume anymore. Gale took over, his tenor cries carrying much farther than mine. More than a few times we heard something rustling in the trees. But it always ran off—a deer, a rabbit, or some nocturnal creature frightened away by the racket we created.

My limbs started shivering in the night chill. After a while— maybe a half hour—I stumbled to the ground. Gale helped me to my feet. "Maybe we should go back, get you some help."

"No!" Anger burned in my veins. "My daughter could be out here. We keep going."

He waited with a steadying hand on my back while I sucked in the cool air. It felt like razors scraping the inside of my lung. Staring into the black void around us made it hard not to succumb to despair. The trees seemed to go on forever. If Buddy were near the trail, we may have a chance spot her. But if she were just twenty feet back into the woods, we could pass by a dozen times without seeing anything in the darkness. And, of course, she might not even be here. She could be somewhere in the city. Or not even in Lincoln at all. I tried to convince myself that maybe Snowman had found her downtown. Or maybe Stick had found her at the other park

We started moving again. By this point I had to use the golf club as a cane. Unfortunately, that slowed our progress. Leaves swirled around me in the glow of the flashlight beams. I didn't know how much longer I could go on. I saw an image of Buddy as a little girl riding her bicycle with training wheels. Then she was a baby crawling across the living room carpet in her pink footed pajamas. I also saw her sitting in the big rocking chair holding Luke in her lap. Other visions of her at different ages came intermittently. If only she would respond to Gale's call.

The trail passed near a creek that flowed below us. I pointed the light down into the water. Something had jumped in. I had to be careful not to fall because the drop-off from the trail to the creek was about twenty feet. Gale shined his light down there too. His beam found the dark object swimming away. "Looks like a beaver," he said.

We pressed on. The woods around the trail thinned and our light fell on some logs and downed trees ten or fifteen yards off the path. Gale called. No response. I don't know why, but I didn't follow when he started walking again. My beam kept roaming the area. It caught something red just above a huge log. I stepped forward and squinted at the object. Whatever it was, it seemed out of place. I tried to yell at Gale, but it came out as more of a croak. Fortunately, he still heard me.

We stepped off the trail and advanced through the brush, twigs snapping beneath our feet. Our lights remained trained on the red. It appeared to be a cone of some sort. We made it to the downed tree, which matched the diameter of a bus tire. As I moved around to the other side, my heart stopped. The red object wasn't a cone, but the top of a hood. A hood that was part of a red-hooded sweatshirt like my daughter wore. She sat slumped on the ground, her back propped against the log.

"Buddy!" I staggered over to her and fell to my knees. She didn't move, her eyes remained shut. I placed a hand on her cheek. "Buddy, please …"

A faint noise followed. It came so softly, I almost thought I imagined it. "Dad?"

"Buddy, it's okay. I'm here."

"I'm hurt."

"It'll be alright. We're going to—" As Gale shined his light over her, I noticed a dark stain that covered most of her sweatshirt's torn right sleeve. Similar marks mottled her jeans, shoes, and the ground below. I examined her right arm, where the blotch was darkest. Her forearm had been wrapped with a makeshift rag. But it had come loose. The cloth was soaked with blood that seeped from a deep gash.

"Oh Buddy, what happened?"

"I fell in the rocks by the creek," she whispered. "Cut my arm…. Think I broke my ankle."

From behind me I heard a case snapping open. Gale knelt down and examined her arm. He wiped clean her wound and affixed a large bandage. "Hopefully, that will stop the bleeding."

"Her other arm?" I said.

He rolled back the sleeve. "It's fine. There are some smaller cuts on her hands. None of them look too bad. We probably shouldn't move the ankle."

"Dad," Buddy said weakly, "I'm really thirsty."

I wrapped my arm around her. "We'll get you some water. We're going to get you home."

"I don't want to die."

"That's not going to happen. I've got you."

She tried to move her arm, but it fell back into her lap.

"Just rest, sweetheart. We're going to get help."

Gale stood. "Well this is fortuitous."

"What?"

He pointed at the trail. Someone with a flashlight approached. Using the 3-iron for support, I struggled to my feet. "Hopefully it's a Ranger or a police officer," Gale said.

"Whoever it is, he can help us." We both shined our light at the approaching figure.

"You arrived at just the right time," Gale called out. "We could really use some assistance."

"I bet you could," came the reply.

The voice riddled my body with most crushing dread I'd ever felt. This feeling grew even worse as my beam illuminated Cole's face.

"So you found the little princess," he said. "Congratulations. I didn't think you would."

"Excuse me," Gale said. "Just who do you—" He cut short his statement upon spotting Cole's gun pointed at him.

"I'm not talkin' to you, preppie, so you just keep your mouth shut. And both of you, get your lights outta my eyes."

We lowered our beams to his waist, further highlighting the .38 in his hand. "What are you doing here?" I asked. "Haven't you done enough already?"

"Me? I didn't do nothin'. I realized that after I got back home. See, nobody but you and me knows what happened in that dugout. Hell, nobody but you and Toni knows I was even there. That gets me thinking that *you* were the one who shot Toni. All I have to do is go back and put a bullet in your head so you can't tell nobody otherwise. Then I'd put the gun in your hand and make it look like a murder-suicide. Two exes who couldn't handle the stress of losing another kid."

The shock of seeing his horrible face and hearing his miserable voice paralyzed me.

"So I get in my truck and head back the ballpark," he continued, "but the cops are already there. Then I notice this car pulling out from the lot across the street. Who could that be, I wonder. So I follow it here." He burst out in a sick laugh. "It couldn't get any better. You guys going deeper and deeper into the woods. Calling out every so often to make sure I don't lose ya. It's perfect, the perfect place to waste the Fish. The only reason I didn't do it earlier is 'cause I wanted to see if you'd actually find her here."

"Please," Gale said, "if I may interject. It doesn't have to come to this."

"Who asked you?"

"Zane told me about what happened in the dugout. It was clearly an accident."

Cole's brow scrunched in contemplation.

"You will not be incarcerated for anything that happened tonight," Gale continued. "I have a great lawyer who will see to that. There will be no prison time for anybody, I assure you. Especially when Zane testifies that the unfortunate events at Sherman Field were an accident."

Cole shifted his gaze to me. My overflowing hatred for him prevented me from responding.

"Zane?" Gale sounded like an impatient teacher. "Please explain to the gentleman that you will testify that what happened tonight was an accident."

I would never do that, but I understood Gale's intent. If he and Buddy were going to get out of this forest alive, I had to play along. "Yes ... it was an accident," I said. "I know you didn't mean to shoot anybody."

Cole examined me for a long time, before his mouth twisted into a sneer. "No, I don't trust you. You'll say anything now to save your hide. But once we're talking to the police, you'll turn on me. I've been bitten by snakes like you too many times." His voice grew louder. "You ruined my life this summer. All I wanted was to live in peace with my woman, but you had to show up and stick your nose in our business. Now it's time for payback."

"Fine," I responded. "Kill me. But let Gale go. He didn't do anything to you."

"Yeah, but he's a friend of yours. That means he's no damn good. Plus, I can't leave behind any witnesses." He looked at Gale. "Sorry pal. Collateral damage, you know."

"Damn it, Cole," I barked. "What is wrong with you?"

He stepped toward me, the gun barrel pointed at my chest. "Shut up!"

"You may have already killed an innocent woman tonight. Are you going to kill three more just to cover it up?"

His sneer slithered into a smirk. "What kind of a monster do you think I am? Yes, I will kill the preppie. Then I will kill you. But Buddy here, I'll leave her alone. She can get up and walk right out of here." He glanced down at her. "You can walk can't you, sweetie?"

Nobody said anything.

"Hmmm, looks like she's not in too big a hurry to go anywhere." Cole waved his gun at Buddy. "Might even need some help. Too bad her daddy failed her, yet again."

The reality behind his words crashed down on me. I would die right here, unable to save my daughter. I had failed Buddy. Remembering Toni's last words to me, I realized that I'd failed her too.

Gale turned to me and cleared his throat. "If only Bob Charles were here."

Cole glared at him with a confused look. "Who the hell is Bob Charles?"

It took only a second for Gale's comment to register. *Bob Charles the golfer—the golf club—I'm leaning on a potential weapon.* My grip tightened on the 3-iron, and with the last ounce of energy left in my body, I stepped forward and swung the club at Cole's skull. It connected, the impact sounding like an axe chopping into wood. The gun went off. Blood splattered onto my face. Cole went down. So did I.

My eyes opened. Dark shapes spun around and around. I felt like I might vomit. "Zane, are you okay?" Gale's voice asked from above.

I didn't know how to answer that question. Aside from the spinning, a fire burned in my shoulder and it hurt to breathe. But I didn't notice any new pains. "I think so." My eyes fixed on his flashlight. "What about Buddy?"

"She's fine. The bullet didn't hit anybody. I'm going to call for help."

He set his flashlight down and punched numbers into his phone. I heard his voice, but couldn't comprehend what he was saying. The beam from his light pointed at Buddy. I rolled onto my hands and knees and crawled to her. Given how much the world shook around me, I don't know how I made it even that short distance. I tried to speak, but couldn't form any words.

Then I blacked out.

Epilogue

Six Months Later:

The knuckleball loafed toward the plate with too much spin. And, as is so often the case in such situations, the batter launched the ball into the sky. The players on the field watched in admiration as the baseball sailed high into the beautiful blue expanse, hovering as if it would stay there forever. Gravity finally pulled it back to Earth, where it disappeared into a tree some 430 feet away.

"That's what happens when you mess around with knucklers," I said, walking toward the mound. "Now you're going to have to go fetch it after practice."

The tall kid kicked the dirt behind the rubber. "You threw knuckleballs all the time last season," he protested.

"Yeah, but I didn't have any choice." I rubbed a new baseball between my hands. "I didn't have a ninety-three-mile-per-hour fastball like you. Mix in a decent change with that heat, and you may actually get drafted this summer."

He rolled his eyes and held out his glove. "Whatever."

I thrust my face closer to his. "Stop tinkering with junk balls, Meat. You don't need 'em." I dropped the ball into his glove.

"Better listen to him, Stephens," Curtis bellowed from dugout. "The Fish used to pitch in the big leagues, you know."

"Yeah, he's mentioned that a couple times," Stephens yelled back.

One of the guys near the batting cage then chimed in. "How can we forget? Coach Fish begins every one of his lectures with, 'Back when I pitched in Cincinnati ...'"

"And he always works in something about winning the Cy Young," another kid added.

"Very funny," I said. "Back when I pitched in Cincinnati, we used to run laps. All the time. Staying in shape like that helped me win the Cy Young Award. And guess what you animals are going to be doing at the end of practice today? Your usual quota of laps, plus five more."

The players groaned and protested to Curtis. "You brought it on yourselves," he said, his eyes on a clipboard. "Shouldn't cross a living legend."

"That's right," I said to the team, "I *am* a living legend. Don't you ever read the papers?" I turned to Stephens. "Alright, three more batters, then let Osterquist take the hill." I walked toward the dugout. "And no more knuckleballs. You have to be a trained professional to use those things."

"Fine," Stephens groused.

I took a seat in the dugout next to Curtis, the head coach of the Nebraska Wesleyan Prairie Wolves. He'll be the first to tell you, he never expected to be coaching a college team. His plan was to manage the Giants for a few seasons and then work his way up the farm system of a big league organization. But when the Central States League folded the previous summer, Curtis was out of a job. So he was quite happy when one of the colleges in Lincoln called during the offseason with a coaching opportunity.

One of his first decisions in his new position was to offer me a job as his pitching coach. I definitely had never planned on coaching a college team. Or a team at any level, for that matter. I was going to pitch in the big leagues a few more years and then get into broadcasting. Or maybe open up a bar where everybody knows my name. But when Curtis called, I immediately accepted.

You may be wondering what convinced the Fish to so readily become an employee of an institution of higher learning. Well, let's go back to Wilderness Park the previous September. As you may have guessed by now, I made it out of the woods alive that night. So did Buddy. And we have Gale to thank for that. After he dialed 911, he carried Buddy over a mile of trail to the parking lot, where the ambulance arrived. Then he led the EMTs back through the woods to where I lay, still unconscious. Though I don't remember any of it, that must have been quite a bumpy gurney ride through the trees.

We made it to the hospital, where a pint of blood went into Buddy and a .38 caliber slug came out of me. Both of us were in rough shape, but we would improve fairly quickly. It was much worse for Toni in the emergency room of that same hospital. Doctors said she nearly flatlined during her four-hour surgery that night. She remained in critical condition for days and serious condition for weeks. Her situation gradually improved through October and she finally got to come home just before Thanksgiving.

Gale really came through for me that night at the park. I'd made fun of him a lot during the season, but looking back, I couldn't have asked for a better teammate. Or friend. I even started calling him Gale Force. He'd earned it. Though I can never really pay him back, I did what I could. Over the off-season I made a few calls and got him an invite to spring training with the Reds. I'm hoping he'll land a roster spot with one of their farm teams. But even if he doesn't, I'm sure he'll find an opportunity to display his considerable talents in some other pursuit.

As for my other friends on the Giants, Snowman started working in the music and video department at a Wal-Mart in Lincoln. He also got his high school rock band together again, though they hadn't landed any gigs last I heard. Dirk Davis signed with an indy team in Chico, California. Since his arrival, air freshener sales in the city have tripled. Larry the Geek found a job with the Cleveland Indians. I don't know what exactly he's doing for them, but I'm sure it involves statistical charts and graphs. Brian Carter is still writing for the newspaper. In November, he and Eileen had a little boy. They named him Bobby.

Cole Hagler survived his encounter with the 3-iron, though he'll never see out of his right eye again. After being hospitalized with a concussion and a fractured orbital bone, he went straight to jail, where he awaits trial for two counts of attempted murder. When the time comes, I will have to testify. I'd rather not relive the events of that horrible evening again, but I'm the key witness so it will have to be done.

I dread the trial even more so for Buddy. Even though her physical condition improved, the emotional wounds lingered for a long time. I hate the thought of stirring up those memories for her. The stress of worrying about her mother in the hospital week after week really took a toll, especially since she blamed herself for what happened. Buddy's frame of mind got a lot better after Toni came home. Having Stick as her pal again helped too. He told me he was okay being "just friends" with my daughter. I was glad to hear that, though I wouldn't mind him dating Buddy someday. You know, maybe ten or fifteen years down the road.

My mother flew to Lincoln last fall to stay with Buddy and me for a couple weeks after we got out of the hospital. Tim Haines came out for a visit too. Their presence helped us deal with everything that had gone down. Tim even convinced me to go to church with my daughter. I sure didn't see that happening, but I'm glad it did. Being in that type of community brought healing to us both and helped me stay securely on the wagon. Get this, I even became a sponsor for somebody else. That goofball Weed got religion (a real religion) and pledged to go clean. So now I'm his Captain Underwear. Bruce, as he now likes to be called, has been drug-free for three months and is talking about going into youth ministry. He still has his stilts and has developed a comedy act to perform at summer Bible camps.

More surprises came with the public reaction to the events of last September. Once the story broke, reporters and commentators started saying nice things about the Fish. Got a bunch of cards and letters from fans across the country. Sidney Cruz even sent flowers to me in the hospital. Inside the card she wrote, "You're still a pig, but at least you've got heart. Hope you get well soon." Below her name, she drew a smiley face and wrote, "Call me sometime."

Baseball clubs sought me out too. A dozen GMs invited me to spring training in '99. The Cardinals, Pirates, and Reds even offered me a big league contract without a tryout. It was a great vote of confidence for an old guy like me to still be wanted, but I had to turn them all down. My place is in Lincoln with my daughter. That's why I was so happy when Curtis called offering me a coaching job right here in town. It's like it was meant to be. Sure the money isn't all that great, even with the baseball clinics I'll be teaching in the summer. But I get to be around Buddy year round, and that's worth way more to me than a big league salary.

Plus, I've started dating someone in Lincoln. I like her a lot and Buddy does too. In fact, before the first date, my daughter came over to my apartment to give me advice so I wouldn't screw it up. She picked out my wardrobe and peppered me with last-second instructions.

"Did you remember the flowers?" she asked.

"Yes."

"Don't forget to open doors for her. We girls like that."

"Yes, Buddy."

"Compliment her hair and her outfit. Definitely say something nice about her shoes."

"I will."

"And don't talk about baseball. Find out what *she's* interested in and talk about that."

"Dang it, Buddy! I've dated your mother before. We were going to proms before you were born. I think I'll be alright."

"I know, but that was years ago. You were young and handsome back then. Now you're … old. So you're going to have to rely on your personality and charm. See why I'm so worried?"

My daughter, ever the wiseass. And for the record, my "first date" with Toni went well. So did the second and third dates. I think this may be going somewhere.

After the World Series last October, *Sports Illustrated* published an article assessing the Hall of Fame chances of current big leaguers. Most of the experts they polled believed I'd make it, but a couple noteworthy exceptions thought I'd fall just short of Cooperstown. In their opinion, if I got 300 wins I'd be a lock, but 293 just wasn't quite enough. Brian Carter recently asked me in an interview if I'd consider going back to try to win those (apparently all-important) seven games. I said no. Not while Buddy is still in school. Maybe I'll think about it after she graduates in a couple years and goes off to college. See if the Fish can still toss the knuckleball.

But really I'm not all that concerned about playing baseball again. The events of last season opened my eyes. There are a lot more important things in life than winning 300 games or making the Hall of Fame. I'm content now and I know I'm where I'm supposed to be. It's been a long time since I could say that. Getting Toni and Buddy back in my life—especially after I'd nearly lost them both—far outweighs anything baseball could ever offer me.

I may never stand atop a pitcher's mound again, but I finally made it home.

About the Author

Kent Krause writes content for online high school history courses and social studies textbooks. He holds bachelor's and master's degrees from Iowa State University, and a doctorate from the University of Nebraska-Lincoln. In addition to his three novels, he has published articles in *Great Plains Quarterly* and *The International Journal of the History of Sport*. USA Book News selected his first novel, *The All-American King*, as a category finalist for the National Best Books 2009 Awards. Kent lives in Nebraska with his wife Jill.

Visit Kent online at: **kentkrause.com**